# THE
# MADONNA

## JENNY BRIGALOW

ISBN: 978-1-8383354-3-4

# DEDICATION

For Tess and Emily, my two amazing voluntary editors and proofreaders. I just couldn't have done this without you. My undying thanks.

# CHAPTER 1

It was cold. The night sky was blanching in the east, smudging softly on the edges of the earth. Grey turned to amber and then to the red of a blood orange. The great sandy desert lit up like a stage, silhouetting the camel train against a dune.

Mia gently pulled her mighty camel, Ashan, to a halt and waited patiently for the rest of the party to join her. In the sharp rays of the morning light, her green eyes sparkled like polished gems. Shifting the small stone in her mouth, trying to ignore her thirst and empty belly, she worried about her companions. It was daylight and they had to find a place to rest.

Whilst it was true they had all volunteered to join her in the journey to Alice, she still felt responsible. In particular her concern lay with Shyboy, whose albino inheritance made him particularly vulnerable to the harsh desert conditions. Volta too was a worry. Whilst he had toughened up considerably in the short time Mia had known him, he had spent most of his life in his mother's palace. Tully, Volta's bodyguard, was made of sterner stuff and D2 (aka The Confessor), assassin and living legend, was probably the toughest of them all. But still, the desert was a dangerous place.

The tattoo of shod feet heralded the arrival of Whisper. Mia turned anxiously, noting that she had dropped condition. "Whisper," she called. The mare strolled over, lifting her soft muzzle to Mia, who scratched her chin gently. Whisper blew softly down her nostrils, eyes peering brightly through the silver veil of her forelock. Love surged in Mia's heart. Whisper turned away, playfully nipping the fat rump of Volta's gelding, Hawk Eye. Mia, reassured all was as well as could be expected, relaxed a little.

Mia glanced at the fast approaching camels. She waited, a sick feeling in her stomach as her companions joined her. Her eyes ran over them one by one. "How's everyone going?" she called.

Tully looked tired but robust. If D2 was suffering she could not tell. But Shyboy and Volta looked haggard, skin papery, eyes bloodshot and lips cracked and bleeding. Panic began fluttering in her chest like moths in a jar. Mia dragged her eyes away from their suffering and looked into the distance. The landscape spread out to the horizon, an endless vista of sand and rock. Anxiety gripped her. They should be there by now. But there was not so much as a hint of the town called Alice.

"We'll make camp here," said Mia. Silently and efficiently the group dismounted. In a short time the small tents were erected and the desert camouflage nets put in place. They did not bother with a fire, there was nothing to cook. As the water bottle circulated around the silent and exhausted group, Mia was forced to acknowledge the seriousness of their predicament. Whilst her travelling companions had been eager to join the quest to free her father from the prison hospital in the north, she still felt responsible. She took the water bottle, faked a few sips and passed the bottle onto Volta who sat beside her.

He glared at her with his brilliant blue eyes. "You're faking it again!" His voice was hoarse, cracking like corn in oil.

Mia shook her head. It was easy to forget that behind Volta's angelic face and golden head of hair lay a mind sharper than a prickly pear. Still, two could play at that game. She opened her eyes wide. "I don't know what you are talking about."

Volta shook the water bottle violently. Tully reached out, plucking the bottle away and took a sip. Undeterred, Volta eyeballed Mia. "You know precisely what I'm talking about. You're not drinking your share of water." He looked urgently around the rest of the company. "Am I right or am I right?"

D2 turned his head, looking sharply at Mia. "Is this true?"

Mia scowled. "No."

Tully nodded.

Mia gave him a look that should have stripped the flesh off his bones.

body sagging with fatigue. He had not spoken a word and his computer sat silent beside him. The young man's usually cheerful disposition had subsided into the muteness of exhaustion. Fear struck with sharp claws in Mia's young belly as she faced the fact that — for Shyboy — the threat of capture was now secondary. She looked into Volta's dirty, tense face. "It is a risk I fear we must take." She looked around the gathering. "If everyone is in agreement?"

Tully looked at her slight figure and remembered, with something akin to awe, how young she was. It was easy to forget. Mia had taken them across the most hostile land on the continent without so much as a scratch. Her determination had never wavered as she carried the burden of responsibility like a veteran of many campaigns. "It's a good plan, Mia."

Mia waited on the others. One by one they acquiesced. The show of solidarity gave Mia renewed confidence. She turned to Volta. "Why don't you go out for a recce? See if you can find some flat rocks for drying the meat."

Volta appeared to be on the verge of protesting but then glanced at the camels. "Good idea," he said.

Mia smiled at him, relieved. She did not want him to witness the calf's death. It would, she sensed, distress him and he had enough to contend with. The memory of his last communication with his mother was still fresh. It still shocked her when she recalled Pavan's cruelty to her son. The powerful owner of the Western Water Company had brutally cut Volta from her life when he had refused to kowtow to her demands. And seemingly without an ounce of remorse. Poor Volta. "Take some water," she said, "and don't be longer than half an hour."

Volta handed her a bottle. "You first."

Mia took it, taking several delicious, brackish, hot swallows.

Without further prompting, Volta departed. For a moment Mia watched him, then turned abruptly to Shyboy. She thrust the bottle into his sunburned hands. "Drink." Guilt overwhelmed her. He looked terrible. This was all her fault. She was failing. But with each small sip, Shyboy miraculously seemed to be reviving. Mia flopped down beside him, peering anxiously into the sculpted face and pale eyes.

He grinned, the skin of his face cracking and splitting. "I like my steak medium rare," he said, his voice rough as grit.

Mia laughed. There was a sharp crack of a gun. Mia leapt up and hurried over to where D2 and Tully were hovering beside the dead calf. Mia made thanks to Sol. With her stomach growling ferociously she began butchering the carcass, mouth watering in anticipation.

# CHAPTER 2

The fire crackled softly, orange tongues of flame licking around the stones. The faint aroma of dried dung lingered in the air. The gathered group took a collective sniff of appreciation as Tully dropped three fat steaks onto the hot rocks. They sizzled tantalizingly. Mia's hair was in danger of igniting as her nose drew her closer and closer to the meat. It was only as she bumped heads with Volta that she drew back to a safer distance. They grinned at each other but their eyes returned irresistibly to the steak as Tully expertly flicked them over, revealing the golden brown underside.

Tully looked around at his rapt audience. "Anyone for rare?"

D2 jumped up, holding out a plate. Tully deftly picked up a steak and deposited it. D2 grinned, teeth flashing in his face and took a large, juicy mouthful. Blood oozed down his chin.

Mia watched, mesmerised, licking her lips. Then started, blushing in embarrassment. Goodness me, what was wrong with her? She hurriedly tore her eyes away and back to the sizzling meat.

Tully was serving up another portion. He handed it over to Shyboy. "Medium rare."

Shyboy's eyes closed in ecstasy as he cut a slice, popped it into his mouth and chewed. Mia noticed Volta was chewing in sympathy. He caught her eye and grinned bashfully, his cheeks suffusing with heat. Mia smiled back, empathising. More steaks hit the rock. Mia waited in a frenzy of impatience, practically drooling. After several minutes, she cracked, picking up her plate and holding it out.

Tully eyed her speculatively. "It'll still be red on the inside."

Mia nodded. "Whatever."

Tully slapped the rest of the steaks down onto plates and handed them out. For several moments there were only the sounds of chewing and swallowing.

"I love camels," said Volta, licking his plate.

They all watched D2 putting away his third steak in awe. Finally sated, Tully doused the fire and they all collapsed beneath their tents. It was mid morning and the heat had built to a ferocious level. It would get worse. But still, the strips of meat spread out on the stones would dry quickly.

Drowsy, but not ready to sleep, Mia's eyes grazed around the camp, lingering on the sooty stones of the fireplace. She wondered where the herd had gone and hoped the horses had found some shade. She fretted for a while about them but finally she drifted off into sleep, exhausted.

When she awoke she sat up, instinctively searching around for Whisper. To her relief the herd was standing in a narrow strip of shade cast from a tall dune, heads low as they waited patiently for the heat to ebb. With her stomach full, Mia began worrying once more about water. The camel's milk would be a blessing but no good for their four-legged companions.

Mia lay back down, eyes wandering listlessly around the camp. Something was niggling in her mind. She looked at the mottled pattern of the nets and at the camels lying peacefully behind Volta's and Tully's tent. Then she looked toward the strips of drying meat and decided to go and see how they were progressing. She got up, wiggled out of the tent and went over, passing the fireplace. And stopped, a thrill of excitement coursing through her. The stones. Of course!

Oblivious to the savage sun beating down on her uncovered head, Mia retraced her steps, crouching down to examine the scorched rocks. She brushed soot and sand off the largest one, hissing in protest as its burning surface caught her unawares. She sucked her sore fingers absentmindedly, thinking furiously. For a minute she sat, still as stone. Then she leapt up and went galloping back to the tents.

"Volta!" she yelled. "Volta, wake up!"

Whipping the tent open, she stuck in her head. "Volta!"

Volta jerked awake. He sat up, staring around in alarm. "Shit!" he said. "Mia, what's happened?"

Mia opened the flap wide and pointed in the direction of the fire. "Volta, can you remember where you found those stones yesterday?"

By now sleep had deserted Volta and he eyed Mia curiously. "Sure. It was in a bit of ridge country. You know, all rocky. A few cacti. Not far really." He scrambled over, looking out at the fire. "Why?"

Mia took a deep breath and then let it out slowly. "O.K. I could be wrong, but I think that the well back at our campsite is dug from the same rock type."

Volta stared blankly at Mia for a moment and then his mouth gaped. "You mean?"

Mia nodded. "I mean that there may be water there, beneath the ground."

"Fantastic," said a voice behind Mia. It was Tully. He was joined by D2 and Shyboy. They all observed her with expressions both anxious and hopeful.

Mia hurried to quash any unrealistic expectations they may be entertaining. "I'm not promising," she said. "Even if there is water, it may be too deep to dig out. It may run beneath an impenetrable rock seam. Or, even if we find it, the quality may be poor. It may be too full of salts and be unpalatable. Even for the camels."

At the thought of the suffering animals, Mia's eyes searched out the horses. Outwardly they looked bright enough, but Mia's sharp eyes noticed the tightness of their skin and sucked-in flanks. Soon they would begin to fail. Mia's lips compressed together in a hard line of determination. She would find them some water even if she had to dig to the centre of the earth.

She turned her attention back to the others and caught Volta staring at her. She felt herself flushing slightly at his attention.

Then he too turned, observing the horses. With a small smile he reached out and took her hand, squeezing it hard. "Don't fret, you will find water Mia. The horses will have drunk their fill by nightfall."

Mia was struck by two things. Firstly, Volta was as concerned for the horses' welfare as she was herself. And secondly, that the young Isbanite was far more attuned to her emotions than she would have given him credit for. And these thoughts in turn led to others. She could not deny his words warmed her inside. That it gladdened her heart to feel his kindness and consideration. Yet, she also felt a surge of anxiety. What was this thing she felt? Did Volta feel it too? But she shied away from this last, unwilling to explore it further.

Confused and distressed, she abruptly withdrew her hand from his. It was a hand, she acknowledged, as work hardened and calloused as her own. As any Overlander's. She could not fail to miss the wince of hurt on Volta's face as she drew away, but pretended she had not noticed. Then she became acutely aware of an embarrassed hush hanging over the company. It was mortifying. Mia felt her face burning but she did not know what to say. Or do.

Mercifully, Tully stepped into the chasm. "So," he said briskly, "is it too hot to do a recce?"

A tiny breeze brushed across Mia's perspiring cheek. Everyone stirred. Gratefully, Mia shook her head at Tully. "It's hot, but the sun is waning and if, as Volta says, it's not far, we can work into the cooler hours."

"Good," said Shyboy. "What do we need?"

In several minutes they were ready and robed, loaded with empty water bottles. Mia's divining rods were stowed carefully in a bag, still swaddled in the cloth Nonna had knitted for her. The camels arose grumbling softly and, with Volta riding at the lead, they set off. The sun had finally begun sinking, its dying rays staining the landscape a deep rose gold. Mia felt a reverent love of the land filling her. It was cruel and unforgiving but it was also untamable and filled with a savage beauty that satisfied some deep need within her.

Mia knew they had arrived at the site even before Volta turned, eagerly pointing to a small tor of rocks. The ground sloped upward, the soft sandy desert floor giving way to grit. As they neared the small rock formation, the grit disappeared, revealing stone scoured clean by the wind.

"This is it!" said Volta.

Ashan sank to his knees and Mia slid to the ground. She carefully took up the woollen package, unrolling it to extract two slender rods. With a rod in either hand, she placed one clenched fist atop the other, aligning them. In the dimming light she looked carefully around at the lay of the land and began to head south-west, back to the lower ground. With every nerve and fibre tuned into her rods, she moved slowly, waiting for a sign.

Concentrating hard, she almost forgot to breathe as she searched. Then the ground beneath her gave way once more to sand and Mia felt a pang of fear. What if she was wrong? It was a prospect too horrible to contemplate.

And then, after several minutes of futile effort, she felt the tiniest vibration. She stopped, deliberately relaxing her body, eyes shut. Trembling with anticipation and anxiety, Mia took another step forward. But the tiny electrical current was lost. Immediately she stepped back and felt the force field buzzing softly. Instinct sent her to her left and to her immense relief, she felt the soft vibration beginning to build. As she travelled on, the two wires began quivering and then slowly rotated in her hands. The powerful current pulled her onward until the rods finally crossed.

Mia stopped and turned to the others. "It is here," she said.

# CHAPTER 3

Tully and D2 worked with a will, but armed with only one spade and a large tin plate it was slow going. After a while, Volta took the spade from an indignant Tully and got stuck in. He noticed that despite his protest, his body guard sank down onto the cooling earth. And likewise, when Mia took the spade from him, Volta did not protest. He collapsed on the ground beside Shyboy, legs and shoulders burning with fatigue. Shyboy patted his shoulder and got up. He went to D2 and a heated (but brief) conversation ensued, resulting in Shyboy's reluctant retreat.

Shyboy sat down beside Volta, shaking his head. "Waste of breath," he said ruefully. "Just look at the man! He's just bloody... brilliant."

Volta smiled, watching the feline hybrid digging. It was an awe-inspiring sight. His desert robes had been cast aside, and he was stripped down to his singlet, his massive muscles glistening like liquorice with sweat. D2 worked like a man possessed. Which, Volta reflected, was perhaps not far from the truth. The terrible pale, puckered scars on the assassin's arms were a stark reminder of the man's suffering. Captured and incarcerated in the prison hospital, the hybrid had been reduced to little more than spare parts for harvesting. His escape had been nothing less than miraculous.

No wonder, Volta thought, he was hell bent on revenge. But Volta could not sit for long watching. He got up, went back and strong armed Mia aside. Ignoring his protesting muscles and parched mouth, he dug with grim determination. D2 was not the only one with vengeance on his mind.

It was nearly dark, yet still they dug. As the hole deepened they could only work one at a time, filling a canvas sheet with sand and hauling it up. No one spoke. All their energy was centred on the tiny well. Mia rested for a while, watching. The thrill of locating the water was diluting as all her old worries resurfaced. What if the water were a league deep? Could they tunnel that far? Even if they had the strength, how would they hold up the walls? Were they wasting precious energy in a futile search?

Then Volta's head popped up, the whites of his eyes brilliant beneath the moonlight. "I got wet sand."

Mia, all her weariness magically dispelled, jumped up and joined the others. "O.K." she said. "Now we have to start to widen it out. A small soak's alright for us, but the camels and horses have to access it too." She paused, collecting her thoughts. "We'll go deep enough to strike the flow, drink enough to keep up our strength and fill the water bottles. Then we'll open it out."

No one argued. Volta dug frantically and D2 hauled up the waste. Excitement built, crackling like ozone in the air around them. The sand got wetter and heavier, until it finally turned to grit and then quickly to coarse gravel.

D2 took over, his massive arms and shoulder muscles bulging with effort. Then his head popped up. "Wet feet!"

There was a burst of cheering and laughing at the news, Tully and Volta pounding each other's backs. Mia and Shyboy hugged spontaneously, grinning like idiots at each other. D2 watched on somberly but the end of his black tail unfurled into sight, twitching suspiciously, hinting at underlying excitement.

Mia dashed over, handing D2 a water bottle.

D2 grabbed the flask and, bending awkwardly in the hole, stooped down. The rest of them quieted and waited breathlessly. After half a minute D2 stood, lifted the flask to his lips, and tipped the contents into his mouth. He swallowed. He exuded the air of an experienced wine taster sampling a rare vintage.

"How is it?" said Mia, almost faint with worry.

D2 smacked his lips together. "Fit for a king." He took another sip. "Wasted on you lot."

Shyboy stared at D2 in astonishment. "Good grief, did you just make a… joke?"

travelled swiftly over the terrain, long legs swallowing up the land. Fed and watered, Mia felt her optimism reasserting itself. They would soon reach Alice. She was sure of it.

On and on and on they rode until the moon slowly slid down the sky and vanished. Mia was struggling to stay awake. Occasionally she would drift off, awakening with a jolt as her forehead bumped onto the front of the saddle. They must stop to make camp very soon, she thought. She began casting around for a possible campsite, but passed three good sites without stopping. And then an unsettling sensation began creeping up on her, washing her lethargy away.

She sat up sharply, looking around at the camel train but in the dim light she could detect nothing amiss. But her senses were singing. "Do you hear anything?" she said to D2, who was padding softly at Ashan's feet.

The assassin did not answer, but he paused for a moment, clearly concentrating. Then he hurried on, catching up. "Someone approaches."

Whisper lifted her head and whinnied.

Tully, ever alert, called out. "What is it?"

Mia could sense the group rousing; she knew without looking that D2 would have his automatic rifle at the ready.

Tully, Shyboy and Volta urged their camels up to Mia, milling around anxiously.

"I think someone approaches," said Mia.

"O.K.," said Tully, "everyone stay calm. It's imperative that we take the time to form a plan of action—"

Whisper took flight, the rest of the herd racing away after her. Letting out a shrill cry, Mia spurred Ashan off in their wake.

"Mia, wait!" Tully urged. But she was gone. He turned to the others. "We must have order! Or we will all perish."

Too late. Volta was away. Tully swore ferociously and looked at Shyboy in desperation. "We must have order!"

The albino grinned. "Apparently," he said, kicking his camel and accelerating away.

Tully watched furiously. "We must have discipline!" There was no reply. "That's the problem with youngsters today," Tully muttered to himself, "no damn discipline." Cursing, he urged his camel into its awkward gallop.

Volta, heart thumping like a jackhammer, flew across the flat sandy landscape, his back and seat absorbing the violent motion of his galloping beast. Ahead, he could just make out the blur that was Mia and Ashan. He looked behind and watched Tully come thundering up behind him. He heard Mia's wild tribal call echoing in the distance and his heart began fluttering fearfully. He whacked his camel, willing it on.

The sun broke over the back of the desert and lit up the world. Volta's eyes widened at the sight unfolding before him. Across the desert came a tidal wave of humanity. A hoard of horsemen galloping toward them, white robes

stained red by sunlight, like a rippling wall of flame.
Unnatural and unearthly. Volta watched the apparition with
growing trepidation. "Mia, stop!" he screamed.

But she persisted in her headlong flight and Volta watched
in helpless horror as she was swallowed up into the seething
mass. "Oh no! Oh no." It was almost a sob. Tully careered
up on his camel. Volta pointed. "We must hurry. We will
lose her."

But Tully shook his head. "I don't think so."

And in a flood of relief, Volta saw that Tully was right. The
horsemen, now rather less threatening in flamingo pink than
flame red, had formed an orderly formation and were
trotting back toward them. A camel led the way. Volta
laughed out loud, feeling foolish. In the midst of the throng
was Mia! Volta shook his head. He should have known.

Mia had brought them home.

# CHAPTER 4

A jubilant Mia approached, two horsemen flanking her. Volta glanced at both, but his attention was drawn to a rider sitting easily astride a black stallion. He was tall, his skin the soft brown of toffee. His hair was as dark as his steeds and he looked out at Volta with the sharp, knowing eyes of the falcon. Dart, thought Volta with surprise and a prickle of resentment. What on earth was Dart doing here?

"I see you, Volta of Isbane," the young man said.

Volta nodded politely, "I see you, Dart of the Overland." But before he could ask the question perched on his lips Mia came to the fore.

"Dart, how is it that you are here?"

"Shamay sent word to the tribes about the threat of war." Dart explained. "The tribes decided to bring forward the annual festivities. They gather at the oasis as we speak. The men came ahead, our women, children and elders are expected soon, travelling with the camel train."

Pleased as he was to see Mia's obvious pleasure in this unexpected news, Via was irked to be met in such a dashing style. And how did that happen? Some of the Overlander men, at least, had arrived ahead of them. They must have travelled as the crow flies at a furious pace on horseback without the need for stealth like himself and his companions. He had always sensed an element of competitiveness between himself and this self-assured young Overlander. And Volta felt uneasy, particularly when Dart was gazing at Mia in frank admiration. And just a suggestion of smug satisfaction. Volta could not forget it had been Dart who had saved their skins when they had been held captive by the dingo hybrids. And in quite some style. The git.

Mia, blithely unaware of the mild antagonism that was developing between the two men, urged Ashan to his knees, sliding off as lithely as an eel. "Volta, the mounted men are here already," she said, beaming up with a smile of pure happiness.

Volta could not resist the intensity of her emotions or the brilliance of her green eyes, sparkling like gems. She was breathtaking. He smiled back. But then he noticed that Dart was not smiling. Instead, his eyes were fixated on Mia. Volta couldn't subdue a sense of satisfaction that it was he who held Mia's attention.

He urged his camel to his knees and slid off, aware of the tiredness in his joints. But vanity forced him to bounce softly to the earth and whistle to his pony, Hawk Eye. To his fury, Hawk Eye looked around, blinked but made no move. Volta whistled again and the brown pony came ambling over

Volta grabbed one and pulled the soft, pliant skin through his fingers. "For drying off, I think."

D2 stalked over to the bath and put a finger into the water. He withdrew it quickly. "Hot." He shrugged off his automatic rifle, dropping it to the floor. Then reaching into his many pockets, he began emptying the contents. Soon pistols, knives, rounds of ammunition, a couple of grenades, nunchucks, discs of terror toxin and a wicked length of chain lay at his feet.

Shyboy reached inside his robe and dropped a small pistol next to the pile. He shook his head. "Not quite the same, is it?"

D2 launched himself, fully clothed, into the water.

Volta, Shyboy and Tully followed more slowly and more suitably attired in their grubby underwear. Volta was amused to see the big black hybrid still had a large pistol peeking out of his jacket. Waterproof, he assumed.

Water beaded, rolling off of D2's bald domed head. He sniffed. "Hot water. Good. Cold water. Very bad." He grabbed the sponge and the weed and began washing himself energetically with the resulting suds, clothes and all. He submerged beneath the water, creating a tidal wave as he burst out again blowing out a fountain. Then he hauled himself out of the bath, his clothes clinging to him like giant kelp. He shook violently. The others watched in fascination as he calmly replaced his armoury amongst his sodden, dripping clothes, and stalked out, leaving a wet trail behind him. A soft wave of dry air rushed through the doorway as he disappeared through the flap.

Volta turned to Tully. "Do you think we should tell him how fluffy and cute his tail looks?"

Tully chuckled. "Mmm. Best not push our luck."

Volta picked up the sponge and the slippery bit of weed and rubbed them together, fascinated by the sweet smelling suds that resulted. He lathered his head thoughtfully. "Do you think this place belongs to the Overlanders?"

Tully rinsed his face and shook his head. "I don't think so. As I understand it, their land lies a little west of here. I suspect this oasis may belong to Fidelus Ferguson."

"He's very rich." Volta mused.

Tully ducked his head beneath the water and came up blinking owlishly, his eyelashes stuck together like starfish. "Sorry?"

"I was saying that Ferguson is very rich."

Tully shook his head dry. "He's Alice's most notorious villain. By all accounts he's wealthier than the Western Water Company and makes our friend The Confessor look like a cheesecake."

Shyboy grinned. "Rumour has it that Ferguson's even got the Agency scared witless."

Volta was impressed. Even more intimidating than D2. Interesting. And the Agency was Isbane's feared secret police service. Rumours about their covert and sadistic practises were generally discussed in whispers. "So, what does Ferguson do? Exactly?"

"Well," said Tully, fastidiously washing behind his ears. "As you know, he's into arms. And just about anything else of importance. A finger in every festering pie, apparently."

Volta absorbed all this as he lay back in the hot water. It was hard to think. The heat of the water seemed to be sucking the energy from his body and brain. He gave up the effort after a while and just soaked lazily. His stomach growled and he opened his eyes.

"Better get out, I suppose," said Tully.

They all nodded but made no move. Shyboy, his hair restored to its normal white, reached out, grabbed his computer and switched it on. "Let's have a quick look at Alice." He tapped fluidly over the compact keyboard and Volta moved forward to take a look.

As an image emerged Volta's lethargy disappeared. "Wicked!"

# CHAPTER 5

The town of Alice was vast and filthy. Volta peered at looming constructions half hidden in smog. The grey fog moved around the edifices in lazy, sullen patterns, licking the sooty brick and smothering portions of the city entirely. But, on the outer edges, the buildings, if one could call them that, were clearer, though no cleaner.

"What are those things?" said Volta, one white wrinkled finger touching the screen.

Shyboy slapped the offending digit away.

Volta grinned as the words, 'don't touch me, you idiot' popped up on the screen in large red letters. "Neat," he commented.

Shyboy nodded.

They peered at the screen again. The tall buildings were slender. Like elongated fingers they did not appear to have any doors, windows or openings of any kind. Each rose

Mia wasn't concerned. She had great faith in her own ability when it came to the horses. "Dart, don't worry. I'm sure we'll get along famously."

Dart was silent, observing her keenly. "How about a wager?"

Mia didn't like the look on his face. She had the uncomfortable feeling that Dart was playing some kind of perverse game. "A wager on what?"

"I'll bet that the filly will buck you off twice before she's broken."

Mia gave him a scornful look. "And what do I get if she doesn't?"

Dart frowned for a moment. "I'll give you my braided saddle cloth."

Mia was delighted. Dart's mother had made that cloth, it was beautiful. She was tempted. "What if I lose? What do you want?"

"Every dance at the Promising."

Mia exploded into laughter. Finally subsiding into hiccups she took a deep breath. "You're on! I expect that saddle cloth to be wrapped and beribboned."

Volta watched silently as Dart nodded curtly at Mia and continued on his way. Betting, Volta understood. But there had been an undertone to this last conversation that troubled him. He said nothing but listened as everyone began chattering about the wager. All around, bets were being laid.

Volta wondered what a 'promising' was. He didn't like to ask. But he was bright enough to understand that Dart's undisguised interest in Mia contributed to his growing sense of uneasiness. He glanced at Mia who, by contrast, looked utterly at home. And why wouldn't she? She was home.

And then he had an epiphany. It hit him like a fist. Quite simply, it was he who was now the outsider. In Isbane it had been Mia. And during the journey from Isbane to the Overlander camp the five of them had quickly formed a supportive group. Each individual had been as necessary as the next. In that time Mia had never indicated she felt that Volta, or any of the others, were different. But here, sandwiched in by her tribe, Volta realised that Mia was not typical of her kind. Without knowing quite how, Volta knew that Dart, at least, was not as accepting. Exactly what this indicated Volta did not know. But it cast a shadow over his spirits. The future had never seemed so uncertain.

# CHAPTER 6

It was an excited and exuberant crowd that gathered around the breaking yard, which was constructed from tyres half buried in the sand. Each tyre was linked to its partner with coarse rope manufactured from prickly pear. The sandy surface of the round yard could have been tailor made for its purpose.

Dart arrived, leading the filly into the yard. She was a fine animal, a pretty dapple grey with a stocky body and fine boned head. Not as nice as Whisper, but then, Mia reflected, few were. The young Arab was already saddled and bridled and stared around at the crowd with pricked ears and bright eyes.

Dart passed over the reins to Mia. "Her name is Chameleon. Good luck," he said slyly.

It was mid-morning and hot. Mia could feel beads of perspiration tickling her forehead and trickling down her spine. She turned, looking into the horse's soft brown eyes and gently laid her hand on the velvety skin of her muzzle. "I see you, Chameleon. Let our spirits be as one."

Chameleon's ears twitched but her eyes did not leave Mia's. Then, in one swift, supple movement, Mia vaulted into the saddle. The horse froze and a hush spread over the watching crowd like an inverted Mexican wave. Mia gathered up the reins with one hand and wrapped her legs firmly around the barrel of the pony's body. Chameleon's head jerked up and she took a stiff step forward. Mia relaxed and the horse stopped still. Again she squeezed her legs. Again the horse stepped away to try to escape the pressure. Mia relaxed. Chameleon halted. Several times she repeated the aide until Chameleon gained confidence, stepping out freely. Mia sat down heavily, drawing the rein. The filly stopped so abruptly that Mia nearly tipped over the front of the saddle. A soft murmur swept over the crowd but she barely heard, utterly absorbed.

In little time she'd taught the animal to turn, stop and go. She felt a wave of satisfaction. Without a doubt Chameleon would be a fine addition to the herd. The filly questioned nothing, her ears waving around as she listened, trying to interpret Mia's signals. Mia ran a hand slowly but firmly up Chameleon's sweating neck.

Then, with one hand holding the reins loosely and the other set lightly on the front of the saddle, Mia made a soft kick with her leg. Chameleon did as Mia had hoped and startled forward, breaking into a canter. Mia remained perfectly still in the saddle, her body sitting softly, following the rhythm of the beat. She made no effort to restrain the horse, waiting for her young muscles to tire under the unaccustomed strain. After several loops of the yard the horse's head dropped abruptly as she transitioned down to trot. Again Mia remained relaxed and soon Chameleon, utterly spent, returned to a loping walk. Mia breathed deeply and gently stroked the horse's shoulder, playing out the reins to allow the filly to stretch and release tension. She sat deeper into the saddle and thought of being still. A few strides from the gate Chameleon stopped, body trembling with fatigue, sweat running in rivulets down her belly and legs.

Mia gathered herself to dismount quietly but a sound caused her to look to the east. The crowd followed suit, a loud ripple of concern spreading through their ranks. And then Mia saw them, and felt an icy finger run down her spine. Hovercraft! Mia feared and detested the flying tanks. They always spelled heartbreak. But before she could process the situation, Chameleon jerked upward, spinning wildly away. Mia could feel the filly's heart hammering, even though she could not hear it over the throbbing noise of the approaching hovercraft. She felt a moment of panic and considered jumping off the frightened youngster. But she knew that if she abandoned her, Chameleon would be spoiled. Mia was still wavering when the fleet was upon them, bursting her eardrums, and whipping up a maelstrom of wind. One of the tyres began rocking. Chameleon let out a shriek of terror and reared. Mia clung on with all her might. Just as Mia felt that she must fall, Chameleon came crashing down to earth, all coherent thought lost. And bolted.

As the line of tyres towered up in front of them, Mia felt a jab of fear. She needn't worry about the Isbane army,

Chameleon was going to crash. They would probably both be killed. A great rush of air shot out of her lungs as she felt the horse gathering herself. They left the ground and Mia watched the tyres beneath her as they went soaring clean across.

The landing was less elegant. Mia was somehow now sitting in front of the saddle, right up on Chameleon's neck. Breathless, she scrambled back awkwardly, praying to Sol that Chameleon didn't choose to shy or buck, because she would surely be a goner. But Chameleon didn't waver from her goal of putting the desert between herself and the predator in the sky.

For several lengths Mia made no effort to control the horse. Her limbs felt watery and weak, and she was flat out catching her breath. But as she recovered from the shock, Mia began looking around to try and gauge where they were. Briefly she glanced behind, scared of what she might find. But she had travelled a long way and the oasis was a just dot on the landscape. Her keen eyes swept the shimmering, golden sand for any sign of moving shadows, afraid the hovercraft might be on her tail. She was a wanted woman, after all.

At last Chameleon began to slow, her breath rasping. Mia drew the rein in a fraction and Chameleon finally fell back into a walk. Mia turned for home, eyes peeled for trouble, expecting to see smoke and fire curling into the sky. She felt sick with fear despite past reassurance that the presence of Fidelus Ferguson in Alice would protect them. If the army hurt more of her people, she would never forgive herself.

They covered the ground slowly, Chameleon utterly spent. Mia found herself torn between anxiety for the filly's well being and a desperate desire to gallop home to see what was happening. Her imagination was running wild, as she envisioned a camp filled with mutilated, suffering people. She thought she could hear the distant thunder of gunshot.

And then two dark blobs materialized in the distance. She stood in her stirrups, shading her eyes to get a better look. With a whistling sigh of relief she sat back, as the blobs turned into horsemen, racing toward her. Frustrated by her own slow passage she could only wait for them to cover the distance.

Volta's heart leapt for joy at the sight of the distant figure plodding across the desert. It was Mia, still on the grey and hopefully unharmed. But his spirits dampened as the big black stallion beside him began accelerating effortlessly away. Volta's mild antagonism toward Dart jumped up a notch. He kicked Hawk Eye in the ribs. Hawk Eye ignored him and continued rolling along at his top speed, a rocking horse canter. Gallop was obviously not on the menu.

"You rotten mule," Volta said. Hawk Eye slowed a little. And then, to underscore Volta's frustration, Tully went sweeping by with a wave.

Volta scowled. It looked like he was coming in third. A heartbeat later, half a dozen armed, mounted men went surging past him. His mouth tightened into a hard line. Make that last. By the time he arrived Mia was hidden, completely surrounded by her escort. Volta slotted in behind. Inevitably, he could make out the tall figure of Dart, distinctive in his black and red cowl. And Volta knew, without seeing, that the young man would be sticking like a leech to Mia's side. Resentment and frustration coursed through him. Truth was, he'd become used to Mia's company. He had taken it for granted. But not any more. Now it seemed to have evolved into a competition.

Laughter spilled out of the tight knit group, carrying on the hot wind. Volta wondered what was so funny. He felt excluded and suspected that — on Dart's behalf at least — this could be deliberate.

"You O.K.?"

Volta was jerked out of his reverie as Tully trotted up beside him.

"I'm fine, thanks," he said. And he did feel better, his sense of isolation fading in the light of Tully's familiar presence.

Tully pointed to the west, toward the camp. The desert shimmered in the heat, rippling like water. "Looks like it was a flying visit. The hovers, I mean. What do you think that was about?"

"They were definitely from Isbane. They were armed hovercraft."

Tully was quiet for a minute, eyes searching the skies. "Do you think they knew we were here? Came looking for us?"

Volta sighed, and nodded. "Without a doubt."

"Still," said Tully. "We're safe. For now."

But to Volta, Tully sounded unsure. While the Overlanders had confidence in the protective influence of Alice and the enigmatic figure of Fidelus Ferguson, Volta was only too aware that at some stage, they would have to leave. And the army would be waiting. The sand guns that they were hoping to purchase, he reflected, were beginning to look more and more appealing.

"When we get back, Shy's got something to show us," said Tully.

Another wave of hilarity wafted toward them. Volta closed his ears and forced himself to focus. "Do you think his fan club will let us have a minute?" Shyboy had become immensely popular since sharing his computer with members of the camp.

Tully smiled. "Shyboy downloaded a heap of games yesterday. They just lap 'em up."

Volta cheered up, suddenly feeling more optimistic. As the party finally swept back into the camp he waited for Mia, wanting to pass on the news about Shyboy. At least, that's what he told himself. He watched as she dismounted and he could see the fatigue in her movements. She lifted the reins over the equally exhausted horse's head and began walking away. Volta hesitated, suddenly unsure.

Then she stopped, looking back. She glared at Volta. "Where've you been? What are you and Tully so cozy about? Come and tell me." She sounded pretty pissed.

Ridiculously happy, he nudged Hawk Eye on, passing a few metres from Dart. He could feel the young man's eyes boring into his back. But he quickly forgot as he joined Mia. There were more important things to think about.

# CHAPTER 7

Pavan's lips tightened in a thin line of disapproval. She pressed her finger hard on the door bell, listening to the deep gongs resonating inside. In a fit of pique she did not release the button, taking great satisfaction in the act. The door opened, revealing a small, scared figure. Pavan scowled down at the woman, who cowered in terror.

Pavan examined the maid minutely, scanning for any signs of hybrid. She was not going to quickly forget Beatrice, a foul hybrid impostor previously — and disastrously — in Wolfram's employ. But while the girl had a mousey countenance, with her small-boned body, brown scared eyes and wispy blonde hair, she did appear to be human. Just. Pavan sniffed and swept into her brother's palatial apartment. The effect was diminished as she was levitated upward, her robes swirling in an undignified manner around her knees.

For his part, Wolfram made no attempt to hide his amusement at his sister's discomfort.

"Turn it off!" Pavan snapped, trying to hold down her skirts.

Wolfram put down his hot chocolate and floated easily to the far wall where he twiddled a small round button. Grinning, he watched as Pavan thudded down. The smile faded as he waddled painfully back to his seat. Without his floatator, Wolfram was feeling once more the full effect of the earth's gravitational pull. His knees were aching abominably, as were his back and neck. He'd have to seriously think about a reduction and knee replacements. An abysmal prospect. He snapped his fingers and the maid came racing over. He pointed to the door and she went scurrying out.

Pavan sat down. "You're getting obese," she said, her voice laden with spite.

Wolfram did not reply but took a loud slurp of his drink, his lips smacking together in satisfaction. He ignored Pavan, knowing this would serve to further irritate her.

Pavan's eyes narrowed. "Well?"

Wolfram's piggy eyes widened in their folds of skin. "Well, what?"

Pavan exploded. She leaned down, slamming her fist upon the table. The hot chocolate threatened to exit its cup. "Don't play games with me, Wolfram. You're in this as deep as I am. Volta and his little friends are in Alice." She paused for breath, leaning into Wolfram's face. "What are we going to do?"

"First, you're going to get out of my face and compose yourself."

Pavan sneered, but backed off.

Wolfram nodded. "That's more like it." Despite his calm exterior he was secretly shaken. Pavan appeared to be on the verge of a meltdown. This was not good. "It's true, they are at Alice. But we know that the Overlanders meet there regularly to trade. All we have to do is sit tight and wait it out. They'll move on. Then we can sort this out with minimal fuss."

Pavan shifted in her chair uneasily. She knew she had to tell Wolfram what she'd done, but quailed at the prospect. He was going to be rightfully furious. If the Directorate found out she'd acted without their approval she'd be toast. The Isbane governing body gave her a long rein but there were still limits. She swallowed. "I'm afraid it's too late for the niceties."

Wolfram froze, his eight hundred and eighty year old brain on red alert. "What have you done?"

Pavan looked away, drumming her long golden fingernails on the table surface. "I sent in a reconnaissance team this morning."

Wolfram felt as if the air was pressing down and squashing him. Momentarily he was speechless. He just sat. The silence built up like an invisible force field. Finally he shook his head. "You fool. Whatever possessed you?"

Pavan glanced at him, a small quiver of anger flickering in her chest. The fury that had prompted this foolish action was not completely extinguished. To be outsmarted by a bunch of mutant monstrosities was humiliation enough, but Volta's disappearance had left her open to snide comments and disrespectful sniggering behind her back. It was intolerable. For the first time in her long life she felt vulnerable. She felt afraid. She wanted to drop a great big bomb on the lot of them. Alice and all. Bloody Fidelus Ferguson was expendable. Everyone was expendable.

She lifted her hands, palms up in a conciliatory gesture. "I'm sorry."

Wolfram observed her minutely. An apology was the last thing he'd anticipated. He doubted it was sincere but decided to play along. "Apology accepted. What's done is done. We must try to minimize the damage." He reached across the desk and pressed a small button. A compartment in the ceiling opened silently and a computer dropped slowly to the table. In seconds Wolfram mailed a message. They sat waiting, both preoccupied with their own thoughts.

The machine bleeped and a face appeared. It was a man. He was handsome, with short dark hair, streaked white at the temples. He looked at them with piercing blue eyes, hedged with thick black lashes. "What are you playing at?" he said.

"Ferguson, how are you?" said Wolfram, jovially.

The blue eyes narrowed. "Pissed."

Wolfram smiled ingratiatingly. "Of course you are. Quite understandable, I'm sure."

Ferguson was silent for a minute, his mouth tightening a fraction. "Who authorized the hovercraft? That was out of order."

"A terrible mistake, Ferguson! A simple misunderstanding. A case of the old Chinese whisper phenomena. You know how it is?"

Ferguson lifted a finger, pointing at his audience. "This little 'mistake' has impeded business. And undermined my authority. I'll be after compensation." He paused and smiled. The smile did not travel to his eyes. "Or worse."

Wolfram bowed his head. "Compensation! Of course. A few water bonds will help smooth things over I'm sure. You know, oil a few cogs and all that."

"A few water bonds?" Ferguson laughed contemptuously. "My family is upset. Threatened. Scared. And when my family is upset — I'm upset. I want three hundred thousand bonds. Today."

Pavan gasped. The presumptuous little oik. She'd give him three hundred thousand bonds! She tried to stand but found herself restrained by her robes. Irritated, she turned, trying to see what the problem was. Her temper was not improved when she realised that Wolfram was gripping her beneath the table. For a few seconds she strained furiously, but aware she was missing the moment, gave up. What she had to say could be said just as well sitting down.

But Wolfram beat her to it. "Three hundred thousand? More than fair. I'll see to it."

Ferguson jerked his head in a gesture of acceptance and the screen went blank.

Wolfram let his sister go.

Pavan stood up jerkily. "Three hundred thousand? Are you insane?"

"You can afford it," Wolfram said softly. He watched her swelling with indignation. It cheered him up immensely.

"I'm not handing over a single bond to that… to that… terrorist!"

Wolfram smiled, his teeth bared. "Well, I'll leave it to you to tell him so."

Almost spitting with fury, Pavan swept out of the room.

She'd pay, of course. She knew it. Wolfram knew it. And Ferguson knew it.

# CHAPTER 8

He did not know what day it was. He did not even know where he was. Why he was still there remained a mystery. Sometimes he felt less substantial than his own shadow. But still he waited. He had not given up hope. He did not dare to.

He looked at the off-white wall. There was no choice. Unless he looked at the off-white floor, or the off-white door. He whistled a jaunty tune. The sound comforted him. And his mind filled with a picture of his daughter, laughing up into his face. But the whistling ceased abruptly. Her features had become a little blurred. Indistinct. Panic squeezed in his chest but he swallowed it down. It was inevitable, really. Besides, everyone had their off days.

He sat up a little straighter, his keen ears picking up a sound. He stood and paced to the door. Breakfast. Although, he rationalised, there was no way of knowing if it was morning or night. A wave of grief and longing swept over him. Every atom in his body ached. It ached for the sight of the sky, the smell of the sand and the sound of loved ones. At first he had believed that, in time, the tearing agony of separation would recede. It hadn't, but it surprised him less.

A sound broke through his preoccupation. He pressed his ear to the door. Yes. It was definitely a food trolley. He could recognise the heavy rumbling of the wheels and its constant pausing. As the trolley approached, the stops and starts became louder. The food itself, although nutritionally adequate, was not appealing. Sheer willpower forced him to keep eating. He had to keep his strength up. What really drew him irresistibly to the door was the source of the trolley's locomotion. Quite simply, another living person.

There was a faint scratching sound and the flap in the door fell open. The man was so tall he had to bend down to look through. There was no one there. But then a figure, carrying a tray, came out from behind the tall trolley and into sight. And a thrill went through him.

She lifted the tray, poking it through the small gap. But he did not take it. For a few seconds she did not move. She did not look at him, her eyes focusing on a spot somewhere at her feet.

The man brought his hand in a graceful gesture to his forehead. "I see you, Woman of the Desert."

He could see her startle. The tray wobbled dangerously. He resisted the impulse to steady it. Scared that if he did, she would be gone. Then she looked at him. Man and woman both stared. Green on amber. Her face was taut and drawn, the muscles on her arms starkly visible beneath the pelt stretching over her emaciated frame. Her hands were thin and clawed but dexterous. He smiled, closing his eyes to inhale heartbreakingly familiar scents. Of earth and smoke and open space. Of sun. For a moment the confines of his cell peeled away and he was alive again, riding flat out across the desert.

Then a sharp sound bought him back.

"Take it!" The woman tapped the tray again. Her voice was dry and rough. The amber eyes urgent.

He sensed her distress and reluctantly took the tray. "I thank you," he said.

She blinked and then the flap snapped shut. He could hear the trolley moving on.

For a minute he stood stock still, the tray hovering at chest level. When he could hear the trolley no more he put the tray on his mattress and sat down. Automatically he inspected the tray. Nothing new. A thick gruel, which he thought was sorghum. A sludgy drink coloured a pale pink. A cup of bright orange water. Absent-mindedly he picked up the gruel, scooping the plastic spoon through it. But the spoon didn't make it to his mouth. He dropped the spoon and got up, pacing around. The unexpected communication with the woman filled him with an odd sense of expectation. It was as if she were... an omen.

She pushed the trolley on. Stopping and starting. She tried not to think and not to see. The airless, windowless place scared her. Sometimes she could barely breathe. Constantly she had to resist the urge to abandon the trolley and run. Despite the dense population, the place was eerily quiet. Every time she opened a door flap she dreaded looking in. She feared the dead, hopeless eyes. Although they never spoke she could feel the waves of anguish rolling off them. She could literally smell their fear.

She despised herself for being part of such a horror. Anger crashed around in her chest. What sort of world was it that reduced her to this? To relieve her stress she imagined walking out and walking away. Far away. Her spirit lifted and then came crashing down. There was no escape. She must feed her children. They were all she had left. They must survive. Although what the future held for them filled her with foreboding. She felt almost as imprisoned as those locked in. Every day she came back. She coped by reducing her thoughts to the trolley and the trays. There was no room in her life for pity or empathy. Life held out none to her.

She tried to focus on the end of her shift. Exhaustion waved over her, but she pushed it aside. She would take the boys out hunting. They must learn to kill effectively. If anything happened to her — with an effort she pushed this thought away. The trolley wheels rolled around in different directions, bringing her to an abrupt halt. She kicked the two offside ones wearily, too tired to be irritated. With a small jerk the trolley rolled on. Time stood still. Down the endless corridor she travelled. The trolley grew lighter, her stride increasing as the pile of trays slowly diminished.

She flipped open the second to last flap. Automatically she lifted the tray, her mind already focused outside the building, on the long trek home. With a sigh, she pushed the tray in. She let out a loud yell, the tray banging to the ground in a sticky mess as a hand gripped her wrist. Instinctively she pulled back, drawing the clutching hand toward her. She tried prising the fingers off. It was a small hand. Slowly, slowly the little fingers unfurled. And finally let go. The hand hung limply for a moment and then slowly withdrew.

Trembling with shock, the woman tentatively bent down, peering in from a safe distance. A pair of soft brown eyes looked back. It was a hybrid. Through a mop of curly brown hair a pair of long, soft ears were just visible.

"Help me," said the child.

The woman froze, shocked. Slowly the child slid down a wall, slumping onto the cold floor. But the woman could not respond. A child! In this place! It was incomprehensible. Her mind reached out to her own, half-grown boys. Panic filled her. They were not safe. Nausea curdled her stomach. She forced herself to look again at the pathetic shape on the floor. Against her will, a wave of pity wiggled its way forward. She tried to shove it away. It was sad, yes. But what could she do? Why should she care? Even if she did, who would listen? She had her own worries. Didn't she? Who cared for her? No one. That was who. If she said anything she'd lose her job. At that thought sweat broke out over her body. She shook her head. She could do nothing for this little scrap. She'd just walk away. But still her hand held the flap aloft.

The little body moved. Thin arms wrapped around bony knees and the hybrid began rocking. It was a strangely terrible sight. Backward and forward she swayed, emitting a high whistling sound that the woman doubted a human would hear. She could not move her eyes away from the desolate sight, aware she was witnessing a depth of misery to which she had mercifully been spared.

Slowly she leaned in until her lips were level with the opening. "I see you, child."

The child visibly stiffened.

"I see you, child."

The small ears lifted, two eyes peering up suspiciously. The child blinked. And smiled.

The sound of a door banging sent the woman flying back. The flap locked down. Heart pounding, she glanced furtively down the corridor. A bed with wheels was navigating toward her, pushed by two nurses. She grabbed the trolley and with a vicious jerk, set off. Such was her agitation that she nearly forgot to deliver the last tray. To her relief the occupant of the room took the tray without incident. She hurried to the lift. She shuffled in beside another member of staff. Neither acknowledged the other. They travelled in silence as they plummeted down to the kitchen.

Finally she clocked out, passing through the security scanner. As always, she waited tense with fear for the green light to glow and for the door to open. As the door hissed aside she sped through. Only as she heard the soft suctioning behind her did she breathe again. She lifted her head and looked up at the sky. She sucked in a lungful of dry, hot air. She shook herself and set off down the hard packed earth of the road. As always, much of her fatigue washed away and she travelled swiftly. The stench of the camp came drifting to her long before she saw it. But the acrid smells of poverty no longer worried her. Indeed, it just smelt like home.

She veered around the camp, keeping a watchful eye on the makeshift tents, plastic lined boxes, abandoned containers and concrete pipes. Fires smoked sullenly and rubbish spread untidily. There were hundreds of inhabitants, but it was surprisingly quiet. Individuals tended to hunker down, withdrawn and hostile. An occasional harsh, angry shout could be heard, but the atmosphere was one of slow, simmering desperation.

Past the camp, she headed out into the mountainous terrain. There was a little cover in the shape of stunted bushes and trees, as well as the undulations of the land. Despite this she stopped often, eyes searching and nose questing the air. With infinite patience she travelled to her camp. Each day she chose a different path. Each day she worried. What if she had not been careful enough?

Finally she paused, scanning the landscape. Satisfied, she pushed through a crop of spiny bushes, dropped down onto a rocky ledge and peered into the depths of a cave. Three pairs of identical eyes looked back. Seconds later she was submerged beneath bodies as her children greeted her. She tried to push them off but little hands crept under her armpits and tickled, reducing her to hysterical helplessness.

"Stop!" she gasped.

Finally spent, her young sons, grinning toothily, let her be. She lay still for a few minutes to regain her breath. She could feel their eyes upon her and for a brief moment her troubles melted away. These were her boys. Three bright, healthy, exuberant bundles of energy. There was nothing that she would not do for them. She sat up and grinned back, her nose wrinkling up. She patted her faded green trousers and slipped a hand into a deep pocket. Like a magician she pulled out three plastic sachets and tossed them neatly toward her young. They jumped up, catching them mid flight.

She sat back against the cool stone wall of the cave and listened as they concentrated on preparing the contents. A simple procedure of adding bottled water and stirring. Personally, she thought that the gluey drinks were horribly sweet. But the boys loved them, and were still fascinated by the novelty. Sometimes she worried that it was unwise to take the packets which were described as 'out of date'. She didn't understand this, but understood they were destined for the bin. She did not consider it stealing and would not have worried much if it had been. But she did worry that she may get found out. She relaxed a little as the boys settled down to devour the strange mixture. There must, she thought, be something good in them, for the boys looked well. Better, she knew, than herself.

"Bidgee, Paroo, Woomba."

The boys ceased licking out their cups, looking up with hopeful faces.

"Today we will hunt."

There was an explosion of yipping and general high jinks as the half grown boys let off steam. They had spent almost fourteen hours hidden in the cave, waiting for their mother to return. Their strong young limbs twitched and ached for action. Besides, hunting was the best!

By the time they were dressed and armed they had sobered up, slipping out of the cave like shadows. As she climbed, the woman stumbled, dislodging an outcrop of shale and soil. She steadied herself, found her balance and looked down for a better foot hold. Something caught her eye. She bent down and picked up a stone, holding it up to the light. She let out a gasp of superstitious fear and wonder, for trapped within the depths of the black rock, was a brilliant red streak of lightning.

Out in the sunlight she paused, calling the boys to her. One by one they examined the magical stone, their eyes wide. They gasped when the sunlight caught on the surface making the stone blaze with power.

The woman finally stowed it away in her clothes but continued to ponder on it as she led her sons to the hunting ground. It was as if the destructive force of a storm had been trapped in its hard core. It was both beautiful and awesome. She felt that it must have worth beyond her own understanding. It was light in the darkness.

Even while she hunted, her hand unconsciously reached for the small, hard lump at her waist. Luck was with them. In a short time they caught a large goanna. Meat enough for several days. She smiled to herself as the boys strutted ahead, chunks of lizard hanging over their underdeveloped shoulders. They had done well. Their father would have been proud. The smile died. The sun beat down on her head. Back at the cave she collapsed onto the sandy floor. With the stone clutched in her hand she fell into the dreamless sleep of the exhausted.

# CHAPTER 9

The man sat quietly. There was little else to do. Occasionally sounds would penetrate his cell but he took little notice. Everything was familiar. Each bump, tap of foot, rumble or voice. His hearing was acute but becoming more so as time went by. He could pick up the tiniest variation of noise. He had begun to distinguish the different footfalls of the people who moved around him. He pondered on the desert woman. She was new to him. He wondered what had brought her to this alien place. Her presence triggered memories of life from before. Some things forgotten, returning. The sweeping, upturned wings of the eagle. The vivid colours of the women's tunics as they danced. The smell of horse. It bought a small measure of comfort. He lived in terror of forgetting, for he felt that when his people were lost to him, he would be lost to his people.

His eyes opened, tension stealing through his body. His face fell into grim lines. As tightly sprung as a cornered snake, he waited. The heavy, deliberate footfalls continued toward him. He held his breath, senses questing. Then, as the footsteps grew louder, his body unwound in a fluid motion and he stood. He waited. They might not stop. But seconds later the steps ceased and he heard the ping of the security pad being pressed.

The door swung slowly open to reveal a man dressed in white. White shirt, white pants and white shoes. His skin was pale, like uncooked dough and his facial features slack. Blackheads peppered his nose. His rubbery lips formed into a snide smile. "We can do this the hard way, or we can do it the easy way," he said softly.

It was a face that the man had learned to loathe. With every atom of his being the man longed for the cool weight of an automatic rifle in his hands. He knew he could slaughter this creature without an ounce of remorse.

But nothing of this internal stress was evident. The vivid green eyes narrowed slightly. His people had never bent to tyranny and he did not intend to be the first. His heart began accelerating as chemicals exploded into his bloodstream. Abruptly he lifted his chin and the ululating war cry of his people burst into the room. It echoed eerily down the long empty corridor beyond the open door. The sound died away and for a second there was a hush. Then voices raised and a rhythmic banging reverberated as dozens of inmates responded to the man's defiance.

And that was the thing that really pissed off Nurse Emeric Elapid. This prisoner's strange, almost psychic connection with the other scum. Elapid could deal with the inmate's arrogance, his pride, his delusional beliefs and his violence.

But this uncanny campaign of resistance really gave him haemorrhoids. Corridor Eight in Block Seven was the only area in the facility where such anarchy existed. And Elapid planned to eradicate it at any cost. There would be no insurrection on his watch. He glanced quickly behind him and reassured, stepped smartly into the doorway. Three nurses followed, hard on his heels.

But the prisoner was ready. He could sense their twisted excitement and despised them for it. He stood lightly on his bare feet, muscles taut with anticipation. In some strange way he had almost come to welcome these confrontations. Whilst he realised he could never win, these sporadic incidents made him feel real. Made him feel alive. The loud shouts and bangs on the other cell doors gave him a bizarre sense of belonging. The paralysing loneliness abated.

Nurse Elapid pointed at the man's chest, jerking his chin toward the doorway. "Move it out."

The prisoner stood his ground.

Elapid took a tentative step closer, the last confrontation's bruises and broken fingers firmly lodged in the forefront of his mind. Hence the reinforcements. He pulled a plastic syringe and small dart gun from his pocket. Quickly he fed the syringe into the mechanism, twisting the safety catch free. "Out! Now!" he said, smiling.

The prisoner eyed the mechanism warily. Something new. He watched as the nurse took another step, more confident now, unclipping a stun gun from his belt.

The prisoner lashed out with one foot and the stun gun flew from the nurse's hand, ricocheting off the ceiling, whereupon it was neatly caught by the prisoner. Elapid cursed and looked frantically behind him. But he need not have worried, his panting staff were surging in around him, stun guns quivering. "Get him!"

Eager to please, they raced in. Thirty seconds later they retreated, two dragging the unconscious body of the third.

Elapid was delighted. The dart of terror toxin was not exactly a banned substance, but it could only be used under extreme provocation. By his reckoning, one unconscious and two crippled staff was provocation enough.

The prisoner had received a number of nasty wounds. His cheeks and eyes were swelling. His lip was split and blood spattered his clothes. He waited, eyes locked onto the only nurse still standing. He was very aware of the open door, the snivelling staff and the one remaining obstacle. He weighed the stun gun in his hand and launched himself forward. As he did so, he felt a soft mist of cold on his face. His eyes closed involuntarily, stinging and sore. He dropped the gun, rubbing at his eyes.

Aware of movement, he forced his streaming eyes open. It took half a minute for his vision to refocus. His whole body jerked in shock and a wild scream ripped from his throat. "Mia!"

He went berserk. He fought to get out of the cell, slamming, punching and kicking, trying desperately to get to the trolley on which his child lay. Pale and still. "Mia! No!"

Then something hit him hard just above his right eye. He fought on blindly, but his legs sagged as his brain finally quit. His breathing became shallow and rapid until his green eyes began rolling up into his head. "Mia," he whispered.

Silence ensued. Elapid and his intrepid crew stood back from the body warily, gasping for breath. They looked as if they'd just failed a crash course in survival. If he'd been conscious, their prisoner would have been well pleased.

Elapid was secretly shaken. Things had not gone according to plan. He dropped to the ground, wincing as a couple of fractured ribs grated together. Two fingers found a pulse in the prisoner's neck. His relief was profound. While his superiors did not begrudge him his fun, the death of an inmate was not welcome. Elapid was cunning enough to realise that this particular patient was special. His premature demise would definitely blight any future chances of promotion.

With a conscious effort, the nurse pulled himself together and sent one of the others limping off to get a trolley. As he waited, the quiet began to get on his nerves. He could visualize the rest of the inmates sitting in their cells. For a moment he wondered what they were thinking. But this unnerved him. He was not an imaginative man, but even he could sense the hostility trapped within those walls.

When the trolley arrived he helped haul the inert body up. The body was strapped down. Without a word Elapid pushed the trolley up the corridor. As he pushed he began to invent a plausible story to explain the damage.

When he reached the theatre doors, they slid open. A gowned and masked figure came out, observing the trolley. A frown wrinkled up the man's forehead. "What's the meaning of this?"

Elapid shrugged his shoulders. "Man went crazy. I've got injured staff. One's out cold. Had to resort to the toxin."

The surgeon did not reply but his steady gaze did not waver.

Elapid began to sweat. "Ask anyone. This one's been trouble from the start."

An eyebrow raised.

Despite the mask, Elapid sensed the surgeon's disbelief. "Ask the others," he muttered, his pale eyes looking every which way but at the ones in front of him. He hastily shoved the trolley through the gap. The doors slid silently shut in his face. He cursed for a few seconds and retreated back down the corridor.

Inside the surgical theatre the staff peered anxiously at the unconscious man. The atmosphere relaxed as vital signs checked out O.K.

"He's tough," said a woman's muffled voice from behind her mask.

The surgeon grunted. "Just as well."

The team worked quickly, removing blood, spinal fluid and skin samples. Two of the team unrobed and took the man back to his cell, placing him on his mattress.

The man awoke and opened his eyes. He thought he'd heard
the door close but he couldn't be sure. The front of his head
was throbbing and his back hurt. He sat up groggily, his
head spinning. For several moments he just sat. Finally thirst
pushed him to his feet. He staggered over to a shelf built into
the wall and poured a drink from a jug. The water slid down
his parched throat. He felt a little better.

He undressed and observed himself minutely. There were
the usual puncture marks in his arms and a few raw looking
patches of skin on his stomach. Awkwardly he bent his arm
behind his back and his fingers groped up and down the
length of his spine. Toward the bottom he found a small
dressing. He ripped it off and felt a wound. The area was
tender and aching. After a few more minutes he was
satisfied that nothing else was amiss. Still, it was enough.

These invasions of his body filled him with foreboding.
They always left him depressed and anxious at his own
helplessness. He sat cross-legged on the bed, pondering on
the incident. What did they want? Why didn't they just ask?
He had no idea, of course. He sensed they were removing
his blood and skin. But he could not imagine what they had
done to his spine. Most frightening was not so much what
they had done but what else they planned to do.

At moments like this he could feel despair perching like a
predator on his shoulder. He began to give prayer to the
ancestors. He reached out to Sol, asking for strength. He
prayed for his loved ones. He smiled as the ancestors
gathered around him, speaking words of kindness. They

spoke of days long gone and of days to come. They spoke of the Overlander way. Entranced, he listened.

How long they remained he did not know. But when they left, he felt at peace. Able to cope. He could feel the courage of his people, past and present, surging through his blood. This led him to thinking about his own children, his blood. His future. In the end, he would never really be gone. He would live on through them. He knew that Mia had not really been here, that it had been some kind of hallucination. A cruel trick. What sort of people were these? Who were their ancestors that they could have sunk so low? In what did they believe? He shook his head. He almost pitied them.

He tilted his head, listening as a trolley came rumbling down the corridor. He remembered the Woman of the Desert. Throwing on his clothes he hurried to the door. Patiently he counted the stops and starts as the trolley made its laborious journey. Finally it paused directly behind his cell door. The flap opened and a tray slid through. He took the tray, bending down to peer through the slot. She was there.

The woman looked nervously up and down the corridor. All was quiet. "I see you, Man of the Desert," she said, her voice low and husky.

The deep lines of his face softened. "I see you, Woman of the Desert. I am Valley."

"Tacker," she said. "My name is Tacker."

He opened his mouth to reply but the flap shut. He stood still, listening as the trolley rolled away. The clattering noise finally faded. Then he paced over to his bed and sat down, his eyes glancing listlessly over the tray. More of the same-old-same-old. Corn bread, beans and a pink drink. Then he spotted something slipped under the edge of his plate. A small, oval rock. He picked it up curiously. He held it cupped in his hand as if it were the greatest treasure upon the earth. He felt its hardness, its enduring toughness. He lifted it to his nose and inhaled its earthy scent. Rolling it around, he admired its proportions. And then he gasped as light caught on the black surface. Deep inside the rock, red lightning flared, sending a rainbow shimmering across the wall. It was so beautiful. Magical. He smiled and looked at the door.

His fingers touched his forehead. "I thank you, Tacker, Woman of the Desert," he said softly.

# CHAPTER 10

Volta could not believe his ears. "You have got to be kidding!" He spat out each word, every syllable a vehement protest.

Mia giggled.

Volta gave her a look that should have melted the flesh from her bones. She had the good grace to cover her mouth and look at her feet. But her obvious amusement did not improve his temper. "Whose idea was it?"

Volta looked from face to face, his scowl deepening. They all looked guilty. But his gaze lingered on Tully who suddenly seemed fascinated by a fly that was crawling slowly up his left hand. His gaze travelled to D2, Shyboy and to Mia, but then slid irresistibly back to his bodyguard. Tully was whistling softly under his breath and watching the insect avidly. Volta sniffed loudly and pointed. "It was you." This time, it was not a question.

Tully continued to scrutinize his hand, despite the fact that the fly had disappeared.

"Tully!" said Volta loudly.

Tully jumped visibly and looked at his young charge with an expression of injured innocence that would have impressed both a judge and jury. "Yes?"

Volta, however, was not taken in. After all, he was the master of deception."This was your idea, wasn't it?"

Tully did not reply and Volta could almost hear his man's brain buzzing.

Ultimately, Tully sighed. "Yes, it was my idea."

Volta crowed victoriously. "Hah! I knew it!" He sat down on a large woven mat in the middle of the tent. For a moment he forgot his angst in his delight at getting one up on Tully. A rare occurrence. Slowly the rest of them settled to the floor around him.

Mia picked up the dress, shaking it out gently. The filmy material floated momentarily in the air and then settled softly onto the ground with a sigh. "Honestly Volta, it'll look lovely with your eyes."

Volta eyed the dress as if it were about to make a full frontal assault. He shook his head violently. "Not going to happen."

Tully tutted with exasperation. "Volta, you've seen the news. You've got a bounty of two hundred thousand water bonds on your head. It's a fortune by anyone's reckoning. Too much temptation for many."

This irritated Volta. "What about your bounty; it's almost as much! I don't see you offering to dress up like a girl."

"I'm too ugly," said Tully.

"True," said Shyboy.

Volta's mouth twitched, but he held back the smile with steely determination. The vision of Tully in a dress was pretty hilarious. He — however — had absolutely no intention of making a spectacle of himself. Already he could envision Dart's lively amusement. Capture seemed preferable to humiliation.

Then Mia cleared her throat and raised her head. "Volta, please listen. You can't go to Alice without a disguise. It's too dangerous."

"Hang on," said Shyboy, thrusting his hand into a bag and pulling out what Volta thought was a dead animal. Shyboy shook the furry thing and thrust it at Volta.

Volta startled and leant away.

Tully rolled his eyes. "It's just a wig, doofus."

Volta was not much wiser. "What's a wig?"

"It's false hair," said Shyboy. To demonstrate he jumped up and jammed the furry mop onto Mia's head.

Mia parted the curly black hair and peered out. "I'm gonna wear some army pants and a shirt, and Shy's lending me a pair of wrap-around shades. I'll be practically invisible."

She looked so bizarre that Volta started grinning. "Looking like that, you'll be practically certifiable."

Shyboy hastily turned the wig around. Volta collapsed into fits of laughter. Even D2 grinned.

Mia glared at them. "What? What's so funny?" She turned to Shyboy. "Pass me a mirror."

There wasn't one but Shyboy kindly snapped an image of Mia on his computer.

Mia peered anxiously at her picture and nearly dropped the laptop in horror. She rounded on Tully. "I look like a freak! I'm not wearing that!"

It was true. The black wig made her skin unhealthily pale. The fringe sat low over her eyebrows giving her features a furtive expression. It was not, Volta thought happily, a good look.

Tully lost patience. "It's not a beauty pageant. It's a disguise. Besides, everyone's freaky at Retrospectro."

Volta felt a little less resentful. In truth the huge bounty on Tully, D2, Mia, and himself had shaken him. It was sheer luck that Shyboy had so far evaded identification. Volta understood that a disguise was essential if he wanted to go to Alice. And he did. The idea of being left behind was intolerable. After all he'd heard about the infamous nightclub, Retrospectro, and its owner, The Madonna, he was in a lather to check it out.

He looked at Mia again. She looked mutinous. He grinned to himself. In all honesty, he felt he'd be a much better looking girl than Mia would a boy. And besides, Mia's wrath and indignation acted as a salve to his wounds. He decided to be magnanimous and rise to the occasion. While he might look a sight, Mia wasn't exactly going to shine either. There was a certain amount of comfort in that. To say nothing of Dart's exposure to a less than lovely Mia.

He stood, his face heating up. "I'll wear the dress."

Tully pretended he hadn't heard. "What was that?"

Volta sighed, holding out his hand. "The dress. I'll wear it."

Mia dropped the wig on the floor. "It's not fair! Volta will look gorgeous in his outfit. I'll look hideous!"

For a moment Volta was offended. But then the full ridiculousness of their predicament hit him. He snorted with laughter.

Mia glared at Volta. Then she looked at the wig on the floor. It looked like a dehydrated rat. What would people think? She sniffed and forced herself to be more honest. What she really meant was, what would Dart think? And, irritatingly enough, what would Volta think? She looked at Volta who had picked up the wig and put it on his own head. He looked ridiculous. She was determined to be cross. Her eyebrows swooped together in a fierce scowl. How dare he make her care about how she looked!

How dare he complicate her life.

# CHAPTER 11

Mia's crotchety mood dissolved as the meeting continued. She soon forgot her angst as Shyboy switched on his computer. She peered eagerly over Volta's shoulder to take a look at the first tangible evidence of their strategy. Well, she thought, Shyboy's strategy really. The man was a genius with computers.

Shyboy took a deep breath, closing his eyes briefly to centre his thoughts. Then he relaxed and pressed a few buttons. The screen flickered and a 3D image popped up, rotating slowly. Several pairs of eyes followed, expressions varying from sickened, to saddened, to furious. A second viewing did not diminish its impact.

Mia looked away, unable to bear Beatrice's battered and tortured image any longer. She was still shocked by the capture and subsequent torture of Beatrice, a Mutant Liberation Front (MLF) member who had infiltrated Volta's uncle's home.

Shyboy looked around slowly. "I know… it's horrible. But stop for a moment and consider the powerful impact it has on all of us. It is my belief that it will be no less emotive for others. My idea is simple. I'll break into mainstream media sites and insert this image. I think I can ensure it appears every time a user opens their page." Shyboy looked around at his audience. "What do you think?"

There was a palpable silence. Mia didn't comment as she had no experience with computers. She contemplated the others, trying to gauge their emotions.

Volta spoke first. "Shy, it's brilliant. It has almost unlimited potential."

Tully and D2 concurred.

Looking relieved, Shyboy continued. "I thought that we'd just post the image first. No explanation. No nothing."

Volta nodded. "And then what?"

Shyboy clicked at the pad. The 3D image reappeared with a caption printed below. 'I am Beatrice'. Shyboy looked around anxiously. "What do you think?"

Tully smiled at the young man. "Bloody genius."

Mia was impressed. "Everyone will be intrigued. How could they not be?"

Volta leaned forward, staring at the image, his brow creasing in concentration. "So," he said, "each new release will tell just a tiny bit more. Sort of like a story without end."

"That's about the sum of it," said Shyboy.

"Shy," said Volta, "are you sure that your posts won't be traced?"

Shyboy's pale blue eyes glittered with mischief. "Not a hope. I am — though I say so in all modesty — brilliant."

Tully looked around the group. "So, does anyone have any objections?" No one volunteered any. "Go ahead Shy. Let's get this thing rolling." He checked his watch. "We'd better get ready, it's time for the sand guns."

Mia leapt up in such haste that she accidentally bumped Volta's head.

"Ouch!" Volta exclaimed. "If you want my attention you only had to ask," he joked.

Mia forced a smile but felt her face burning. Whether her embarrassment was due to Volta's words or his close proximity, Mia wasn't sure. "Sorry," she muttered. "Best go get ready." She grabbed the wig and hurried out. As she walked, she thought about her disguise and felt resentment welling up inside her. She was going to look a fright!

Suddenly she wondered when it was that her appearance had become so important to her. And — more worrisome — why? Two heads flickered through her mind's eye. One black as a raven and the other as gold as the underbelly of a kestrel. She sighed and pushed the uncomfortable subject aside as she wove her way through the throng of tents.

As she finally reached her destination, Mia became acutely aware of the campsite. The multitude of bodies, the smell of smoke, the cries of excited children, the distant whinny of a horse. Tears came unbidden to her eyes. All this was hers. Her people. And it reinforced to her the importance of what was happening. She felt ashamed of her petty preoccupation with her appearance. Today would be the beginning of something big. Bigger than her. Bigger than the MLF. Bigger than even the Overlanders. It was the beginning of change. Would she be worthy? Or perish in the attempt?

Inside, Mia laid out her clothes. She wished Nonna was there. Truth was, she felt increasingly anxious. Going to Alice had been an abstract idea up until now. Exciting and exotic. But the reality was more than a little daunting. Alice. A lawless and dangerous place by all accounts. And that was under ordinary circumstances. But she and her companions were going into that place with a bounty on their heads. Even disguised, the risk of capture was scarily high.

Mia sat down abruptly on her bed, her legs like custard, heart hammering and perspiration beading on her body. She was afraid. Really scared. What if she never saw her family again? Her mother, grandmother, cousins, aunties and uncles? She hadn't said goodbye. Not properly. But then she thought of her father. Her Da. Out there, somewhere. Alone. Waiting. Without the sand guns her people would never be safe from the forces of Isbane. And they must be secured before she headed north to find her father. Was she going to give up so easily?

Trembling, Mia stood up. She took deep breaths, holding them and letting them out slowly until she felt the weakness in her limbs abating. She looked down at the faded army shirt, fatigue pants, a length of cloth and boots. Feeling stronger, Mia stripped down and took up the long strip of fabric. After a moment's thought, she proceeded to wind it tightly, effectively flattening her chest. It was uncomfortable but not unbearably so. The shirt and trousers fit fairly well but her boots felt strange, having hardly been worn.

Lastly, Mia bound up her hair and pulled on the despised wig. She peered into the tiny mirror hanging above her bed and didn't know whether to laugh or cry. In the end she settled for a resigned sigh. With the wrap-around glasses tucked into a pocket she left the tent, heading to the men's quarters.

As she hurried, she found to her surprise that she was smiling. She couldn't wait to see what Volta looked like!

# CHAPTER 12

Outside the men's tent a crowd had gathered. It quieted as Mia made her way to the entrance. Mia heard a few chuckles as she squeezed past. Determined to be mature, she ignored them. Mia desperately wanted to see if Dart were amongst the curious but forced her gaze steadfastly forward.

She paused outside the drop of canvas that acted as a door. "Knock, knock," she said.

The curtain whisked open and D2 peeked out. He nodded and lifted the curtain aside, then beckoned her in. Mia found them all standing tensely in a huddle. At the sight of Mia they made a greeting.

Mia couldn't help staring at Shyboy who had adopted the tribal uniform of her people, plus a pair of black shades. His usually white hair had been coloured pale brown and his hands and face artificially darkened. But Mia's eyes slid involuntarily to Volta. He looked very self conscious, dressed in nothing but his undies. His bare chest looked very pale in contrast to his sun kissed arms, face and neck. Still, Mia noticed that, although as lean as goanna steak, his stomach was tightened into muscular ridges and his chest had muscled up considerably.

So engrossed was she with these fascinating details that she failed to notice that Volta was observing her with equal curiosity. When her eyes met his, she blushed and backed away, choosing to watch proceedings from a safer distance.

Volta took the dress proffered by Shyboy and shook it out. He eyed it critically for a few minutes. The colour, a deep midnight blue, pleased him. Ideal for his colouring. The style was simple, with a round neck and long sleeves, cinched in at the waist with a full skirt sweeping elegantly to the ground. Volta held it up to his front, looking down.

Someone, Tully he suspected, let out a long, low whistle. Refusing to be baited, Volta ignored him. Then he looked around at his audience anxiously. "Do you think it will fit?"

Tully nodded. "Some of the women have let out all the seams and inserted a couple of extra panels."

Volta did not feel convinced. The dress looked very small to him. "It's going to be snug."

"Hang on," said Tully, digging around in a bag. "I nearly forgot this."

Volta stared at the object dangling from Tully's hand. It was weird. A bony, rigid thing with strangely delicate decoration. He took it, holding it by one pink strap. "What is it?"

"Well," said Tully, "it's a corset."

Volta turned it in his hands; it was both satiny smooth and iron hard at the same time. "What's it for?"

There was an explosion of laughter. Volta observed Tully and Shyboy suspiciously. Clearly something was amusing them. Volta looked at the pink thing, aware that this was the source of their hilarity. He waved it in Tully's face. "So?"

Tully sank to the floor, tears brimming in his eyes. Shyboy could only shake his head helplessly. Even D2's lips twitched.

Mia came forward, shaking her head at the men. "Volta, it is a woman's undergarment that makes the waist smaller and emphasises the…" She paused, her face burning. "Chest." She took the garment from him, holding it to her abdomen, and sucked in her breath to demonstrate.

At her words Tully and Shyboy pulled themselves together. Still grinning, they looked at Volta. Hoping, Volta surmised, for a tantrum. "Thank you, Mia," he said, with all the dignity he could muster.

Mia handed the corset back. Volta examined it again minutely. Then he grinned. "Looks like a form of torture." He turned it this way and that. "Which way was it again?"

Clearly disappointed, Tully stepped in. "It ties up at the back."

Volta wrapped the cool, strange article around his torso. But it wouldn't meet at the back. "It's too small," he said.

"Hang on," said Tully.

Next thing, Volta felt a knee settling in the small of his back and saw Tully's hands grasping two pink cords dangling innocently from the bottom of the corset.

"Breathe in!" Tully commanded.

Volta breathed in.

Tully began hauling ruthlessly on the cords.

And to Volta's amazement he watched his waist slowly growing smaller. "Bloody hell," he gasped.

"Another big breath," said Tully.

Volta's eyes popped with indignation. "I can't."

Tully rewound the pink cords firmly around his hands once more. "Don't be a wimp. You've got to suffer for beauty."

Volta's head whipped around and he opened his mouth to retaliate. But Tully ruthlessly seized the moment, leaning back and yanking the cords once more, effectively cutting off Volta's words. And — it seemed — his ability to breathe.

And it was over. Panting with exertion, Tully nimbly tied the knots and stood back to admire his handiwork.

"Are you alright?" Mia asked Volta. "You look a bit… pale."

"Just a bit — breathless," said Volta.

Shyboy laughed. "Why, Volta, even your voice sounds different."

Volta eyed him sourly. "I'm sure that will give me great comfort when I pass out from oxygen deprivation."

Tully came to him, holding two wobbly pads carefully in his palms.

"What are they?" Volta asked.

Tully shook them softly. "Boobs," he said.

Volta sighed but allowed Tully to push the two convex jelly pads into place. Before Volta could inspect the effects, Tully dropped the dress over his head. With a little jiggling and wiggling the garment slid into place. There was a hush. Volta looked around impatiently.

"Well, how do I look?"

But their varied responses were lost as Shyboy pulled a strawberry blonde wig over his head and began tugging it into shape. Volta's hands tried to explore his new hair but yelped as Shyboy rapped the back of his hands with a hairbrush.

Then there was a movement at the entry. "Are you ready?"

It was a woman's voice.

"Come in," said Mia.

Volta watched as a girl, not much older than Mia, entered. She carried a woven basket in one hand. She smiled. "I see you, Mia of the Overland."

"Trina!" said Mia, obviously pleased. "What are you doing here?"

Trina lifted her basket. "I have come to paint the Isbanite." Then she made a funny little face. "I have come to make him pretty!"

Volta wasn't sure what to make of this last. But he soon found out. Trina asked him to sit and she settled before him, staring at him for what felt like an age. Then she opened her basket and took out tiny pots and an array of delicate brushes. It did not escape Volta's notice that she was very pretty. She had the dark features typical of her people, with wide doe eyes and dimpled chin.

"Close your eyes," she said.

He did. It was a strange experience. The paints smelled sharp and the paint brush felt soft. Trina worked quickly, making light strokes about his eyes, cheeks and even his lips. The tent was utterly quiet. Volta could hear only the rustle of Trina's robes and the clink of the pots.

"There," said Trina finally. "Open your eyes."

Volta did as he was bid and found he had a rapt audience.

Volta stared back impatiently. But no one spoke. "Well! Say something!"

Mia spoke. "You look… lovely."

Trina thrust a mirror into Volta's hands. He peered at himself. For several seconds he said nothing, leaning this way and that, trying to get every angle possible. His eyes stared back at him, big and blue, framed in black lashes. His cheek bones looked high and hollow and his lips lush. He put down the mirror and took Trina's hand. "Thank you!"

Laughing, Trina began packing away her things. "You are most welcome, Volta," she said.

Volta grinned broadly. For him, dressing up was a new and novel experience. He realised he was enjoying himself. He stood up, sashayed over to Mia, dropped a curtsey and peeked coyly from beneath his eyelashes. "Young man, would you do me the honour of a dance tonight?"

Mia rolled her eyes but did not look displeased.

Volta quickly pulled on a pair of sandals. They were very plain by comparison but there had been nothing else to fit. Besides, the long skirts would hide them.

Shyboy cleared his throat and looked around at the assembled company. "Everyone ready?"

There was a clatter of plastic and metal as D2 began strapping a formidable armoury onto his body.

Shyboy tapped a canister hanging from the huge hybrid's belt. "Is that really necessary?"

"What is it?" Asked Tully.

Shyboy turned to address him. "It's an Apocalypse Incendiary Device. Not quite antimatter, but close enough."

"Cool," said Volta, acutely aware of his funny, breathless new voice.

D2's massive hand closed protectively over the canister. "In Alice, Apocalypse essential. Alice is a very bad place."

At the mention of the fabled town Volta felt a shiver of anticipation ripple down his spine. Alice. At last.

# CHAPTER 13

It was the time of day that was neither dark nor light. The power of the sun was diminishing and a cool breeze brought the promise of the cold to come. The water darkened and waves lapped softly upon the sandy shore. Above, the sky slowly faded and small stars began peeking out. Mia trembled slightly, but more from excitement than anything else. The Overlanders were gathered together around the lake and an unnatural hush spilled across them. A baby wailed half-heartedly and was quickly comforted. Mia could hear the soft crunch of the horses at their grain and the slower grind of the camels. Like everyone else, her eyes were fixed on an invisible point toward Alice. Beside her, Volta watched and waited.

A soft gasp travelled through the desert people. Mia's mouth opened, green eyes widening. Children broke the silence, talking rapidly in their piping voices, pointing up at three large bubbles of light bobbing through the darkening skyline. They moved silently, shimmering in transcendent beauty. As they travelled closer they grew larger. By the time they were half a kilometre away their dimensions were clear. Each globe was the size of a small tent.

Finally they floated to the ground and were still. Up close the giant bubbles were quite astonishing. Inside, Mia could see two clear plastic seats, high backed with broad armrests. The shell was sparkling clean and shining, the surface rippling with rainbow colours. She could just make out the soft tones of music. Simultaneously the doors of the globes opened with a soft whoosh. Mia could smell the artificially scented air that escaped, and she wrinkled her nose, unsure whether or not she approved.

Then the globes spoke in soft, feminine tones. "Ladies and gentlemen, welcome to Bubble On The Double. The floating flavour in travel. Please climb aboard." A clear ramp slowly played out of the entry of each bubble.

Volta didn't hesitate and stepped up. Mia paused, looking back toward the camp, a surge of anxiety filling her. She didn't want to leave.

Then Volta's voice cut into her thoughts. "Hurry up, Mia!"

Finally she stepped up and entered the strange vehicle. Volta had already settled himself into one of the big chairs. Mia turned as the door closed behind her. She looked out and saw the others already in their bubbles. Shyboy waved. She waved back.

"Please be seated," said the bubble. "Next stop, Alice."

Mia staggered and sat down heavily in the empty chair as the bubble lifted off the ground. She floundered for a moment, convinced the soft chair was swallowing her whole. Lifting herself up a little she felt the chair re-inflating beneath her. She watched, in growing trepidation, as the earth began receding. Soon the ground disappeared from sight. She felt extremely insecure, not fully convinced that the pretty plastic globe was strong enough to carry its two passengers. Her fingers gripped the armrests and she could feel her pulse beating rapidly in her neck.

Volta bounced out of his chair and began to poke and prod the vessel.

Mia's fingers gripped the chair convulsively, squeezing her eyes shut as a bead of perspiration rolled down her forehead. "Please don't," she begged, opening her eyes a smidgen.

Volta looked at her, clearly astonished. "I don't believe it!"

Mia's eyes opened a fraction more. "What?" she said weakly.

"You're actually… afraid."

She glared at him. "Of course I'm afraid, you dingo dropping. This is not natural. One should be on the ground, unless climbing a tree, or riding a horse. Sol gave us feet for a good reason." She closed her eyes tight shut again. "One should not… float. We shall perish," she said resignedly.

Volta shook his head, as if confused. "But… you are never afraid!"

His words shocked Mia. Never afraid! If only that were true. "Volta, of course I am afraid. I get afraid often. I am afraid this thing will burst and we shall plummet to our deaths. I am afraid of Alice. I am afraid for my Da. I am afraid of the army." She shook her head slowly. "Sometimes I cannot count all the things in this world that I am afraid of."

Volta was staring at her with an odd expression.

Mia felt herself flushing. He thought she was a coward.

"I had no idea, Mia. You always seem so… fearless! But, if it's any consolation, it's reassuring to know you are afraid of things that you should be afraid of." Then he leaned over and took her hand, patting it gently. "Excepting this occasion. It's alright Mia, it's really quite safe. This company is very reputable. It's safer than camels."

Mia stared out, looking into the night sky. Far below she could just make out the fires burning in the camp. A wave of vertigo made her head spin. She looked at Volta and took a gulp of air.

"Just think, we'll be in Alice soon," Volta continued. "I can't wait to meet Fidelus Ferguson and go to the club where we're meeting his contact, The Madonna."

Distracted from her imminent doom Mia sat up a little. She realised her hand still lay softly in Volta's. She wasn't sure whether this was a good thing or a bad one. She chose to ignore it, for the moment. After all, he was probably just being kind. "Remind me again why we can't just meet Ferguson?"

"No one meets Ferguson."

Mia puzzled over this."Well, if no one's met him — how do we know he exists?"

Volta frowned. "Well, people have met him in the past, I suppose."

The bubble suddenly lurched to a stop; it quivered for a few seconds and then surged on. Mia gripped Volta's hand tightly. The darkness beyond the circle of light filled her with foreboding. Her eyes closed and she swallowed. "We're going to fall."

Volta laughed. "No, we're not. Look at that," he said, pointing.

Getting a grip on herself she opened her eyes and stared out the window into the adjacent bubble. She frowned in confusion. Inside his bubble, Shyboy was swaying, contorting and jerking in a most peculiar fashion. Then Mia got it. "Oh, he's dancing! He's brilliant, isn't he?"

Volta nodded. "He certainly is."

Then they both looked at their clasped hands. Mia faked a cough so she could cover her mouth.

Volta pretended not to notice.

There was an awkward pause. Mia watched Shyboy again but her mind returned to the earlier conversation about Fidelus Ferguson. She wondered what sort of man he was. He lived outside the law. He was a renegade. An anarchist. It occurred to her then, for the first time, that this was how others might view her own people. It was a strange thought.

But also comforting, in an odd way. Perhaps Fidelus Ferguson would prove to be not so different after all. Besides, ultimately the important thing was his independence. This man was beyond the control of The City.

She peeled her eyes away from Shyboy, and looked back at her companion. "What will we do afterwards?"

Volta was silent for a moment, clearly considering the question. "You mean, after we get the sand guns?"

Mia nodded.

Volta grinned. "Well, first thing, I'll take this corset off. It's murder." Mia grinned back. "Then, well, I guess we'll head north. Find the prison hospital."

*The prison hospital.* The words filled Mia with apprehension. It was a terrible place. She knew this because D2 had told them. D2 with his mutated and scarred body, resulting from his long incarceration in the hospital. Although *hospital* was not an appropriate word. In reality the patients were prisoners whose sole purpose was to provide body parts, blood and skin. It was an illegal but lucrative market. And that was where her Da was. Mia screwed up the courage to voice a fear she'd been harbouring for days. "What do you think our chances are?"

Volta looked away, frowning. "I don't really know. After all, who would have bet we'd make it this far?"

Mia watched his face carefully, trying to read him. She sensed that while he did not lie, there were things he was keeping to himself. The decision to go to war weighed heavily upon her. Her people, long committed to a policy of pacifism, had only agreed when violence had been done to them. While it had been a collective decision, Mia knew her own input had influenced the outcome. But then, what else could she have done? She thought of Farro lying dead in the sand. She thought of her father, locked away within the walls of that terrible place. Of The Confessor, scarred inside and out. Of the tribes, free and independent. And added to the equation the inexplicable desire of The City to decimate them all. They could run and fall. Or fight. And perhaps Volta was right. The five of them had overcome overwhelming odds. Perhaps their luck would hold.

The bubble continued to bounce lazily through the sky. Mia, wrapped up in her thoughts, forgot her fears. She gasped in shock as the bubble stopped abruptly, making her rock in her seat. She grabbed onto the squashy arms and stared around in panic "What's happening?"

Volta peered out. "It's alright, I think we're there."

Mia sagged back in relief. Thank goodness.

"Prepare for departure. Have a lovely bubbly day," said the bubble.

Mia jumped up. "Not likely," she said.

The door swished open. They stepped to the ground and gawked around. They were in some sort of terminal. A couple of dozen bubbles were neatly parked in rows. Tully and D2 landed and joined them. They waited impatiently as Shyboy arrived and alighted.

"Nice moves," said Volta cheekily.

Shyboy bowed, then stood with a shiver. "It's cold."

It was. The temperature within the enclosed terminal must've been artificially controlled, as it surely could not be that much cooler than the desert they had just left. They looked around, trying to see which way to go. The large terminal was dwarfed by towering black buildings. It was eerily quiet. There were no signposts and not a soul in sight.

D2 primed his gun and glared around in the dark, his eyes glowing.

Mia edged unconsciously closer to the others. "Where's the entry?"

There was a loud pinging noise and then an explosion of light as a lift door swished open. For a second nothing happened and then two heavily armed men strode out. Gagging, Mia stepped hurriedly back as the men passed them, assiduously avoiding any eye contact. She placed a hand over her nose and mouth and held her breath. The men stank. It was dreadful. Positively rank. She caught Volta's eye and he shook his head, his wig undulating softly.

The men soon disappeared into the darkness, their footsteps fading. Mia looked around at the others. "Who in the name of Sol were they?" she asked.

No one seemed to know. But no one looked happy.

# CHAPTER 14

Mia tried to put the dirty, unkempt men out of her mind. But she couldn't. The encounter had unsettled her. Why did they smell so bad? Of death and corruption. What had they been doing in Alice? She could not imagine. The incident felt like a bad omen. Some of her enthusiasm for the place was effectively dampened.

D2 lowered his gun and looked briefly into the dark landscape then back at the lift door. "Looks like that's the only way in. We'd better hurry."

Rather reluctantly Mia followed Volta inside. The lift was utilitarian, grey plastic floor to ceiling. The five of them fitted in quite comfortably, with room for approximately half a dozen more bodies. There were no visible panels or buttons.

Tully rubbed his beard. "What now?"

Volta shrugged. "Dunno."

D2 spoke. "Retrospectro."

The lift vibrated softly, the doors swished shut, and they began to drop.

Tully grinned a little nervously at D2. "Good work!"

Mia felt her stomach clenching as a familiar anxiety filled her. In her experience, down was never good. It brought back the dark days of Isbane city and the claustrophobic confinement within the prison. Her overactive imagination began conjuring visions of what lay below.

It seemed simultaneously like no time and eternity until the lift finally stopped. The doors opened and they pressed out eagerly. All but D2 stopped, gazing around in undisguised wonder. Mia's immediate response was relief. The horrors her mind had conjured on the journey down were happily not translated into reality. Alice was... amazing.

Looking around, Mia's immediate impression was one of space. She was reminded of the inside of the ruined church in Isbane. Huge pillars reached up to the ceiling, forming into wide arches. As she gazed around at the vast space, Mia wondered just how deep in the earth they had travelled. It was an unnerving thought. The vast underground dwelling was lit with green, luminescent light, emanating eerily from the pillars and ceiling.

Volta stepped forward and touched a pillar tentatively. "What sort of light is this?"

Tully and Shyboy took a closer look, but neither seemed to know.

The place heaved with activity. All around them people went surging past. No one gave them half a glance. Mind you, Mia reflected, it was hardly surprising. Even Volta's costume, which had seemed so exotic, now looked commonplace by comparison to the present company's code of dress. It seemed to be a case of 'anything goes'. The only thing that everyone seemed to have in common was a spectacular array of weaponry.

They set off, walking slowly. Mia stared as a woman went sweeping by on a hovering board. Beneath the lights the woman's white gown glowed leafy green, the multi-tiered skirt fluttering as she glided by. In one hand she pulled a small mobile cannon and in the other she held a tether attached to a frilly lizard, zipping along on his own board beside her. Its frill was fanned out with fear, and Mia felt sorry for it. Her attention quickly latched onto a man and woman, both dressed in shocking pink suits of what might have been scorpion skin. There were children racing around, ignoring or oblivious to the entreaties of their parents. Their clothes varied, some wore snug fitting overalls, others the loose shirt and pants of the desert dwellers. One child wore a beautiful emerald top embroidered with shiny gems, paired with gauzy baggy pants. Others wore an ill-sorted mismatch of articles, which revealed much wear and tear and not a little dirt.

Mia watched them curiously. Their exuberance and energy matched that of the youngsters back in the camp. And Farro. She felt a sharp stab of loss. With an effort she forced her eyes further down the passage and saw that they approached a crossroads.

Volta tapped her on the shoulder to get her attention. "Look at the floor."

Mia looked down and immediately became conscious that the ground was vibrating beneath her feet. The floor was dark and grainy. She stepped forward, watching her foot sink into the springy surface. Fascinated, she watched as, stepping back, the floor surged up and down in rippling waves.

"Weird," said Volta.

Mia looked around and saw that the hundreds of mobile people created a constant swell of movement. It was as if the floor were a living organic mass. "Weird" barely covered it.

Shyboy came to join them. "Which way?"

D2 pointed north.

"Come on," said Tully.

Looking left, Mia discovered a whole new dimension. A mass of people were swarming in and out of an astonishing number of stores. Mia was constantly distracted by strange sights and sounds. Each window held a fascinating display of goods. The street was a kaleidoscope of mouth-watering "stuff" to try and to buy.

Mia came to a rude stop as she bumped into Volta.

"Would you look at that?" he said, staring through a window into a brightly lit store, barely acknowledging the collision.

Mia, intrigued, peered in. It was a very strange place. There were no displays, clothes, or other goods. Instead, plush chairs in bright primary colours lined the square room. In many of the chairs sat women. It took Mia a few minutes to note that all the women were hybrids. But not like D2. Not catlike at all. But still familiar. As familiar as Whisper. "Horse hybrids!" she said softly to Volta. "What are they doing?"

A young hybrid woman took a pew close to the window. Mia watched in amazement as a shop assistant settled on a small cushion on the floor and picked up a hoof. Then she produced a pair of cutters and neatly trimmed the hoof. Next a file rounded out the shape. The assistant picked up the other hoof and repeated the process. Then she put the tools away and disappeared briefly, returning with a cabinet on wheels. A brief conversation ensued, a selection seemed to be made and the girl set to work again. Grasping a hoof, she bent over and proceeded to hammer a sparkling diamante into the hard surface.

In a matter of minutes the job was done. The finished effect was very glamorous. Two rows of glittering stones, overlaid with clear varnish. The customer smiled as she examined her tidy toes.

Mia jumped as a hand settled on her shoulder. But it was only Tully.

"Come on, you two," he urged.

They hurried on, catching up with the rest of the crew.

Shyboy gave them an exasperated look. "Stay with the program!"

Mia nodded, embarrassed. "Sorry," she said.

Shyboy smiled. "It's a lot to take in, I know."

Volta nodded. "You're not kidding. This place is… galactic!"

They set off once more, Mia determinedly refusing to be distracted. She restricted her attention to the back of D2's head. D2, she felt sure, wouldn't be distracted by pony girls and lizards on wheels.

But she was wrong. D2's head began turning. Left. Right. Left. Right. Then he looked back over his shoulder. There was something in his demeanour that sent a frisson of alarm tingling through Mia's brain. When the assassin slowed, Mia was not surprised. Clearly something was troubling him. And anything that troubled D2 could not be ignored.

D2 moved aside, pressing to the sides of the tunnel and the rest followed. Huddled close to Volta, Mia glanced nervously around. It struck her then that this part of the neighbourhood was not as salubrious. Gone were the glamorous stores, the pretty displays, the sweet scents and the exciting bustle of the well-to-do. The atmosphere here was drab. There were only a few stores. And those were filled with poor quality goods. Cheap but not very cheerful. Other businesses existed but they had no windows. Or had windows blacked out and barred. No one lingered, hurrying on to their destinations.

Shyboy was looking around, a tight expression on his usually happy face. "What's wrong, D2?"

The big hybrid did not answer. He seemed to be listening intently. Mia caught Shyboy and Tully exchanging alarmed looks. What was happening? She couldn't decide whether not knowing was a good or bad thing.

A long, sibilant hiss of sound came from D2. "Fur farm!" Then, cursing and spitting, he lunged away.

It took Mia a moment to compute D2's words. *Fur farm.* Then her stomach roiled as she understood. She knew what the terrible stench had been emanating from the two dishevelled men. She turned to the others. "Those men —"

But Volta had already got there. "They smelled like death," he said.

Shyboy and Tully looked ill but did not argue.

After a second of shocked stillness, Mia rallied. "Hurry!"

They hurried, racing flat out after D2. They came to a ragged halt, all staring around, looking for the assassin.

"Where's he gone?" said Volta.

Then Mia spotted him, paused at the entry of an alley. Even from a distance, she could see the tension in his huge frame. "I think he's found something," she whispered.

The others exchanged nervous glances and nodded. In silent assent they set off again, keeping close to the sides of the tunnel, stopping behind D2. The assassin turned to them.

The look on his face was so ferocious that Mia was not the only one to take a step back.

D2 did not seem to notice their collective cowering. "Down here," he said, pointing.

Mia tiptoed cautiously forward and peered around. Mean and dirty, the alley was an uninviting proposition. But that was not the worst of it. Mia backed away hurriedly, dry retching. "Sol, it stinks!"

"Come," said D2. And he disappeared around the corner.

They hastened after him, although Mia had a very bad feeling about it. But what else could they do? She did not need to know what a "fur farm" was to understand it was not a good thing. The sickening scent of decay and corruption boded very ill indeed.

And then she heard it. A high-pitched, muffled screaming. It was dreadful. Every bit as bad as the sounds she had heard in the city prison.

"Shit, did you hear that?" said Volta behind her.

But before she could respond another scream spliced the air. With a snarl, D2 burst into action, his hands priming his weapon as he moved. Heart accelerating, pulse pumping and adrenaline flowing, Mia's hands were already unhitching her crossbow, sliding a bolt home.

Unheeding of danger they tore down the narrow path. They moved at such speed that Mia had only a vague impression of refuse bins, dark windows and an underlying atmosphere of menace. Another scream broke over their heads as they slid to a halt. The alley had ended in a singular brick wall. There were no windows or doors. Just solid stone. D2 was frantic, slamming his gun against the wall in frustration.

Then they all froze as an angry spitting and hissing sound came from a boarded window to their left. In less time than it took for Mia to assemble this information, D2 had raced across the alley and launched himself straight at the window. There was a dreadful cracking as boards popped and splintered. D2 disappeared.

Heart in her throat, Mia followed. In three short strides she vaulted through the jagged hole. The others poured in behind her.

The room was lit by a single dim light. Four men faced their unexpected company with expressions of horror. D2 snarled, his face twisting with rage. His neck muscles swelled, blood pumping visibly into his upper arms. The veins of his neck stood out like writhing snakes. The whites of his eyes made him look crazy. Indeed, at that moment, Mia reflected that he probably was. For half a second his eyes raked the four men, then he grabbed the nearest around the neck, lifting him bodily off the ground. The man's face went magenta, his feet kicking feebly. D2 shook him like a rag. Then he stopped and shoved his face up close to his victim's.

"Where are they?" said the assassin.

# CHAPTER 15

The room was silent save for the belaboured breathing of the man. His mouth opened but all that came out was a dribble of spit.

Shyboy stepped forward and tapped D2 on the shoulder. Mia watched fearfully as D2 spun around, snarling loudly.

Shyboy only smiled ruefully, apparently unperturbed by D2's rage. "D2, I think he's passed out. Best let him go."

D2 looked impassively at the man, grunted, and dropped him. He landed with a thud, his head bouncing in a hollow drum roll. D2 trod on the body as he advanced on the other three men, who looked ready to pee their collective pants.

As the huge hybrid reached out for his second victim, the man began backing up to the wall, gibbering in terror. "That way, that way, through there." He jabbed frantically with one shaking hand.

Four heads swivelled to where he pointed. Mia frowned; the stained wall offered no answer. But then she realised that there was a door, however it had no visible handle.

"Open it," D2 roared.

One of the men scurried over and slid a small plastic card into the gap between the door and the wall. There was a loud click and the door swung open excruciatingly slowly, revealing nothing but blackness. Even D2 jumped back half a pace as a wild figure burst through the opening. Mia stared.

It was a hybrid. A cat hybrid like D2. She was black as well but slight and very thin. She wore nothing but a large, tattered plastic bag. The visible parts of her body were covered in fur so fine and shiny, that Mia longed to reach out and stroke it. In a little pointed face two golden eyes gleamed like pumpkin lanterns. Her small hands were clutching a long piece of pipe that was shedding bits of brick, plaster and mortar. She must, Mia guessed, have pulled it from its fixture.

The slender girl stood panting, her eyes gazing around the room. Then, as she fixed on the three terrified men, she let out a feral scream, raised the pipe and went careering toward them. Suddenly the room seemed very small and there was a mad scramble as everyone tried to get out of range.

The hybrid girl pounced at the first man, spitting loudly. He yelled and ducked, his hands held protectively over his head. His companions did not move to aid him. The pipe made a strangely formidable weapon. Mia held her breath, waiting for impact. But it did not come. Time seemed to stop. The girl stood as if frozen. Only her chest moved, rising and falling rapidly. It seemed to Mia that she was paralyzed by some inner conflict. Unable to conclude the act of violence she had started.

Then the hybrid's long, lithe tail curled out, the tip flickering. The tail grasped the pipe, curved it down through the air and walloped the cowering man over the head. He went down.

"Nicely done," said Volta, in approving tones.

The pipe fell to the floor with a clang. Mia watched in dismay as the fragile figure of the girl folded softly to the floor. Her head drooped and her shoulders began shaking. She was crying. It was the sound of utter desolation. Mia did not know what to do. The hybrid wept, tears running and melting into her shiny, black pelt.

Mia glanced at the cowering men accusingly, wondering what they had done. Whatever it was, it was bad. Very bad. She glanced at Volta. He looked every bit as anguished as she felt. He must have felt her gaze for he glanced sideways, caught her eye and shook his head.

It was D2 who moved hesitantly to the weeping girl. He dropped onto his knees, his heavy weaponry clanking and jingling. He put out a huge hand and touched the top of the velvety head.

"Where?" he said softly.

The girl lifted her golden eyes and blinked the tears away. She stood up, reached and grasped his hand, her own as tiny as his was big. She pointed to the doorway but did not seem able to speak. D2 turned and addressed Shyboy.

"You watch these," he said, pointing at the men. "The rest, come with me."

No one questioned. Each sprang into action, following the two hybrids through the door and into the dark space beyond. Mia could hear nothing but as she stepped warily through the doorway, her nose wrinkled. The stench was indescribable.

Tully sniffed loudly. "Scorpion scrotums! What in Hades?"

There was a brief crackle and the room lit up. D2 held up a red flare. Mia looked around. It was another very ordinary room. Their shadows towered above them like watchful giants. There were no windows, no furnishings or decoration.

Volta spotted the trapdoor first. It was in the corner, half open. D2 handed the flare to Tully and grasped the round ring sunk into the centre of the cover. He lifted it, tossing it aside as if it were made of cottonweed. They all peered down rough-hewn steps. Mia's heart sank like a stone in her chest. Down. A strange malaise seemed to settle about the company. No one seemed inclined to make the first move. Perhaps, Mia thought listlessly, none of them wanted to discover what was down there. She certainly didn't.

D2 stepped forward abruptly, shook himself and began descending, the girl on his heels. The spell broke and one by one Tully, Volta and Mia followed. Mia did not like being last. She had an attack of the jitters, glancing behind, half convinced there was something there. The dancing, flickering shadows from the moving flare formed into misshapen ghouls, with long curled fingers and twisted faces. The stairwell was steep, the steps unevenly spaced. The atmosphere was dry and cool. The stinking, cloying odour grew stronger.

"Stop!" It was D2.

"What?" said Volta.

D2 held up a hand. "Quiet."

They all froze. Mia strained her ears. At first she could hear nothing. After a few seconds she recognised the soft thudding of her own heart, the low buzz of the flare and Volta's rapid, shallow breathing. For a brief second she thought she heard something else. She held her breath, but could discern nothing more.

D2 took off again. His pace increased, any thought of stealth erased, as he went crashing down the steps two at a time. Then they came to a violent stop. Mia thudded heavily into Volta, his wig tickling her nose. She extracted herself, apologising.

Volta didn't reply, he turned to her, his breath ragged.

Alarmed, Mia peered into his painted face. "You O.K.?"

He managed a small nod of his head. Even in the red, hazy light he looked very pale.

She watched him struggling for breath and worried he was going to pass out. But his respiration slowed and he managed a strained smile. Mia peered over his shoulder, trying to find an explanation for the sudden stop but could see nothing beyond D2's massive frame. And then the assassin moved on. It went dark. The flare had died.

A crackling sound bought a renewed surge of light. Mia looked around a low-ceilinged room packed with long racks from which articles of clothing hung. Perhaps it was a storage room for one of the shops up above.

Ahead D2 started snarling. It was a raw, primal sound that made the hairs on Mia's arms stand erect. Instantly alert, Mia pulled out her bow, searching for the enemy. But she could not see anyone.

"What is it?" she said in an urgent whisper to Volta.

Volta pointed to one of the racks. "Take a closer look."

Mia took several steps and examined the long rows of clothes. She reached out and ran a hand down one soft fold of material. In the red light it was hard to discern the colour, but it was dark, a little mottled. It was incredibly soft and supple. It was fur. At first its source escaped her, as her brain tried to assimilate the facts. Her head snapped up as D2 let out a deep rumbling growl. And everything fell into place. She dropped the fur guiltily. She was stroking the beautiful hide of a cat.

"Holy shit," said Tully softly.

Mia felt sick. She watched apprehensively as D2 strode between endless racks of furs. His arms swept out violently as he went, racks falling with a loud clatter, furs flowing softly onto the dusty floor. Volta and Mia looked at each other and wordlessly followed.

Abruptly the racks ended to reveal a work room. Mia stared around in horror. The purpose of the work benches and machinery was only too clear. Anxiously she looked at D2, who was crouching in the far corner, the little hybrid hovering at his shoulder.

Tully, being taller, could see what had gained the assassin's attention. "Not good," he said.

With a lump forming in her throat, Mia followed her companions over to the two hybrids. She gazed anxiously over D2's shoulder at a row of cages. The smell was rank. Dirt and terror. At first she thought they were all empty but a frantic hissing bought her attention to two that were inhabited. If one could call it that. They were cats. One cowered at the back of its prison, its ginger ears flattened to its head, teeth exposed. The other sat back on its haunches, muscles rippling beneath a pure white coat. It hissed in fear and fury.

Mia put a hand to her mouth. She could recall all too clearly the encompassing terror of close confinement. Her heart contracted with pain. Did the creatures know their fate? She could hardly believe otherwise. A hard core of anger knotted in her chest and she glanced at the hybrid girl. No wonder she was beside herself.

D2 reached out and pulled at the first cage door. The ginger cat opened its mouth in silent protest. But the cage was locked. D2 cursed and then extracted a pistol. The first shot made Mia leap into the air, her heart pumping like a wild thing. The second shot merely caused her to flinch.

Another shot and both cages sprang open.

"Are they alright?" asked Mia.

By way of an answer both cats burst out of their cage and streaked away, heading for the exit.

D2 turned. The look on his face was terrible to see. "Go." He said.

# CHAPTER 16

As one, they turned and fled. All but the young hybrid, who remained, standing stoically at D2's side. Mia took the lead. At the steps she paused, looking anxiously back. Her heart dropped. Volta was clearly struggling. He was puffing violently, Tully perambulating him along. Mia had to suppress a desire to yell at them to hurry. As they finally joined her on the stairs the sharp crackle of gunfire assaulted the stillness of the cavernous room.

They all froze, hypnotized by the sound, which seemed to go on and on forever. Then there was a brief lull, broken by a sullen thud. Smoke and bits of debris hurtled toward the watching group. It was only as D2 loomed out of a thick brown smoke that Mia took off up the staircase, the others on her heels.

Halfway up, Mia's nose began tickling and she sneezed. Something soft settled gently across her nose, and she rubbed it off. Behind her, the rhythmic rat-a-tat of a semi-automatic sang D2's swan song. The air became close and stuffy. Her eyes, nose and mouth felt as if they were stuffed full of wool. Coughing and dry retching, Mia burst up through the trapdoor. Volta and Tully were not far behind. At the first sight of them Mia gaped. They looked like hairy ghosts. The fur coat collection — it seemed — was extinct.

Out of the stairwell it seemed unnaturally quiet. Only the odd, muffled bang could be heard. Mia rubbed fur from her face, sneezing sporadically. Volta, still breathless, nodded toward the door. Mia followed him into the front room.

Shyboy, still standing guard over the furriers, eyed them with interest. "Been busy?" he grinned. Then his eyes narrowed. "Scorpion scrotums, you're a mess, Volta. Look at that dress."

Mia looked at Volta. Shyboy was right. Volta was a sight.

Volta glanced down. "Damn it!"

He brushed vigorously at his skirt, sending fur floating up into the air. But the midnight blue dress seemed hairier still. Volta stood straight, flicked back a lock of his long, blonde hair and grimaced. "It couldn't be helped," he said. "It was terrible down there. D2 went ballistic — but you'd have done the same."

"What in Hades is down there?" Shyboy asked.

Volta's painted face hardened and he turned to the prisoners who sat in a neat line against the wall, heads drooped and eyes to the ground. Then he looked back at Shyboy. "These men are in the fashion industry. Designer wear." He paused. "If anything feline is your fancy."

Shyboy didn't get paler. He couldn't. But his face flushed. He shook his head. "No wonder D2's lost it." Then things must have come together in his head for he jerked as if he'd been shot. "But, the girl," he said, "the little hybrid, surely you're not telling me that she —"

"That's exactly what I'm telling you," said Volta.

All eyes then turned to the prisoners, who seemed to be trying to melt through the floor. A muffled explosion carried into the room and white smoke came drifting up through the trapdoor into the neighbouring room.

Mia eyed the men. They were truly disgusting. "D2 must be about done," she said. "Can't begin to imagine what his next move will be." She turned conversationally to Tully. "What's your best guess?"

Tully appeared to mull the matter over for a minute. "Not sure. Still, whatever it is, it's not going to be pretty."

Shyboy nodded. "It's going to get ugly alright."

Another loud boom echoed around them and a dark figure materialized from the resulting smoke. Mia watched, a touch afraid, as D2 stalked across the floor, the tip of his tail whipping back and forth. The girl followed a few footsteps behind, almost white with dust.

Without a word D2 bore down on the prisoners. He stopped short, looking keenly at them. The man on the far left passed out, slumping to the ground with a thud. D2 grinned. It was not a warming sight. He looked over his shoulder at the hybrid. "Shoo, come here."

*Shoo.* It was an unusual name, Mia thought. But nice. She liked it.

Shoo sauntered over to D2. The two hybrids just stared down at the two, still conscious, men. At that moment, Mia was very thankful D2 was on her side. He was indeed a fearsome sight. Beads of sweat began to gather on the foreheads of the two conscious prisoners who were now visibly trembling. Mia was glad. They were despicable.

D2 looked briefly at Shoo. "What will it be?"

Shoo tipped her head slightly to the left, fixing her great, golden eyes on the big hybrid. She shrugged slightly. "No plan for bad man," she said.

D2 looked at the men again. Then he reached into his heavy coat and pulled out a short, serrated knife. It gleamed in the dull light. He waved it in a lazy circle. The prisoners looked green, their eyes following the knife's projectile. D2 took a small step closer. The ragged sound of the men's breathing filled the room.

D2 snarled softly. "Like you," he said softly, "I have an avid interest in fashion."

Mia and Volta exchanged stunned glances. Since when?

D2 continued. "Yes, I've been contemplating a new coat for my friend here." He waved a massive hand at Shoo. "Funnily enough, I couldn't see anything downstairs that appeals." He leant down toward the men, who seemed to cease breathing. "But I think you can help me out there."

Both men just stared, obviously trying to work out the nature of this unexpected offer. When D2 continued to observe them expectantly, one managed a small nod of his head.

D2's smile widened, his large pointed teeth brilliant white. "Excellent, I thank you." He twirled the knife between his fingers. "I am really most grateful. Man skin is so hard to source these days."

There was a loud silence as the assassin's words sank in. Mia was just about to broach a loud protest when a hand gently grasped her wrist. It was Shyboy. He shook his head a fraction. She stared at him in confusion before realisation hit her.

Relief flooded her. D2 was just playing with the men. Thank goodness! She relaxed and settled in to watch.

The two prisoners, however, did not seem to doubt their large captor's sincerity. One began to sob. The other collapsed on the floor and squirmed on his belly, begging for mercy.

D2 eyed them distastefully. He looked at his companions. "Does anyone know this 'mercy'?"

Shyboy shook his head. "Never heard of him."

"Or her," interjected Volta helpfully.

D2's smile vanished. "Me neither." With one fluid movement the knife was airborne. It flew, arcing in circles and plunged into the sleeve of the nearest man.

He let out a shriek of terror, and then subsided into sobs when he discovered the blade simply pinning his sleeve to the ground.

D2 retrieved the knife and glared at the prisoners. "Be warned, if there is a next time, I will skin you alive," he said.

Shoo sauntered over to the exit and vaulted out of the window. D2 followed. Without a backward glance, the rest clambered back out into the alley.

Mia glanced at Shoo, who simply stared back, her long, black tail weaving back and forth. "Are you O.K.?"

By way of an answer, the little feline hybrid turned to D2, gazing up at him with a fierce intensity. "Shoo likes you," she said. And then, in less than an instant, she was gone. No more than a shadow, fleeing up the alley.

"I'll be…" said Shyboy in wonder as he watched her leave. Then he grinned. "Looks like you've got a fan club, D2."

D2 pretended not to hear.

Mia, suppressing a laugh, looked around at the others. "Time's getting on. We need to clean up before we go to Retrospectro."

Shyboy nodded. "We passed a public restroom on the way here."

Mia was glad to go. Relieved to leave the stench and fear behind. Back in the main thoroughfare Mia was thoughtful. She wondered how the girl, Shoo, had come to be caught. Perhaps she had heard the distressed animals and followed the men to the horrid factory. Or maybe they had hunted her down deliberately. A sickening thought. How terrified she must have been, sitting in the darkness amidst the stink of slaughter. Mia hoped she was safe now. Safe amidst her family.

She startled from her reverie as they slowed. They had reached their destination. She cast around for the right words. *Restroom.* That was it. The men peeled away as she went through a green door with the black silhouette of a woman on it. She looked around with interest. Like the rest of Alice the place was packed. Women were busy adjusting their hair, clothes and makeup. Despite the varied and colourful costumes, the room seemed very white. White shiny floors, white shiny walls, white shiny cubicles, with white shiny toilets. Mirrors reflected her image tenfold. It was not a happy sight. She barely recognised herself. She had looked hideous before. Now she looked hairy and hideous.

While Mia was aware of the glances that passed her way, no one seemed perturbed by her odd appearance. They must, she decided glumly, just think she was a very ugly woman. At the sink Mia was momentarily mesmerized by a number of small white machines whizzing frantically around the room, even scooting up walls and hugging the ceiling. One bumped into her feet and stopped. The word 'Dirtbuster' was emblazoned on its shiny shell.

Mia let out a squeal of shock as the Dirtbuster shot up her leg and began buzzing busily over her clothes.

A glamorous woman applying orange lipstick at the mirror beside Mia glanced over. "It's a Dirtbuster, dear," she said. "They digest dirt and germs. Very handy."

And sure enough, as it ran around, the machine left a strip of clean cloth in its wake. As soon as her army fatigues were good as new, the robot was off and away. Mia washed up quickly and wondered how the others were faring. Were there Dirtbusters in the men's bathroom too? And were the men as accepting of Volta as the women had been of herself?

She hurried out, eager to find out.

# CHAPTER 17

Inside the pristine white room Volta shoved his way toward
the wall and peered into the mirror. What a sight. His
makeup was smudged, his wig looked prematurely aged, and
the lovely blue dress was grey. He was going to need some
major sorting. It was hard to know where to start. Such was
his preoccupation, he didn't notice anything amiss. However,
when he glanced back into the mirror he flinched in shock.
Behind him, leering over his left shoulder, was a very big,
very ugly man. He had a bald pate, with dark hair fluffing
out of protruding ears. His nose resembled a squashed
sausage and scars latticed his cheeks.

"Can I help you, darlin'?"

Suddenly Volta became acutely aware he was not in the
right place. Heat suffused his face and his mouth flapped
uselessly. What an idiot. His discomfort increased as he
became the centre of attention. Movement to his right
brought reinforcements as Tully, D2 and Shyboy shouldered
their way toward him.

The ugly mug leaned down and grinned, showing several stained, chipped front teeth. His breath smelt like a drainpipe. Then Volta let out a yell as a hand clamped onto his left buttock. Aware of his blunder, he upped the pitch of his voice a couple of octaves. "Unhand me you uncivil brute!" he fluted.

The man stepped back in confusion. "'Ang on a minute," he muttered.

Volta's brain went into overdrive. If the man was suspicious it wouldn't take much to reveal Volta's true gender. Which was worse, he wondered, to be a woman in a man's toilet or a man dressed as a woman in a man's toilet? A tricky one.

The ugly man's eyes boldly traversed over the tightly laced contours of Volta's figure.

Volta, embarrassment giving way to resentment, scowled. The man's perusal was insulting. A flicker of anger stirred in his gut. "What are you looking at?" he said, in his husky voice.

The man took a step forward, reaching out toward Volta's chest. Volta's eyes widened in shock as he realised the intent. Panic and fury reared up and he lashed out, Volta's right fist smacking the man high on his nose. The sausage flattened and began bleeding copiously. For a minute the man froze, shocked. Then he spat a dark wad of blood at Volta's feet and roared a protest. He charged at Volta but had barely taken a step before D2 waded in.

D2 caught the bully firmly by the back of his coat, lifting him calmly off the ground.

The man struggled and swore and kicked. D2 took absolutely no notice. After a few moments the man quit. He hung sullenly, his nose dripping blood down his chin. He glared into the mirror at his captor's reflection. "Put me down."

D2 shook his head. "Say sorry to the lady first."

By way of reply, the man spat again. D2 shook him enthusiastically, splattering blood across the walls.

Volta stepped back hastily. He'd never get blood out of the dress.

D2 stopped shaking.

The man glowered at Volta. "Sorry," he hissed.

D2 dropped him.

The man straightened his clothes and observed D2 cautiously. "What's your bleedin' problem?"

D2 made no reply.

The man turned to the rest of the crowd looking for support. "He's got no right to treat me like that!"

Tully looked up from the sink, water trickling off his beard. "He's got every right," he said, "that's his mother you're molesting."

The man's jaw dropped open, looking at Volta and then at D2.

Volta dusted down his dress and nodded. "It's true."

The man glanced back at D2, doubt and amazement fighting for prime position on his battered face.

D2 was eyeballing Tully who had become very busy at the sink.

Volta figured it was time to make a hasty exit. "I must go find the ladies," he said. Without a backward look he sashayed out the door.

Outside he found Mia waiting anxiously.

"You idiot! Stop smiling and get in the ladies," she hissed furiously.

He followed her through the doors and looked around curiously. It was packed and very clean. It smelled pretty too. He wondered why men's toilets weren't as nice.

"You are a sight!"

Volta glanced at himself glumly. It was true. He snatched in a breath of air as something whirred up his skirt but then he relaxed. "Dirtbuster! That's handy."

"Best go into the toilet," Mia whispered. "Take off the wig and give it a good shake."

It was a good idea. Inside the cubicle he whipped off the wig, gave his scalp a good scratch, shook the blonde tresses and then slid it back on. Back at the sink he was relieved to see the wig sat straight. Mia came closer and proceeded to poke and preen until his hair resembled something of its former glory.

He washed carefully around his eyes leaving the makeup, but the rest he had to wipe away. The effect wasn't quite the same and Volta turned anxiously to Mia. "How do I look?"

Mia grinned. "Gorgeous."

The Dirtbuster departed, leaving the blue gown none the worse for wear. Satisfied it was as good as it was going to get, Volta pointed to the exit. "Let's go!" he said, suddenly excited. Grabbing Mia's hand they hurried out.

They found the others waiting in a huddle outside. Shyboy looked them over and nodded his approval. "Everyone ready?"

There was a general murmur of assent, and they set off, D2 in the lead. As they travelled the crowds seemed to increase, the floor beneath them quivering softly. It made Volta feel a little queasy. But he soon forgot as he stared around at an endless array of weird and wonderful sights. He apologized hastily to Mia after he accidentally stood on her toe whilst staring at a group of women dressed in gauzy, flowing robes. A wispy veil of material covered their faces and he could hear them chattering as exuberantly as a flock of apostle birds. Alice, he decided, was both strange and fascinating. He found that he felt oddly at home. Less of a stranger.

Whilst he enjoyed being with the Overlanders he couldn't escape the fact that he was a guest. A very welcome guest, but a guest all the same. And he couldn't ignore the fact that not all the tribe's people were thrilled by his presence. It was no good pretending that Dart, despite his outward courtesy, was happy. There was an underlying hostility, an unspoken challenge. Volta suspected he knew why.

He glanced at Mia beside him, her face illuminated pale green beneath the black wig and glasses. Yes. He had a fair idea. Trouble was, he wasn't sure what to do about it. He knew what he'd like to do. But not what he should do. And of course, the biggest question of all was whether or not there was any point in doing anything anyway. It was very tricky. Still, he thought, at this point in time Dart wasn't there. And he, on the other hand, was. He grinned happily.

Tully caught his young charge's expression. "What are you smiling about?"

Volta twitched guiltily and looked at him. "Just practising a few winning ways," he muttered.

Tully smothered a laugh. "Good idea."

They could hear Retrospectro long before they could see it. Muted, electronic music throbbed around them, its insistent beat drawing them in. Volta felt his heart accelerating, as if the music itself was laced with some kind of drug. They all picked up the pace and pressed through the crowd. Volta noticed two large double doors ahead. As they approached, they swung slowly open. A burst of music broke over their heads and a wispy, white vapour floated out, curling lazily in a bright beam of light.

They hurried toward the open doors but to Volta's intense irritation they began swinging shut. Ahead, Volta heard D2 cursing. The hybrid began to labour his way through the crowd, who seemed to be in no hurry at all. But, despite the added muscle power of Tully and Shyboy, the doors sealed shut in their faces.

Tully banged loudly on the door.

A small window appeared and a bored face peered out."What?" it said rudely.

"We want to come in, please," said Tully.

"Sure you do," said the face, "so does everyone."

Tully frowned. "Well, can we come in?"

The face nodded. "If you know the password."

Tully looked blank. "A password?"

"Yes, yes," said the face, "the password."

Tully turned to the others, clearly exasperated. "Any ideas?"

D2 stepped up to the window.

The face looked at him. "Password?"

D2 reached into his long coat, withdrew a shiny gun which he poked into the window. His finger released the safety catch. The doors opened.

As they stepped through into a golden light the face reappeared, attached this time to a body. "Welcome," he said, "to Retrospectro."

Volta stared around, music assaulting his eardrums, eyes dazzled by colour and movement. He felt a shiver of anticipation running through him. So much depended on this moment.

May Sol be with them.

# CHAPTER 18

The Madonna leant back in her chair and observed herself in the mirror. With a flick of a soft brush she added a little more shading beneath her cheekbones. Satisfied, she paused and went back to the array of screens that lined the wall of her dressing room. She pressed a button, rewound one image and watched it again. Clearly she could see the group outside the door. She watched the black hybrid extract his gun and her pathetic employee hustling them through the door. Her painted lips pursed together. It would be his last shift.

There were two ways into Retrospectro. Invitation or bribery. Her face softened a little at this latter thought. Big fat wads of water bonds. She reran the scene, peering at the pale man. There was something familiar about him. She looked at the blonde haired girl behind him, at the wide blue eyes and innocent expression. She felt troubled, but couldn't say why. Something flickered on the perimeter of her consciousness. She reached toward it, but it slipped away, out of sight.

There was a respectful knock on her door. "Five minutes to curtains, ma'am."

Curtains. Butterflies wafted soft wings through her abdomen. She turned away from the screen. She would think about this later. For now, there was only the stage.

It was showtime.

Inside the club it was warm. Much warmer than in the long corridors. The whole place seemed to vibrate with the energy of the dancers moving on a huge suspended platform. Soft clouds billowed around them. As disjointed as marionettes in the strobe lights. There was no discernible dress code, but the music seemed to mould them into one pulsating mass. An arc of a rainbow, shimmering and brilliant, connected the dance floor to the lower level. People glided up and down. Other than skeletal metal trees, leafless and black, the area below was bare, unless you counted the crush of bodies gathered to quench their thirst. The whole place was heavy with perfume.

Mia stood with the others, adjusting to the noise and light. She looked around curiously. There were pictures on the walls, giant posters of people that Mia sensed belonged to the past. A handsome man with black hair and a white suit snarled down at a forgotten audience. In another, two men and two women in tight bodysuits with wide-legged pants smiled sweetly. At the far side of the room a huge picture hung, covering two thirds of available space. It was a woman dressed in blue robes, sand rippling beneath her feet. For a moment Mia wished she were outside, with the uncompromising expanse of the desert spreading before her.

Suddenly the lights began to dim, the music fading. As if it were a signal, the dancing people began descending the rainbow elevator, jostling cheerfully for space. Mia could hear the excited timbre of their voices.

Beside her she felt Shyboy moving restlessly.

"Come on, or we'll end up at the back," he yelled.

Mia was unsure as to his meaning, but followed willingly enough, Volta and Tully stepping in behind. Caught in the throng they were drawn into the crowd who gathered, staring up expectantly at the large picture. The lights dimmed until everything became shadowed and bleary. The voices hushed, murmuring like a softly running stream. Around her Mia could feel the tension build. She felt hemmed in; aware that the sheer force of numbers would prevent her leaving if she should need to.

Then the picture on the wall shifted a fraction. It began to rise, revealing a stretch of darkness behind. As one, the crowd began chanting. Mia listened, as the voices swelled in the dim light.

"The Madonna!" they cried.

Mia, a little awed at the outpouring of emotion, waited in breathless anticipation.

A single circle of light, pale as a new moon, spilled across the stage. The crowd stilled. The atmosphere thickened, as silent as a tomb. Music drifted from all around. Not the hyper blend of synthetic sound. This was something simpler. Softer. Easier on the ear. Then a figure unfolded into the light, swathed in soft blue cloth. The figure did not move, but the music began gathering and Mia could feel its rhythm stealing into her blood. Without realising she began swaying gently. Her eyes fixated on the stage. For half a beat, the music paused to surge up again. The blue cloth melted away.

Centre stage, in a black corset and high-heeled boots, The Madonna took control.

When it was over, Mia felt a wistful sense of loss. Around her the crowd was cheering and calling, but the picture slid down and the stage disappeared. Eventually the crowd gave up and drifted away, many leaving the club but some stopping at the long bar for a drink. The club seemed diminished somehow, the rainbow less bright and the leafless trees starkly sad.

Shyboy looked around. "We have to get backstage somehow."

It was true. But they all looked blankly at each other. No one had anticipated any difficulty in this matter. The night club had seemed like such a social place. A stage show so accessible, that finding an opportunity to get a moment with The Madonna had not seemed an issue.

Mia looked at the place where the show had been. It was hard already to believe it had even existed. Only the rubbish on the floor left any real indication of the recent performance.

"Well," said Tully, "let's get a drink before we start to look like we're up to no good."

They all moved to a bar and Volta ordered drinks for them all. Mia had to turn away as the barman started flirting outrageously.

Volta, not one to miss an opportunity, smiled sweetly. "Tell me, how could a lady get backstage?"

The barman filled a tall glass with a flourish and put it on the counter. "Only one way, and that's by invite."

"Bollocks," said Volta, in a most unladylike manner.

The barman gave him a funny look but said nothing.

Mia took her glass gloomily. She sipped and sat up in shock. Melba! Then she remembered that she was no longer a child. As a member of the Sister Council, she was entitled to the alcoholic beverage made from fermented camel's milk. She took another sip, trying to look as if she drank it every day.

No one spoke in the steadily emptying club. Mia guessed that like herself, they were all worrying about their next move. She felt a flare of impatience. She was increasingly concerned for her father. Da was a prisoner. His fate lay in the hands of scientists who sought to expose the secret of divination. D2 was living proof that such men cared little how they achieved their goals. Da was in danger. They must make a move. Soon.

A voice cut through the air. "Shyboy!"

There was a shocked silence and Mia saw D2 and Tully's hands reaching for weapons. Mia looked around, her heart hammering. Who was it? Who could possibly know them in this far distant place? A thousand possibilities burst into her brain. But then Shyboy stood up and Mia saw that he was smiling.

"Palomino!" said Shyboy. He looked around at everyone. "It's cool. Pal's one of us."

Mia understood. MLF. Thank goodness.

It was a young woman. A very pretty young woman. She was beautifully dressed in a close fitting coral pink skirt and jacket. Honey blonde hair curled to her waist and her skin was like toasted almonds. And then Mia realised that she had seen her before. In the shop. Mia's eyes skimmed down a pair of long, shapely legs and — sure enough — found two neat, diamanté studded hooves.

"I know her!" Volta exclaimed.

Mia nodded at Volta. "Yes, we saw her earlier in the shop."

But Volta was shaking his head. "No. I mean — yes. I mean, I just realised. I saw her in the Poor Quarter at the Pony Follies, the first time I met Shyboy. She's a singer and dancer."

Something in Volta's tone of voice made Mia frown. She looked at him, a flicker of jealousy unfurling as she noted the look of frank admiration as he stared at the dancer.

"Guys," said Shyboy, "this is Palomino. Worked at the Follies."

There was a round of greetings. Palomino shook hands. She paused at Shyboy. "What are you doing here?" she said softly. "I have heard — things."

Mia could guess the "things" she had heard and exchanged a look with Volta.

But Shyboy seemed unperturbed. "Palomino, we've come here hoping to get an audience with The Madonna. But we're not having much luck."

The pony girl patted Shyboy on the arm. "Well, your luck's just changed." She pointed to the far side of the room to where the stage was hidden. "I've just been backstage. I worked with The Madonna for a while, but I'm married now and..." she paused and put one hand unconsciously on her belly, "well, I'm expecting."

"Congratulations. When is the baby due?" Mia asked. For her people, the birth of a child was a momentous occasion.

"Who's the dad?" said Shyboy.

Palomino laughed. "Baby's due in seven months. The father is Fidelus Ferguson."

There was silence.

Palomino's smile faded. "Something I said?"

Shyboy looked at the others, his eyes glinting with glee. "Palomino, tell me I'm not dreaming. Did you just say that the father is none other than Fidelus Ferguson?"

Palomino eyed them warily. She took a small step back. "Is that… a problem?"

Shyboy laughed, throwing his hands in the air. "You kidding? It's brilliant."

Palomino looked around the group, her eyes searching their faces. Then she reached out and grabbed a stool. "I think you'd better tell me everything."

The telling took a while.

Palomino listened patiently, sipping at her drink. When Shyboy had finished, she put her glass down. "So, cutting to the chase, you all came here to see Fidelus?"

There was a round of agreement.

Palomino smoothed a few creases from her pink suit and tossed a lock of mane out of her big grey eyes. Without a word she dug into her bag and drew out a gauzy veil, draping it over her head. It floated softly, making her features slightly fuzzy. She looked at the group. "Well, hurry up! We'll be late for dinner."

Mia, her heart leaping and bounding like a jackrabbit, hurried after Volta. She could scarcely believe their luck. And she was — she realised — absolutely starving.

The Madonna stepped back from the screen as the group disappeared out the door. She shook her head, troubled. She sat down in front of the mirror and began applying cold cream to her face. Methodically she removed the heavy stage makeup. For a while she sat, contemplating the result. Then her lips twitched into a small smile. It looked like Fidelus was going to have some guests for dinner. Life was taking an interesting turn.

# CHAPTER 19

It did not take long to reach their destination. Palomino and Shyboy talked nonstop all the way. Within ten minutes they had left the shopping centre behind, the stores giving way to dwellings. Palomino stopped outside a stone door. This seemed so improbable that Volta ran an investigatory hand down its surface. It was cool and smooth, but not stone. Just an artful imitation. Palomino placed her fore finger onto a soft pad of green gel and the door buzzed open.

Volta entered behind Mia, very curious to see what the home of the infamous Fidelus Ferguson looked like. He'd been anticipating a dark, dirty dungeon, filled with armed guards, wicked weapons and torture implements. But he could not have been further from the truth. It was an airy, bright room. Its dimensions were circular, the roof domed and smooth. Green light washed the walls. A lush array of plants grew along tall lattices. A wild tangle of vines curled around a window looking out onto a tree-lined valley, which sloped steeply down to a stream. In the centre of the room was a large pond, its surface covered in lily pads and large pink flowers.

As if driven by some invisible force, Volta crossed the floor, bending down to look into the water. He could feel the others behind him, and caught the murmurs of their muted conversation. He put a finger onto the surface of the water, breaking the tension, sending small ripples rolling away.

He reared up in shock as a head burst through the lily pads. A spray of water made Volta retreat hastily backwards.

Palomino however had no such qualms. She hastened over to the pond. "Biddy, you wicked child, get out of that pond!" She plunged one arm in up to the elbow and pulled a small wiggling body out of the water.

Volta gaped. It was a little girl. Naked and plump she laughed, her black hair crinkling and beading with droplets.

She flung her arms around Palomino, soaking her. "Meeno, I wuv you!" she lisped happily.

Palomino placed the child onto her left hip and glared down at her. "Meeno loves you too, but would love you more if you'd stop swimming in the pond."

The little girl buried her head into the woman's shoulder, peering up with one large, dark eye. "Biddy is — oh — so — sorry."

Palomino's stern expression dissolved and she grinned. "I wish I could believe you."

Biddy giggled and then put a hand guiltily over her mouth.

Palomino put her down. "Go get dry."

Biddy scampered away, dripping all over the floor.

Palomino smiled around at her guests. "That... was Biddy."

Volta wondered whose child she was. It seemed unlikely that she was Palomino's, who he thought was expecting her first baby. Perhaps Fidelus Ferguson had been married before. Doubtless he'd find out sooner or later.

Volta left the pond and made his way over to the window. A soft breeze wafted through, radiating the rich aroma of rainforest. Birds were chirping and shrieking, invisible in the canopy. The scene was disorientating. Common sense told him that he was hundreds, possibly thousands of metres beneath the earth. But he felt like he could climb out of the window into the broad branches of the tree outside.

Shyboy joined him. "Wow," he said. He poked a slender finger through the window. The scene flickered and wobbled. Then it stilled. Shyboy gently removed the finger, creating another wave of disturbance.

"What is it?" said Mia.

Volta could hear the awed tone in her voice.

Shyboy turned to her. "It's an incredibly sophisticated 3D simulation."

"Amazing isn't it?"

Volta turned at the sound of an unfamiliar voice. It belonged to a tall, slender woman. Like Palomino she was beautiful.

Her skin was the rich brown of a coffee bean. Her hair was braided tightly over a perfectly sculpted skull. She smiled, showing two rows of perfect teeth. "Hi," she said, "I'm Sybil; it's good to meet you."

There was a round of greetings. Sybil looked at Palomino. "Dinner's about ready... if everyone is hungry that is?" She looked over the company. "Perhaps you'd like to tidy up first?"

Mia immediately felt like one of the little grey grubs she had sometimes found in rotten logs. Sybil, by contrast, was immaculate. Groomed to perfection. Mia was woman enough to be aware of the admiring glances being cast in Sybil's direction. She scowled, wishing she at least looked like a girl.

Volta nodded. "I think we'd all appreciate that."

Mia couldn't subdue the uncharitable thought that Volta would have been agreeable to serving up his own liver for dinner. Still, he was nearly as pretty as their hostess.

Another woman entered the room, holding up a large ladle, dripping on the floor. Mia's bad temper tripled. Another gorgeous thing. Brilliant. The woman was untidy, it was true, with hair half in and half out of a ponytail, apron askew and wearing oddly matched socks. But her blue-black hair framed a face of delicate beauty, her long almond shaped eyes emphasized by black, thick lashes. She waved the ladle enthusiastically. "Are you changing for dinner?"

Sybil smiled serenely. "They are indeed."

Without another word the cook turned lightly on one socked foot and left.

Sybil smiled. "That was Coco. Come along, I'll show you the facilities."

"Sister," said Palomino, "shall I find some articles of clothing suitable for our guests, while their own things are cleaned and pressed?"

Sybil ran a scrutinizing eye over the slightly embarrassed assembly, pausing for several seconds on Volta, and then smiled. "I'm sure we can manage something."

Volta felt a small ripple of unease, suddenly convinced that he had been discovered. He looked at Tully who met his gaze with a small shrug. Volta sensed his bodyguard was not unduly anxious, which was reassuring. After all, Palomino was definitely on their side. It seemed unlikely they would be betrayed by her family. And besides, he couldn't wait to get out of his corset. It was murder.

He filed out of the room, curious to see more of the subterranean house. All the rooms were curved or round, airy and bright. Beautiful tapestries adorned the walls. Without being told, Volta knew that they were very old. Small niches carved into the rock walls held ornaments — rare, curious and lovely.

At a doorway Sybil paused, indicating to the men to enter. With a small smile, Volta disappeared through the door. Mia followed Sybil, finally passing through a doorway hung with long strands of green beads. They tinkled softly, clinging to hair and clothes. Mia looked around in delight. The room was painted azure blue and the floor was unmistakably timber. A tree spread overhead, a wide hammock hanging between two large branches. Several soft, stuffed owls observed them with big, round eyes.

"This is Biddy's room," said Sybil. She pointed to a small door. "The bathroom is just through there. I'll show you how the shower works before I go."

The "shower" was a small white tiled room, with two large silver buttons set on the back wall. Sybil pointed to the one on the left. "To start the shower, just press that button. When you're ready, the other button will stop the process." Sybil looked at Mia. "This shower is one of Coco's more recent inventions. She's been itching for someone outside the family to try it out." She smiled. "I'll go and organize you something to wear, I won't be long," she said, leaving the room.

Mia peered into the shower room, agog with curiosity. But then she frowned, eyes scanning the space She could not see any wash cloths or towels. Or the sweet smelling soap she liked so much.

Sybil reappeared with a bundle of clothes in her arms.

"Sybil," said Mia apologetically, "I'm sorry, but there is no cloth or soap or towel."

Sybil put the clothes on the hammock. "You won't need anything for the shower." Then she pointed at the clothes. "These should fit. I hope the colour is to your liking." And she left.

Mia inspected the dress, a simple shift of dark green which was pleasing to her. Besides, snake skins would have been an improvement on her present get up. With a groan of relief she hauled the hated wig off her head and stepped into the shower room, shutting the door behind her.

After a few moments of hesitation she undressed, pressed the button and waited. A compartment above her head slid open. But nothing happened. Perhaps the water had run out. Then Mia noticed a strange, soft, tickling sensation on her arm. She looked down but could see nothing. But within half a minute it was apparent that the dirt on her arms was beginning to mysteriously melt away. Then her hair began rippling and curling. Startled, Mia put a hand to her head but could find no explanation. The tickling sensation began spreading over her body until she began to giggle. Amazed, she watched as she grew cleaner, grease and sweat magically vanishing. As soon as she was clean she pressed the other button. The small compartment above slid shut. Bone dry, she returned to Biddy's bedroom and redressed.

There was a knock on the door and Sybil looked in. "When you're ready, Fidelus will see you."

Mia nodded and checked her image in the mirror. Her green eyes stared back. Would Fidelus Ferguson help them? What would they do if he wouldn't? The prospect of failure was nauseating.

As she left the room she found that she was trembling. They must succeed. They simply must. Whatever the cost.

# CHAPTER 20

Volta wondered if the rest of the party felt as nervous as he
did. If they did, no one betrayed the fact. Tully rocked
gently back and forth on his feet and whistled softly under
his breath. D2 and Shyboy were on the computer, playing
cards.

There was a gentle tap on the door and all heads turned.

"Come in," said Volta.

Sybil poked her head through the door. "Are you ready?'

By way of mutual assent the men stood and made their way
over to the door. Volta glanced into a full length mirror on
the way out. The lightweight jumpsuit fitted him well. It
could have almost been made for him, except it was a little
roomy around the chest. He breathed in deeply, happy to be
free of the restrictive costume. Mind you, he felt oddly
vulnerable without his disguise. He hadn't realised how
much confidence it had given him. It had provided a strange
sense of freedom. In the costume he had shed many of the

ideals that had ruled his young life. He grinned to himself. He enjoyed being a rebel.

Outside, Mia waited. Volta smiled involuntarily. Mia's hair waved softly around her face, the green eyes highlighted by a pretty dress. It occurred to him that she was not just beautiful. There was something else. Some unique aura, vital and arresting, that held one's attention, drew the eye and fascinated. Even here, deep beneath the earth, she bought with her the elements of her beloved desert. The light seemed to shine from within.

He was rudely pulled out of his reverie by Tully, who flicked him on the ear. "Move it, lover boy."

Volta glared at him, trying to think of a suitably cutting remark, but his brain failed him. He resorted to a stony stare, which Tully seemed to find even more amusing. Fuming, Volta followed the crew down the corridor.

Sybil paused and waited politely for them all to gather. She knocked loudly on a door, and opened it for them. "Please go in, I'll be back shortly with drinks."

She stepped back and D2 strode through the door, the rest crowding in behind. Volta looked around curiously. It was a shabby, untidy room, not what he'd expected at all. A large desk took up most of the space, its marked and battered surface covered in pens, papers, books and empty cups. The desk was valuable, being timber, but was scarred and stained. A chair sat behind the desk and several more were crowded together in front. The floor was bare, save a scattering of rugs. Whitewashed walls, soft green beneath the lights, were covered in framed pictures. Many of them were photos of The Madonna.

Fidelus Ferguson was standing with his back to them, dark head bent as he examined a computer screen. Alerted by the interruption he pressed a button, killing the screen, straightened up and turned around.

Fidelus Ferguson examined his visitors with undisguised curiosity and they, in turn, examined him. There was a wide silence, broken by Ferguson. One hand gestured toward the seats in front of the desk. "Please, be seated."

Volta noted the infamous renegade spoke in mellow, resonant tones. The diction was clear and crisp. Not at all what he had expected. He was handsome too, with brilliant blue eyes and grey, flecked-black hair.

There was a flutter of activity as the group sat down. D2 had to remove a few items of hardware to wedge himself into a seat.

Ferguson moved over and looked down at D2's toys. He inspected D2.

D2 stared back.

Volta noticed the tip of D2's tail flicking softly and a wave of anxiety washed over him.

Ferguson bent down and picked up a small grenade, lifting it to his eyes and rolling it thoughtfully in his fingers. He looked back at D2. Then, to Volta's enormous relief, he held out a hand. "I am in exalted company, it would seem. You must be The Confessor. "

D2 took the hand and shook it. "D2, to my friends."

Ferguson nodded and stood back. Perching on the edge of the desk, he sent books and documents cascading to the floor. Ferguson seemed not to notice. "Palomino has spoken to me of your circumstances. I understand you are seeking... hardware."

Shyboy nodded. "That's right. Sand guns."

Ferguson lifted one dark eyebrow. "Sand guns. An unusual request. An expensive commodity."

"Can you get them?" said Tully.

Ferguson's fingertips drummed on the table. Volta could practically hear their host's brain whirring. And then his heart plummeted. He knew, at that moment, that Fidelus Ferguson was not going to help.

Ferguson ran a hand thoughtfully up and down his cheek. "I can get them."

Shyboy leant a little closer to Fidelus, his eyes narrowing in concentration. "But, will you?"

Fidelus stood up abruptly, papers and pens showering down. "Probably not."

Volta felt anger flare in his abdomen. "May I ask, why?"

Fidelus gazed at the ceiling. He shrugged. "War is bad for business."

Volta jumped as Mia came to her feet. Her face was paper white, her eyes wide with fury. Her slender frame trembled under the weight of emotion.

"Bad — for — business." Mia spat out each word as if it were poison on her tongue. She stepped up to Ferguson, standing on tiptoes until her nose was level with his chin. Then she jabbed him in the solar plexus.

Volta was not the only one to wince.

"You are a contemptible human being," Mia continued. "I could kill you!" She sank back onto her heels and stepped back. "But I won't, I will curse you and I will lay the spilt blood of my people at your feet."

Volta stood up, suddenly afraid. The others followed suit.

Fidelus Ferguson looked down at Mia, a peculiar expression on his face.

Then the door opened and Palomino looked in. Volta could have kissed her.

She smiled. "A drink anyone?" Then she frowned at Ferguson. "Is something the matter?"

Mia turned, hands on hips. "Yes, there is something 'the matter'. Your husband won't help. We've been wasting our time."

Sybil entered then.

Coco arrived. "Dinner is served," she announced. She looked around the room, and her smile faded. "What's happened?"

Palomino was glaring at her husband. "Fergie, is what's happening."

The women exchanged knowing glances and turned on Ferguson. "Are you upsetting the guests, Fidelus?" said Sybil, dark eyes flashing.

Ferguson seemed to deflate like a punctured goat's bladder. He retreated behind his desk. But there he seemed to regain some confidence. "This — ladies — is business."

Palomino smiled sweetly. "Oh, but Fergie darling, your business is our business."

The young woman's endearment seemed so strange that Volta had to turn away to hide a smirk. He didn't dare look at Tully.

Ferguson looked furious, he opened his mouth and then shut it again. His piercing blue eyes swept over the company, stopped at Mia, and then moved on. "Ladies," he said, his tone pained, "I think we should retire for dinner."

In strained silence the party moved back to the dining area, an oval room with pale green silk walls and slate floors. A table was tastefully set out with terracotta dishes and a fern green tablecloth with white linen napkins. Silently they all sat. Little Biddy bounced in and climbed up onto a chair. Her chin just appeared over the top of the table.

Sybil tutted. "Biddy, go and get your cushion."

Biddy scowled, reminding Volta strongly of Mia.

"I'm a big girl," said Biddy, and picked up a fork. "Don't need cushion."

Ferguson sat down.

Biddy looked at him beneath long black lashes. "Isn't that right, Daddy?"

Ferguson said, "Biddy, do as Sybil tells you."

Biddy dropped the fork, her bottom lip quivering.

Without another word the planet's most infamous individual scooped the child up and sat her on his lap. The tears miraculously dried up.

Sybil rolled her eyes. "You spoil that child."

Ferguson appeared not to hear as he popped a morsel of meat into Biddy's open mouth. He then filled his own plate and began eating.

Palomino smiled at Mia who, seemingly recovered from her outburst, was deeply involved in a salad of greens. "Mia, we have a business proposition for you."

Mia blinked. She looked around the table. "Who is 'we'?"

Sybil picked up the baton. "That would be Palomino, Coco and myself. Owners, managers and chief bottle washers of the Coco Company and blissfully wedded wives of Fidelus Ferguson."

Volta wasn't sure if he'd heard right. Had she said 'wives'? Plural?

Mia looked as baffled as Volta felt. She looked slowly at each woman in turn. "You mean, that you are all married to the same man?"

"Yes, indeed," said Sybil, "I'm sure you would agree that such a bad man needs at least three good women to keep him in order."

Volta eyed Ferguson nervously. But a small smile was playing around the man's lips. The renegade looked at his wives, who smiled back sweetly. Then Ferguson sighed, put down his fork and gave Biddy a banana. It was not, Volta decided, exactly a white flag, but near enough.

Mia looked at Palomino. "What kind of business proposal?"

The three wives exchanged loaded looks. Palomino turned once more to Mia. "Mia, you have something that we need."

"What?" said Mia.

Volta had a hunch, but waited patiently.

"Water," said Palomino, confirming Volta's suspicions.

Volta looked at Mia, curious as to her response.

Mia shook her head slowly. "No," she said firmly. "I do not have water. I merely have the ability to find water, if it is there."

It was, Volta thought, a good answer. Mia, like her father, had an affinity with water. An innate ability to locate hidden water courses. It was the reason that Mia was hunted. Scientists were convinced the answer lay in the green-eyed diviner's DNA. Once identified, the knowledge could be utilised for profit.

Coco leaned across the table. "So it's true, you are a diviner."

Mia sat very still, her eyes moving from each of the expectant women arrayed around her. She chewed at her mouthful of salad. She peeked briefly at Ferguson and finally put down her fork quietly. "I am."

Volta was impressed by her cool. He could tell that the wives shared his sentiment. He glanced at Ferguson and caught him eyeing Mia speculatively. The renegade's expression made Volta feel unsettled, but he was not sure why.

"So Mia, we were hoping that we could trade water for guns," Sybil said. "What do you say?"

"I am an Overlander first," said Mia softly. "And a diviner second. I am not saying yes or no. This is a decision that can only be made collectively. I must discuss the matter first with the Sister Council."

Volta was pleased. Whilst this exchange was not conclusive, he felt that overtures were being made. And he wondered if the Overlanders would agree. Their need for weapons was great. He guessed the Ferguson wives knew this. But the

Overlanders had their own code of honour. They may view the idea with abhorrence. He wondered what Mia felt.

He looked at Mia, and his throat tightened as he noted the dark smudges beneath her remarkable eyes, and a tightness around her lips. She looked tired and anxious. Hardly surprising, for Volta knew this offer would effectively stretch out the negotiations. Which meant the journey north would be delayed. A situation that he knew would grieve Mia. And her grief, he realised, was his grief.

He decided it was time to change the direction of the conversation. Volta caught Sybil's eye. "Tell me Sybil, why are the lights down here green?"

Sybil waved her spoon toward Coco. "You should ask the resident genius. It's Coco's design."

Coco smiled. "It's not so clever really. The lights are green because it is a product of bioluminescence."

Tully grinned and butted in. "Bio what?"

Coco shook her head. "Sorry. Behind the glass is a vast colony of fungi that release light through chemical reaction. It works both to provide light and as a recycling plant for human waste. Our waste feeds the fungi." She paused and gazed at one of the glowing cylinders. "Of course it is only a backup system to the main supply of energy."

"What is the main supply?" Shyboy asked.

Palomino smiled at him. "You are."

Shyboy looked puzzled and Coco took pity on him. "You must have noticed the floors."

Volta snapped his fingers. "Of course — it's brilliant. It's the production of electricity through the constant movement of thousands of feet." He turned to Coco. "The dance floor at Retrospectro?"

Coco nodded. "Yes, it's a significant contributor. The whole of Alice is self-sufficient in power and light."

Volta looked at Ferguson who raised an eyebrow and grinned, making him suddenly seem much more human.

Palomino must have caught the exchange. "That's right Volta, you have guessed correctly, we are the brains and Fergie is the brawn."

Volta waited for the infamous renegade to react. But Ferguson merely rolled his eyes and bounced Biddy on his knee.

"How does the shower work?" Mia asked.

Volta's ears pricked up. It had been a weird experience.

Palomino giggled, glancing at Coco. "You don't want to know."

Of course then everyone wanted to know very badly indeed, Volta being no exception.

Palomino filled them in. "It's Coco's latest invention. The shower releases millions of genetically modified white blood cells that literally eat the dirt off. It works brilliantly but is a hard concept to sell."

Volta could see everyone trying not to be obvious as they inspected bare portions of skin. He was acutely aware he was in the company of intelligent, highly resourceful people. But Volta also sensed they were used to getting their own way. Despite the warmth and generosity they had received, he felt an underlying prickle of caution. In particular he sensed that Mia had become the centre of their attention. Was it the water? Or was it something else?

# CHAPTER 21

With a stomach full of good food, Mia was feeling very sleepy. She had no way of knowing what time it was. Through the arched doorway she could see light streaming through the windows. Except they weren't windows. It was a disorientating experience. A burning desire to leave the underground city filled her. She longed to suck the dry desert wind into her lungs and to feel the strong back of Whisper beneath her. In her chest, a strong resentment toward Fidelus Ferguson was still burning.

It had shocked her to the core that any individual could be so callous, so absorbed in himself. But then she thought of the wives and little Biddy who all seemed happy and content despite Ferguson's formidable reputation. They seemed not the least bit cowed or disadvantaged. In fact, quite the contrary. It was a lot to think about. She had initially been surprised by their offer, but now realised that she was being naive. It seemed that water was what everyone wanted. And people would stop at nothing to get it. Yet, it was a way forward. A valid bargaining chip for her people.

But she also felt impatient. Every hour that passed was an hour she was not on her way north. She was determined to get back to her people as quickly as possible. The prospect of returning and sharing the burden of responsibility comforted her a little. She looked around just in time to catch Biddy stuffing sweet biscuits into her father's mouth. His cheeks bulged like a desert rat's. Biddy, giggling, picked up another. Fidelus winked at Mia with one wicked blue eye. Mia looked away hastily, trying not to be amused. But something softened within her, as she remembered another small child on another father's lap, safe and loved.

"Biddy! Enough!" said Sybil.

Biddy released her father's top lip, dropping the biscuit guiltily.

"Honestly Fergie, she is as wild as a mountain goat," Coco chided.

Ferguson hastily swallowed and began tickling Biddy beneath her armpits. The child, screaming in delight, wriggled off her father's lap like an eel. He shook his head. "She's not wild, she's happy and free."

Three pairs of eyes bored into his.

Ferguson sighed, bent down and poked Biddy. "Behave," he said sternly.

Biddy blew a loud raspberry and Ferguson collapsed into a fit of laughter.

All three wives berated him loudly.

Mia caught Volta's eye and exchanged a furtive grin.

Shyboy cleared his throat and the noise dropped away. "Thank you for your hospitality," he said, "but we must not intrude upon you any longer."

Palomino looked at him. "You can't go yet. Stay the night. You must see the orchards before you go." She paused and looked imploringly at Mia.

Mia's heart sank. It would be the height of rudeness to leave now. While these were not her people, a bond was forming that she did not want to fray. She swallowed her disappointment, resigning herself to the inevitable.

Curiously, Ferguson backed his wives up. "I too have something I'd like to show you."

While the renegade seemed to be making a statement in a general way, Mia couldn't escape the feeling that the comment was orientated toward herself. Then she flushed. What right had she to judge others as self-absorbed? She was being vain and self-important. Nonna would be most disappointed.

She looked around at the others, trying to gauge their feelings. D2 shrugged. Tully seemed agreeable as did Shyboy. Volta looked troubled but did not speak.

Palomino clapped her hands together in delight. "It's settled then."

D2 stood. "I thank you," he said. "But I have business to attend to. I will return at sunrise."

D2 left soon after, while the rest of them settled down to bed. Mia slept on a mattress in Biddy's room and the men in the guest room. Biddy was soon fast asleep but Mia could not settle. Her mind buzzed with all the happenings of the long day. To her delight a moon appeared upon the far wall of the room. Slowly it crept upward until it hung overhead, casting moon shadows. Stars twinkled cheerfully. While she knew it was not real, it brought her comfort. As she fell asleep she prayed to Sol that her Da could see the son and the daughters in the sky too.

When she awoke the sun was rising, a flush of red staining the wall as the stars diminished and died. The little girl still slept, an owl clutched in one hand. Mia slid off the sheets and dressed silently, slipping through the door into the hush of a new day. She tiptoed down the corridor and into the dining area. But it was empty. Unsure what to do, she wandered toward the next room but halted abruptly beneath the arched entry.

Volta, dressed in trousers and a black shirt, was kneeling at the water, staring down into its depths. His face was strangely expressionless, with no trace of the mocking humour Mia had grown to expect. There were dark smudges beneath his eyes and she guessed he had not slept. He was troubled and, instinctively, she stepped out toward him. But then stopped.

Why, exactly, she was not sure. Perhaps because she was fearful he would resent her being witness to his vulnerability. Silently she backed away. Then with a deep breath, she clomped back across the floor.

By the time she reached the archway Volta was at the window, running a hand over his chin. He smiled at her, and she was relieved at the warmth of his reception.

"Good morning," he said.

Mia touched her forehead with her fingers, "I see you," she replied formally. She went to stand somewhat self-consciously beside him. "So... what do you think of Fidelus Ferguson?"

"I'm not sure. It's really odd but I keep feeling that I've met him before. There is something familiar about him, but I just can't put my finger on it."

Mia thought about this. "Do you think it could be because you already know so much about him? You know, all the talk. Things you have seen on your computers."

"Perhaps."

Mia looked at him. "Do you trust him?"

Volta sighed. "I really don't know. But I do trust his wives."

Mia nodded, reassured that Volta's assessment of the situation was not dissimilar to her own. "What do you think D2 is doing?"

Volta grinned. "No idea. Doubtless we'll find out."

To her acute embarrassment Mia's stomach grumbled, but the loud clip clop of hooves mercifully distracted Volta.

It was Palomino, still half asleep, blinking in the bright light. "Morning," she yawned.

"I see you," replied Mia and Volta simultaneously.

The young man's unconscious use of her people's greeting pleased Mia inordinately.

Soon they were seated in the dining room, drinking hot chocolate while Palomino cooked up porridge. Mia was savouring the delicious drink when she was alerted to a rumpus in the kitchen. There were several loud thumps and some very unladylike language from Palomino, followed by several yowls of pain.

Mia and Volta bolted into the kitchen where they found Palomino half in and half out of the back door. Mia raced over and stared in astonishment. Palomino was hanging on to one end of a loaf of bread whilst two hybrid kittens had a hold of the other.

Mia did not know what to do. Whilst it was obvious the kittens were stealing, Mia couldn't help but notice the fragility of their tiny wrists and eyes too big in the little faces. A vivid vision of her people's recent suffering flooded through her.

Palomino turned to Mia. "Help me!"

But Mia was conflicted. She did nothing.

Volta, however, had no such problem. He reached out and grasped Palomino's hand. "Let them have it," he said softly.

Palomino's big grey eyes popped with indignation. "Are you crazy? They're stealing!"

Volta nodded. "I know. But what choice do they have?"

Palomino's mouth opened to protest, but shut again. She looked at the two kittens who had frozen, still clutching their prize. Her hand relaxed. "Shoo! Scram!" she advised them.

They didn't argue, scooting across the small yard, up a pot plant and over the high wall.

There was a strained silence back at the breakfast table. Mia was deeply embarrassed. She put down her spoon into the empty bowl. "I'm sorry, Palomino."

But to her relief, the girl smiled. "No. It's me that's sorry. Sometimes it is necessary to see the world through a fresh pair of eyes. You were quite correct in your reluctance to help me. It's just that the feline hybrids are considered an infestation in Alice. A pest to be rid of. I am ashamed of myself. And I hardly dare think what your good friend, D2 would have made of that little scene. Of course I can spare a loaf of bread."

A loud clattering of feet heralded the arrival of Shyboy and Tully. The latter with Biddy perching precariously on one shoulder. Sybil and Coco followed close behind, chatting quietly.

Palomino smiled a greeting. "Would anyone like to come shopping with me?"

Mia decided it was a Sol sent opportunity to try and make amends. "I'll go," she said.

A short discussion followed, in which the men decided to forgo the pleasures of shopping to spend the morning evaluating the response to Beatrice's email.

Breakfast finished, Mia joined Palomino and they set off, walking back toward the wide avenue of shops and stores. As they passed the alley where the furrier's lair had been, Mia paused, pouring out the story to Palomino.

When she had finished, Palomino's beautiful young face was troubled. "So, you're saying that the furriers were not just capturing cats but hybrids too?"

"Yes," said Mia. "There was a girl there."

Palomino paled. "I had no idea. I never imagined—"

But Mia wasn't listening. Her eyes were fixated on a familiar broad back and black shaven head. D2. But that was not all. He had a companion. It was Shoo. And as the pair disappeared out of sight, Mia saw that behind their backs, their tails were entwined.

Mia couldn't wait to tell the others. Who'd have thought!

# CHAPTER 22

Mia felt she had never been so tired in her life. Not even after a week in the desert, on minimal rations. Palomino, on the other hand, seemed inexhaustible. She went into shop after shop, never wavering in her interest. The hybrid girl examined each store's contents minutely, taking delight in every purchase. Mia trailed after her into what felt like the millionth shop. She looked around at the display. Head coverings crowded every available space in a dizzying array of shapes, sizes and colours.

"Mia, what do you think?" said Palomino, putting a hat on her head.

Mia looked at the wide black and red hat. "It's very... nice. But it would blow off in the wind."

Palomino took the hat off. "True," she said. "But I've got a lovely dress that it would go with."

Mia realised that Palomino would buy the hat anyway. In the same way she'd bought a dozen or so other articles, which to

Mia seemed to be nothing but bothersome objects to be hauled around. Frankly, she was bored. Now, if they'd seen something useful, like leather, or a saddle cloth, or even water bottles, it would've been different.

Palomino put the hat back. "Mia, don't you like shopping?"

Mia froze, her tongue tied in a knot. She didn't want to say that she loathed an activity which Palomino so obviously adored. She didn't want to offend or spoil her new friend's pleasure. "Of course I like it," she lied.

Palomino snorted down her nose. It sounded so like Whisper that Mia grinned.

Palomino observed Mia carefully. "Are you sure?"

Panicking, and desperate to reassure, Mia glanced frantically around the store. Mia thought most of the hats were ridiculous. They wouldn't have lasted from sunup to sunset in the desert. Most didn't serve any useful purpose. But she persevered, her eyes darting around. Then something caught her eye. A scarf. But it was the colour that really drew her attention. A rich burnt orange. Suddenly she knew that it would look exactly right on her mother. She moved closer, picking it up. She ran it through her fingers, enjoying its slippery smoothness.

Palomino pounced. "So, you like the scarf, Mia?"

Mia smiled. "Yes," she said.

Palomino twitched the scarf from Mia's hands and marched triumphantly to the counter. The purchase was made and the garment placed into a bag.

Mia took it shyly. "I thank you. My mother will wear it for the ceremonies."

Palomino let out a long sighing breath, her honey hair rising and falling about her pretty face. "I'm parched. Let's get a drink."

Mia nodded. She could have drunk a lake dry. Several moments later she sank gratefully into a chair and dropped the bags at her aching feet. The delicious aroma of clean water floated in the air. She was delighted to hear Palomino ordering two. And tea.

Mia watched Palomino re-examining her purchases. Mia was pleased to see Palomino so relaxed and happy. Perhaps shopping had its rewards. At this thought, she picked up her bag and pulled the scarf out. It was lovely. Vibrant and rich.

A carafe of water and a pot of tea materialized on the table and Mia put the scarf away and tried the water. It was cold and delicious.

"So," said Palomino, "what kind of ceremonies?"

Mia thought for a moment and had another drink. "Well, when the rest of my tribe join the camp there will be the Joinings, the Promisings and the Namings." Palomino nodded encouragingly, so Mia continued. "The Joinings are those men and women who are at an age for family responsibilities. The Promisings are those who the Sister

Council have chosen for future Joinings. The Namings are as they sound. The time when a baby is officially made one of the people."

Mia looked at her companion who was sitting, staring silently. Something in her expression made Mia uneasy. She put her glass down carefully. "What is wrong?"

Palomino took a sip of her drink and Mia noted that she looked very uncomfortable.

Mia tapped the table top impatiently. "What?"

"I'm sorry, Mia," said Palomino. "It's just that, well, I'm a bit... surprised."

Mia was mystified. "Surprised by what?"

Poor Palomino looked extremely awkward. "Well, if I understand you correctly, I think you said that your marriages are... arranged?"

Mia sagged inwardly with relief. She'd been scared she said something really bad. She nodded enthusiastically. "Oh yes, of course, it has always been so." Again she sensed some pent up emotion in her new friend. Impatient now, she shook her head. "I see you are upset, but I must be very stupid, because I do not see why."

Palomino bit her lip and flushed. "Mia, again, I am sorry. I must explain. It's just that for us, marriage or 'Joinings' are a matter of individual choice. We marry who we love."

Mia was shocked. "But how could I know who is best for me? Surely, the Sister Council is most wise? They only seek to create harmony and happiness."

Palomino frowned. "But Mia, what about... love?"

"What do you mean by 'love'?" Mia asked.

Palomino seemed to consider this question for a while. Then she sat up, leaning in toward Mia. "Love is a very strong feeling," she said. "A strong emotion. Love for a person makes you want to be with someone, to help them, support them, and when they are not there you feel sad."

"But Palomino," Mia said, "I feel all those things for Da, Nonna, Mother, Whisper, my aunties and—" Mia stopped abruptly as heat surged into her cheeks. She had been about to include Volta's name on the list. She took a strategic sip of her drink to cover her confusion. "And my people. So, you see, it will be easy to love my chosen one also."

"What if you did not want to marry the man the council chose?" said Palomino. "Would they force you?"

Mia was aghast. "Force me? Of course not! The Sister Council can only make the suggestion. But no man or woman would be forced into a Joining. Those that Join can be Unjoined, but it is very rare. As I said, the council chooses well. Why would they do otherwise?"

Palomino took a long drink, her expression pensive. Then she placed her cup down carefully. "Mia, do your people ever Join outside your own tribes?"

Mia stared down at her feet, uncomfortable but not sure why. "It has not happened for many generations."

Mercifully Palomino was distracted. "Look! It's D2," she said, "with a... friend."

Mia saw that the young woman was right. It was D2, still in the company of Shoo. D2 carried a huge wrapped parcel slung over one shoulder.

"Come on," said Mia. "Let's see what they're up to."

Palomino and Mia got up. Mia's head was full of their recent conversation. It had unsettled her. She did not doubt that the Overlander way was the best way. Did not their very survival prove that? Her belief and trust in the Sister Council was absolute. It had never occurred to her to question. Indeed, it had never occurred to her that there was any other way. But the unusual Joining habits of the Ferguson family had alerted her to alternatives. And today Palomino had questioned the Overlander way. Mia was filled with confusion and apprehension. Had she been subconsciously subduing an attachment to Volta? For the first time she dared to consider him as a potential partner. Could it be possible? But sense told her that a Joining with an outsider (even one so undeniably attractive) would not be necessarily welcomed.

Once her tribe arrived at the camp, the celebrations would begin immediately. The land could not support the vast numbers for long. The lake, whilst bountiful, must not be depleted. The tribes must soon split up and disperse. She felt a wave of longing for Nonna. Of all the women, she was the wisest. She would lay her head in Nonna's lap and share her troubles. Nonna would listen.

Relieved by this decision, Mia relaxed. They were almost back at the dwelling. She craned her neck looking for D2 and Shoo and spotted them as they disappeared through the front door. Soon Mia stepped over the threshold, thoroughly relieved to be back. The room was empty except for Biddy who was dog-paddling happily around the pond. She waved at them briefly and carried on.

Palomino shook her head. "Sybil will give her what for if she catches her."

Mia giggled as Biddy disappeared completely, the water lapping dangerously close to the edge. There was no sign of anybody else. But then the sound of voices drifted through and Mia set off to investigate.

As she travelled the voices became clearer, and she realised that there was a vigorous conversation in progress. Intrigued, she found herself in the kitchen, where D2, Shoo, Volta and Sybil were crowding around a bench top. There was a pungent aroma in the room. With the exception of Shoo they all appeared to be talking at once.

"What is it?" Mia asked, announcing her arrival.

Volta and Tully turned to greet her.

"Look!" Volta grinned.

Mia inspected the bench top. Still half wrapped in a canvas cloth was the biggest fish Mia had ever seen. Its dead eyes looked glassily at her; it spread over the whole surface of the bench, silver scales shimmering in the light.

Mia looked at Shoo who seemed delighted with herself. She was purring and patting the fish. She looked at Mia with her golden eyes. "Big fish for big dish," she said.

Coco pulled a huge pan out of a cupboard and eyed it. "That should be big enough."

"What are you doing?" asked Mia, catching D2's eye.

His black eyes were unfathomable. "Feeding an army," he said.

There was a round of laughter.

But Mia wasn't sure whether D2 was joking or not.

# CHAPTER 23

The orchard was amazing. Mia and Volta followed Sybil up and down the rows of trees. Their trunks and branches held many small, waxy, pink flowers and several gourd-shaped fruit. The leaves were long and green, with new growth of deep salmon pink. It seemed impossible that anything could grow so well beneath the earth. Mia breathed in, her nose filling with the rich organic smell of earth and slowly rotting mulch. Several loud clicks caught her attention and she looked upward toward the domed ceiling and cried out as a spray of misty water rained down. The green leaves sparkled beneath the artificial lights.

"What are they?" she asked.

"Cocoa trees," Sybil volunteered. "Cocoa beans are in big demand. For hot chocolate and confection."

Mia could fully understand this. She loved hot chocolate which was a rare treat.

Sybil sniffed a flower and continued. "But they need water. A lot of water. The business is extremely lucrative but our water supply is falling."

Mia nodded. "I see," she said carefully.

Sybil walked on, and Mia glanced at Volta but he shrugged and so she followed.

"But it is not just the business," Sybil continued. "It's Alice. If we cannot find another source, Alice will die. And with it, the last independent community on Earth. The financial rewards for finding water would be... significant."

Mia felt horribly out of her depth. She did not know anything about finance. It was men's business. But at the same time she sensed she should not reveal her ignorance. What should she say?

Then Volta finally stepped forward. "What kind of financial reward?"

Mia could have cried in relief.

A ghost of a smile played across Sybil's mouth, but Mia sensed she was not entirely pleased by the intrusion. "The company was thinking of two hundred sand guns and one hundred and fifty thousand water bonds."

It seemed like a vast amount of wealth to Mia.

Volta, however, did not seem impressed. He snorted imperiously down his aristocratic nose. "Triple the guns and you might be close. But the water bonds are useless. The

Overlanders have little use for them." He turned to Mia. "What do you think?"

Mia felt as if she were walking through quicksand. She felt foolish. But then she sighed, better foolish than a fool. "I cannot say. I must take this idea to my people. I do not have the knowledge to speak."

To her surprise both Volta and Sybil were appraising her with what seemed to be approval.

Sybil bowed her head gracefully. "This is honest and wise, Mia. I'm sure an arrangement can be found that satisfies all parties."

Mia nodded. But she wasn't so sure. The Fergusons wanted to exploit her for their own needs. An idea that was abhorrent. Yet, Sybil had also talked about Alice. The whole of Alice. Which was different.

Sybil looked at her watch and made a small exclamation. "Look at the time, we must go and meet Fergie."

They made their way back through the trees, picking up Tully on the way. Shyboy, Shoo and D2 had stayed behind to help with the fish soup. Mia had been pleased to get away, the kitchen had become very cramped.

It did not take long to get to their destination, a brisk fifteen minute walk that left much of the hustle and bustle behind. The stretch of road was pleasant, faced by well-maintained homes. At the end they met Ferguson who was waiting outside a large double door, wide enough for twenty men. Volta thought the renegade looked extremely pleased with himself and was deeply curious as to what he intended to show them. Ferguson led them into a dirt floored passage that sloped gently downward. It was dimly lit, but the air was fresh.

"Not far now," said Ferguson after several minutes.

Volta's curiosity grew by the footfall. When Mia stopped abruptly, Volta almost bumped into her. But she barely noticed. She inhaled deeply. She turned to Ferguson, who was looking at her expectantly.

"It's not?" she said softly.

The renegade grinned. "Could be. Why don't you go see for yourself?"

Mia did not reply but whirled around and took off like a hare.

Volta tore after her. "Mia! What is it, Mia?" But the answer presented itself as he entered a large cavern. Volta stopped, looking around in delight at the long row of horses installed in stables. Many came to their door, peering out. A few whickered. Enraptured, Volta travelled slowly down the aisle. One beautiful head after another leaned out to greet him. At one stall he paused, running his hand down the neck of a bay stallion. His finely dished face and wide set eyes spoke of his ancient blood lines.

"His name is Baha," said Ferguson, coming toward them with Tully and Sybil.

"Where are they from?" asked Mia.

"I bought them from a distant continent. They are among the last of their line."

"What are they for?" Mia wondered out loud.

Ferguson shrugged. "They are an investment. I plan to breed and sell them."

Mia looked shocked. "What, you mean... to anyone?"

Ferguson nodded. "What else?"

Volta listened and watched intently. He felt pleased on two counts. Firstly, Ferguson had definitely put his size fourteens right in it. Mia was looking at the renegade as if he'd sprouted goat horns. And secondly, from the moment he set eyes on the bay stallion, Volta had wanted him. And, miraculously, it seemed possible. He wondered how many water bonds he had left, and whether or not he could access them. Still, he betrayed none of this, moving away to inspect the rest of the livestock.

The sound of shod feet alerted him and he turned to see half a dozen mounted horses approaching. The jockeys nodded a polite greeting, chattering amongst themselves. They dismounted and led their steeds to various empty stalls.

Mia joined Volta, her face set in a thunderous expression of disapproval. "Did you hear that?" She did not wait for an answer but carried on in a furious hiss. "He sells his horses as if they were jugs of Melba!"

Volta grinned. "Welcome to my world," he said.

Mia glared at him, eyes like chips of stone, and flounced away. Still amused (and not a little pleased) Volta joined Tully to inspect the area from which the mounted horses had come from. It was a huge space, its floor covered in sand, mirrors glittering along the back wall. A chestnut horse cantered in a circle, nostrils flaring, breath puffing rhythmically. Volta glanced at Mia, who looked around, her mouth set in a hard line of disapproval.

Ferguson, on the other hand, stood smiling with delight. He looked at his guests. "Fantastic set up, isn't it?"

"No," said Mia, rudely.

Tully winced visibly, but Mia seemed oblivious. "How can you keep them down here, where there is no sun or summer breeze? Where they can never run as a herd or care for their young?"

Ferguson looked surprised but did not seem offended. "If I turn them out, I'll never catch them again. Besides, they are too valuable, they may get hurt or injured."

Mia sniffed loudly in disdain, but mercifully kept her mouth shut.

They left when Ferguson said that the wives were expecting them for a meal. They retraced their steps, Volta stopping once more to talk to Baha. He thought of Dart on his black stallion and himself on his fat pony, Hawk Eye. It was not an agreeable contrast. Then he envisioned himself astride Baha. He smiled to himself. That was more like it.

Mia was very quiet as they walked back to the house and Volta wished they could find a moment to talk in private. Despite the perils they had experienced during their crazy dash across the desert with the Isbane army hot in pursuit, there had, Volta reflected, been benefits. He had enjoyed unrestricted access to Mia's company. He missed that. How quickly things could change. It felt as if life was conspiring to push them further apart. Volta hardly dared think about where this would all end.

When they entered the house Coco appeared and waved at them. "Just in time to eat."

The kitchen was barely recognizable. Its pristine surfaces and shiny floor were a mess of scales, bones and unidentified debris. Shoo, resplendent in a tall white chef's hat, was at the sink. But washing up did not seem to be progressing. Bubbles kept floating lazily up from the sink which set Shoo off into a frenzy as she tried to burst them.

Palomino was clearing the table, her hooves clopping hollowly on the floor. She paused to smile and greet the others. "It was a huge success," she said. "Over thirty youngsters turned up, plus a number of young mums with kittens. We'll make it a weekly thing."

Ferguson looked horrified but patted his wife gently on the cheek. "Terrific," he said dryly.

Coco giggled.

Volta took over from Shoo and they all stuck in and cleaned up the mess. Soon all that remained was the fishy aroma. His stomach gurgled. He was starving.

Coco called attention. "Everyone for fish soup?"

There were murmurs of agreement and the group retired to the dining table. The soup was good. Full of onions, carrots, potatoes and peas, served with crusty bread, goat's cheese and green salad. The figs in syrup and the dish of thick yellow cream that followed were delectable.

Replete, they all lingered at the table, chatting cheerfully. Ferguson and his family excused themselves and Shyboy took the opportunity to bring everyone up to date.

Shyboy's slender fingers flowed over the keyboard. "We have had an unbelievable response. Over three hundred thousand hits, and several thousand replies. Many of them are from Isbane, but there are a fair few from around the planet and even a couple from the galaxy." He opened up a few messages and read them out for everyone's benefit.

Volta was stunned at the results. It was way beyond expectation. There was no doubt that poor Beatrice had captured the imagination of a nation, and beyond. He looked at Shyboy. "What next?"

Shyboy lifted his hands and shook back the sleeves of his robe, smiling. "Never thought you'd ask." He switched over sites. "O.K. Probably the most asked question has been in reference to Beatrice's identity. 'Who is she?'" he glanced around the table, to make sure everyone was with him so far. "So, I came up with an answer." He tapped a key on the board. The image of Beatrice flickered and faded. The same image reappeared but typed below were the words 'I am the truth'.

There was a collective sigh of approval.

"That's brilliant," said Tully.

"I am the truth." Mia repeated. "It is good."

Volta smiled grimly. "That should put my nearest and dearest in a fine lather."

Tully nodded. "Just turns the pressure up nicely."

Ferguson strode in with Biddy hanging on one arm. D2 stood discreetly in front of the screen as Shyboy shut it down.

"Ferguson," said Volta smoothly, "I guess we should be thinking about heading back to the camp. Mia's people will be anxious."

Ferguson smiled. "Of course, I'll inform the wives."

Mia and Volta exchanged looks, both grinning, it sounded so odd. They all drifted off to their rooms to prepare for departure.

After a very close shave, Volta gasped for air as both Tully and Shyboy jerked ruthlessly on the strings of the corset. His last meal suddenly seemed like a bad idea. He pulled on the sandals and straightened his wig.

They all reassembled in the kitchen. Mia was dressed in her disguise and looked less than happy. She scratched her scalp under the wig. "It's so hot," she grumbled.

Palomino gave her a hug. "It's not for long."

"Are we travelling in the bubble?" asked Mia.

"No you're not," said Palomino. "I've arranged for you to travel in one of our vehicles. Fergie insisted."

Everyone looked cheered by this prospect.

When the other wives and Biddy arrived, conversation broke out. Volta, sensing a drawn out goodbye, made a sudden decision. He'd nip down to Ferguson's den and sound him out about buying the stallion, Baha. He could worry about the money later.

"Won't be long," he said to Tully. Aware of the pressure of time he hurried as fast as his corset would allow, banged firmly on the office door and stepped through. "I'm glad I—" He stopped dead.

Perched behind the desk was a stunning woman in a clinging peacock blue dress and long white gloves. Volta's eyes moved from the woman to the collection of images on the walls. He looked at the woman once more. "I'll be—" and he began to laugh, half out of shock, half out of stunned admiration. It was utterly incredible. But it was true. Fidelus Ferguson was The Madonna.

# CHAPTER 24

Squashed into the small hovercraft, Mia listened incredulously as Volta unfolded his revelation. The Madonna and Fidelus Ferguson were one and the same. It was a lot to take on board. Mia pondered on the subject. It seemed that Fidelus Ferguson was a complicated man. He was a renegade. A man of power. An entertainer. A family man. But which was Fidelus Ferguson? Mia wasn't sure what to make of it at all. She pressed her nose up against the grubby window and saw the lights of the camp beckoning below. Love surged in her heart. She was home.

---

The Madonna sat in front of her computer contemplating the brutalized features of the woman she knew only as 'Beatrice'. Words rippled across the screen. 'I am the truth'. Her lips twitched in a small smile. She had no doubt as to the identity of the creators of the post. The Madonna was many things, but she was not a fool.

The young man, Volta, had left a distinct impression. She suspected this was largely because the youth reminded her of herself when she had been young. Individually their guests had been an impressive bunch. But combined they appeared to be metabolising into something else entirely. The Madonna wondered what the end result would be. It was an intriguing thought.

She looked at the screen again. And came to a decision. She composed a brief email and then decisively pressed the send button. It was risky. Very risky. But she could feel a frisson of excitement as the possible consequences of her actions went sizzling through her brain. The click of the hard drive alerted her, she had not anticipated a response so soon. She waited patiently and grinned at the sight of Wolfram's irate face.

Wolfram snarled at Fidelus Ferguson. It was not the first time he had rued the day they had met. It took considerable effort to keep his temper on a leash. "What the hell do you think you're playing at? Have you lost your mind?"

The Madonna smiled and pushed a loose curl from her face. "Good evening Wolfram, a pleasure to talk to you too," she said softly. She batted her long curled lashes. "You seem upset."

Wolfram looked murderous, a fat red vein throbbing on his forehead. "Take off that bloody ridiculous costume."

The smile faded and the brilliant blue eyes narrowed.
"Respect for The Madonna, if you please." Said Ferguson in
a dangerously soft voice. He watched as Wolfram
swallowed his pride, forcing his features into pleasant lines.
It was most amusing.

"Sorry," said Wolfram, his Adam's apple bobbing furiously
in his fat neck. "I take it that this latest is your idea of a
joke?"

"A joke?" said The Madonna, "On the contrary my good
man, I have never been more serious in my life."

Wolfram's face flushed a deeper shade of purple, his lips
puckering, making small silent mewing movements.

For a minute The Madonna thought Wolfram was going to
cry.

But Wolfram let out a long sigh of air and sat back in his
large padded chair, his fat fingers drumming furiously on the
table top. "You can't simply walk away. I know everything
about you. If I talk you'll be finished. Besides, you need me
as much as I need you."

The Madonna smiled coldly. "Do you really think so?"

Wolfram glowered and leaned into the screen. "I understand
that you are a family man, Fidelus. One brat down and one
on the way." He leaned back and cracked his knuckles. "It's
a dangerous world. I do hope you are keeping a close eye on
them."

"Are you threatening me?"

Wolfram managed to look shocked. "Me? How could you even suggest it after all I've done for you? On the contrary, I'm genuinely concerned for their well-being."

The Madonna observed the man with distaste but concluded that his own instincts were right. The world was changing. Moving on. The Madonna had no intention of being left behind. She cleared her throat. "I'll work out the contract, then I'm out. Can't be fairer than that."

Wolfram goggled. "You can't!" he protested.

The Madonna smoothed a long curl through her fingers and smiled. "Oops! I think I just did." One long, ringed finger pressed a button and Wolfram's image shivered and disappeared. There was a knock on the door.

"Come in," said The Madonna. The wives entered. "Ladies, to what do I owe this honour?"

Sybil hugged her husband briefly, followed by Palomino. Coco came in close behind, a tray of steaming hot drinks balanced on a tray. She pecked her husband on the cheek. The Madonna waited while the wives settled themselves into a chair.

Palomino took a sip, put down her cup and looked at her husband. "My love, we've had a brilliant idea."

The Madonna clapped her hands together in anticipation. "So, do spill the cocoa beans," she said.

Sybil related, with a few informed interruptions, the crux of the plan. The Madonna listened intently, occasionally nodding or making small noises of acknowledgement.

Finally done, Palomino looked at her husband. "So, what do you think?"

The Madonna observed them, eyes gleaming with admiration. "I think you're right — it's brilliant."

Well satisfied, the women swiftly left.

As she watched them go, The Madonna observed cheerfully that Fidelus Ferguson was a very lucky man.

# CHAPTER 25

They were here! Mia leapt out of the hovercraft and raced into Nonna's embrace. She then kissed her mother. "Is everyone alright? Is everyone here?" she said.

Nonna nodded. "All is well. You have missed the council meeting but it was all about the festival. It will be tonight. Everyone is preparing."

Mia looked around speculatively. She had lost track of time in Alice. The sun was sinking and the camp buzzed with preparations for the forthcoming celebrations. Usually the event would have made Mia happy. But this year was different. This time she would be Promised. She wondered, for the umpteenth time, who it would be. Mainly she hoped whoever he was wouldn't be ugly, or skinny. Volta's face swam in her imagination. His skin, once so fair, tanned a golden brown, his blue eyes dancing with glee.

She dropped her head so Nonna wouldn't see the colour in her cheeks. She felt bad, but it was impossible not to compare Volta with all the other young men that she knew. Only Dart was really in the same class, although his looks were striking rather than handsome. He was tall and well made too.

Mia's mother gently stroked her hair. "Mia, my daughter, you must go and get yourself ready. Go with Nonna, all is waiting for you."

Mia nodded, but a lump was forming in her throat. She turned then, her eyes seeking Volta, but she could not see him. She slipped her hand into Nonna's and smiled a goodbye to her mother. Silently they walked around the edge of the camp and into her tent.

"Sit!" said Nonna.

Mia sat.

Nonna picked up a comb, knelt down and began brushing Mia's hair. "Mia, is something wrong?"

Mia jumped guiltily, she had been so immersed in her thoughts. She hesitated and then looked at Nonna, whose eyes were creased with concern. "Nonna," Mia said slowly, "did you love Poppa?"

Nonna's eyes searched her beloved granddaughter's face. She had been waiting for such a question. Such concerns were a part of the Promising. Besides, Mia's secrets were not as secret as she thought. Nonna understood much that may not be apparent to others. She sighed softly and smiled.

"Did I love your Poppa?" she chuckled. "I loved him alright, but on occasion I didn't like him much. When we were first Joined we fought fiercely, for we both had a temper." She paused and looked at Mia who grinned. Nonna's eyes became slightly unfocused, as she thought back. "But I guess over time we smoothed each other's rough spots out, like two stones rolling along a river bed."

Mia was silently pleased with the honesty of her Nonna's answer. After all, as she'd said to Palomino, she didn't have to Join with anyone if she didn't want to. But still the thought made her stomach jitter. In her fifteen years no one had ever done such a thing. She had no desire to be the first. She sat for a while, enjoying the soothing feel of Nonna's hands working in her hair.

Nonna tweaked her hair one last time. "I think you are about done."

Mia's hands went up, tentatively patting her head. Her long hair was gathered on top, twisted around and fixed in place with two slender wooden skewers. The timber sticks were precious, passed on from mother to daughter. Mia looked at her Nonna, her heart bursting with love. "Thank you," she said, her eyes filling with tears.

Nonna tutted. "Don't cry, I've got to do your eyes. You don't want to look like a chicken."

Mia was vain enough to pull herself together. She sat still as her eyes were outlined with a soft kohl pencil and her eyelashes darkened with soot. Then Nonna added a brush of rouge to her cheeks and gloss to her lips. Mia was now officially a woman. She took a deep breath and managed a tremulous smile.

Lastly was her tunic. It was green. Mia loved it. And, she was ready.

Together the two women walked to the festivities where Mia joined a dozen other young women, all identically attired, except for the colour of their tunics. Mia thought they looked lovely, and felt very self conscious as she seated herself upon a woven mat. Several of the girls greeted her and she exchanged compliments. The dancing light of the fire cast an air of mystery about them, making them seem half human, half spirit. With her eyes lowered Mia settled herself down to wait.

On the other side of the fire the young men observed the young women discreetly. Their white robes gleamed red in the fire light, and they wrapped and rewrapped their new head dresses, to remind themselves and others that they were now men. Their high spirits bubbled over into tomfoolery and mock fighting. Hopes were high.

Volta stood in the shadow of a palm tree, a little apart from the festivities, his eyes riveted to the spot where Mia sat. A tight pain clawed in his chest at the sight of her, but he could not pull away. In the dancing shadows of the fire she appeared to be all that she was. A young woman of breeding and status. Desirable and unattainable. He did not look at the men but he was painfully aware that Dart was there. Taller, broader and more self-contained than his peers, he exuded a quiet confidence that made Volta want to rip his head off. Could a man feel more miserable?

A voice lifted over the hubbub, calling the celebration to order. There was a buzz of excited chatter as the crowd gathered around the Overlander's spokeswoman, Shamay, who held the speaking stick. There was silence and she hit the stick three times upon the surface of a large stone. The sound was sharp, the night broken only by the soft clattering of palm fronds and the crackling of fire.

The crowd watched expectantly. Shamay held the silence until the tension was nearly unbearable. Then she turned and nodded over her left shoulder. Another voice cut through the night. Petulant and cross. A woman walked slowly through the crowd, her indignant baby held high in her outstretched hands. Four other women fell in behind her, each with an infant.

One by one the infants were passed to Shamay who invoked Sol's blessing and protection. She marked their small naked bodies with a yellow sun and named them. They were returned to their mother's anxious arms, followed by the enthusiastic clapping and calling of the tribe.

Once the tribe's people had settled, Shamay turned slowly to observe the young women, who sat as if hewn from stone. Shamay lifted her staff. As she did, a great gust of wind whooshed through the gathering. Sand flew and robes flapped wildly.

Mia turned away to protect her eyes. As she did so, she heard the distinct throbbing of an approaching hovercraft. Alarm spread through the tribe, men and women reached for weapons as children were herded away to a safer position. The sound of the hovercraft ceased and the wind dropped.

The Overlanders advanced cautiously, watching and waiting.

Then the door of the aircraft opened and Mia let out a gasp. Quickly, she pushed her way toward Shamay. "It's alright, they are friends," she said. She turned to her people. "It's alright! They are friends!"

The atmosphere relaxed a little, guns were lowered, but voices hummed tensely as three figures walked down the ramp toward them. Mia raced forward to greet them.

"Palomino, Coco, Sybil, what in the name of Sol are you doing here?" said Mia.

Coco lifted her gauzy veil and looked anxiously at the armed tribesmen. "We come in peace," she said softly.

Mia turned and looked at the not-so-welcoming committee. "Sorry! Come with me."

The three wives followed behind Mia, who introduced them to Shamay. As the tribe observed their wise woman welcoming the strangers, they lay down their weapons. Children wriggled away from the restraining grasp of their family and came to stare shyly at the visitors. Many had never seen anyone from Alice.

"We are sorry to arrive uninvited and unannounced," Coco said, "but what we have to say could not wait."

Shamay nodded politely, obviously intrigued. "How can we help you?"

The three Ferguson wives exchanged brief knowing glances. "It is we who may be able to help you," said Sybil cryptically. "We have come to request a hearing from your Sister Council."

Mia was stunned. She was not alone. A shock wave of conversation spread through the tribe. Shamay waited until the rumbles subsided then lifted her hand, asking for quiet. She looked at the three women. "It is an unusual request—" she said.

Mia waited breathlessly.

"But reasonable," Shamay finished.

Mia let out a long sigh of relief.

Slowly the members of the Sister Council drew away from their families and friends. Shamay invited the three wives to join them, and they set off toward the lake and the privacy of Shamay's tent.

Volta poked Mia rudely in the small of her back.

She turned, glaring at him. "What?"

He grinned. "Aren't you in the Sister Council, doofus?"

Mia looked blankly at him for a moment. Then she hurried after the retreating figures. She forced herself to slow down a few metres from the tent, so she could recover her breath and her dignity. Head held high, she pushed the material of the entry aside and entered. She took a seat on a cushion. To say she was curious was the ultimate in understatement.

Shamay, on the other hand, seemed completely unperturbed and opened the meeting with due ceremony. The Overlander women and the women from Alice observed each other discreetly. Nonna's dark eyes sparkled with anticipation. Mia knew Nonna would be taking it all in, recording everything in minute detail and adding any necessary embellishments to ensure a dramatic retelling later that night. The uniqueness of the event was underscored as small cups of Melba were poured, offered to the guests and distributed to the council members.

Coco, Sybil and Palomino sipped politely and a round of small talk ensued. Mia sipped her own drink, barely tasting it, her hand trembling slightly as she gripped the cup. Why were the wives of Fidelus Ferguson here?

Finally, Shamay smiled at the unexpected guests. A hush settled over the assembly. "Please, tell us what brings you here today," she said to the three women.

Sybil replied. "We have come here today to ask for an alliance with the Overlander people. We would ask that the Overlander woman, known as Mia, be joined with us to our husband Fidelus Ferguson."

The Sister Council erupted. Except for Mia, whose mouth dried up like a dehydrated mushroom. Inside her chest, her heart was beating fit to burst. Panic-stricken, she turned to Nonna. The old woman reached out a gnarled hand and Mia grabbed onto it like a lifeline. Was everyone mental? Join with Fidelus Ferguson! It was… absurd. She took a deep breath that shuddered through her tense body. Of course it was ridiculous. The Sister Council would soon set things straight. But as she looked around at the animated faces, a deep sense of unease filled her.

# CHAPTER 26

Mia felt strangely disconnected. All around her, women were talking, gesturing, arguing and occasionally laughing. But no one was standing up and sensibly stating the obvious — that an alliance with a man from Alice — a man that was not an Overlander — was utterly out of the question. Mia felt a pair of eyes on her and looked up to find Shamay regarding her with utmost seriousness. At that, nothing was black and white. Not any more.

Finally the noise settled and Shamay again took control. She smiled at Sybil. "Please, go on."

Sybil smiled back. "We do understand that such a Joining is highly irregular." She paused, looking at her sisters, who both nodded slightly. Sybil continued. "To lose Mia would be a great loss to your people, as she would be a great gain for ours. In my homeland we recognize this and when a woman leaves her people, there is compensation. We call it a 'bride price'. So, in keeping with this, we offer a bride price of as many sand guns as you desire and a dozen blood horses of your choice. Additionally, we also offer the full backing and support of the Ferguson family in your cause. We will stand with you against the powers of the city." She stopped for a second, her lovely face scanning the women seated before her. "Thank you," she finished.

Mia did not know what to say or what to think. It would seem by the stunned silence in the tent that she was not alone.

Shamay filled the gap. "Wives of Fidelus Ferguson, we are deeply honoured by your proposal. I am sure you will understand that we must give this offer as much due consideration as you yourselves have done. By this time tomorrow, we will give you an answer."

The wives arose gracefully, covered themselves with their veils and made their goodbyes. As the last sounds of the hovercraft diminished, a soft murmuring began to wash around the tent.

Shamay stood. "This is a most unexpected development. What do you say?"

Nonna stood. "In normal times this Joining would never be given serious thought. But, these are not normal times. While it grieves me to think of losing one of our own, it is clear that the support of the Ferguson wives and their husband offers many advantages. These advantages may spell out the difference between the survival of the Overlander people and their demise. But of course, nothing is certain."

Mia swallowed down her emotions, forcing herself to listen respectfully.

A tall, grey haired woman spoke next. She was, Mia knew, related to Dart. "If Mia joins with the man from Alice, will she then still be an Overlander?" Her voice was hard, her face unreadable, but the question was undoubtedly a challenge.

Mia felt as if she'd been slapped. Her hurt was so deep that she could find no words to defend herself. She was distressed to find herself in the position of being attacked when she had done nothing.

Shamay's eyes narrowed. "Esther, I understand that you are threatened by this. But Mia is not to blame. While she has breath in her body she is — and always will be — an Overlander. Nothing and nobody can change this."

There was a rumble of agreement and Mia bent her head to hide the tears welling up. Nonna's hand squeezed hers and she returned the gesture.

A younger woman, Saffire, stood. "The Ferguson wives are wise. They see an opportunity to bridge a gap which has been long neglected. Overlanders pride themselves on their adaptability. It is the mainstay of our survival. In changing times, perhaps we too must change." She flushed a little at her own daring, and sat down abruptly.

There was a round of applause and chattering. Mia looked at Saffire speculatively. While it was not what she wanted to hear, there was much truth in her words. The discussion took off, the women weighing the pros and cons of the proposal.

Mia realized that the more talk there was, the less incredible the Ferguson wives' suggestion may seem. After a while, it might (almost) appear reasonable.

Finally Shamay rounded the discussion up. "Council members, we must vote. Those in favour move to the front, those against move back."

Mia, almost faint with anxiety, could not move. All around her, women stood, hesitating and then moving away. Several stood undecided, still weighing things up. A few crossed backwards and forwards. Finally it was still.

"Mia?"

Mia looked up miserably at Shamay.

Shamay smiled gently. "Mia, we are equal in number for and against. Yours is the final vote."

Mia drew in a sharp breath, clutching her hands to her chest. Still, she could not speak.

Shamay came to her. "Mia, you do not have to vote. No one here would judge you badly if you so chose. If you would like more time that is fine too."

Mia looked at her. "Shamay, please tell me, who is — was — my Promised?"

"Dart," said Shamay softly.

Mia nodded. "I need more time, please."

Shamay squeezed her shoulder softly. "Of course."

The meeting reconvened, but Mia did not hear. Vaguely she knew they were discussing whether or not they should bring the issue to the attention of the rest of the tribe or wait until Mia had made a decision. She missed the outcome as her concentration dissolved. Mia was filled with an almost uncontrollable need to be alone. No, not alone. With Whisper.

Someone patted her on the shoulder. It was Nonna. "We are returning to the feast. Come and eat, my child. One always thinks better on a full stomach."

Mia stood up. She felt as if her body was filled with sand. For the first time in her life her appetite abandoned her. "I'll be there in a minute," she said.

Nonna nodded, but her face creased up with concern. "Don't be long."

Mia followed the women out of the tent and headed toward the corral. On the way she stopped at her tent, picking up her sling and stones. Then she ripped her hair out of its intricate arrangement and changed into her robe.

At the corral Whisper whickered to Mia, delighted by the irregular visit. Mia slipped her bridle on and leapt onto the mare bareback. Without thinking she kicked Whisper into a canter, and the mare leapt up and over the prickly barrier, away into the night. She urged Whisper into a gallop, speeding away across the moonlit plain. She did not guide Whisper, letting her go where she would. After several minutes the pace began to slacken, falling back into a walk.

Mia looked up at the sky. At the bright full moon and the stars running in silver rivers. She hugged her arms around Whisper's neck, for warmth and comfort, burying her face in the silky mane. "What shall I do, Whisper?" she said. But Whisper had no answer. Mia recalled the wicked, winking blue eye of Fidelus Ferguson. Could she join such a man? It was hard to imagine. Further, could she live in Alice, beneath the ground? A shudder ran through her. It seemed a dreadful idea. Of course, she really liked Palomino, Sybil and Coco. Their friendship and allegiance was a good thought.

Whisper suddenly stopped, letting out a neigh. Mia was not unduly alarmed as it was a sound of greeting, not fear. But at the same time she did not welcome company. She sat up and kicked Whisper who took off at a brisk trot. But then she hesitated as she heard someone calling her name.

"Blimey Mia, wait up will you!"

It was Shyboy. Mia reined in Whisper and waited. Shyboy was smart, she thought. Maybe it would help to talk with him. With someone on the outside whose thoughts were not clouded by emotions.

Shyboy took shape out of the landscape, ghostlike in his robes. He halted his horse beside her. "Are you alright?"

Mia nodded, but his kindness undid her. To her chagrin, tears spilled down her cheeks.

"Mia, what's going on?" asked Shyboy, a frown creasing his white forehead. "Everyone at the camp is going ballistic. Dart looks like he's going to burst a blood vessel."

Mia wiped her face furiously. "Palomino and the other wives want me to marry Ferguson," she said.

Shyboy looked like he'd been slapped with a dead fish. "No shit! That's so… unexpected." Then his face split into a grin. "Blimey cubed Mia, but you are a popular girl! Ferguson, Dart and Volta. Maybe you should take a leaf out of old Ferguson's book and marry 'em all."

Mia felt as if she'd been shoved flat on her back. "What do you mean, 'Volta'?" she said, unable to stop her tongue.

Shyboy's smile faded. He hid his face momentarily in his hands, shaking his head. "I'm sorry. I assumed that you knew. I mean, it's hard to miss."

Mia glared. "Stop talking in riddles, Shyboy. What's hard to miss?"

"Well, you and Volta. You're just crazy over each other! I mean, it's obvious."

Mia was devastated. "Volta's crazy about me?" She wanted to cry and laugh all at the same time.

"Mia, of course he is. Didn't you know?"

Mia shook her head, stunned by her own stupidity. Of course Volta hadn't said so in actual words. But now — in retrospect — she could see how small gestures, kindnesses and warm moments could be construed as affection. She stared helplessly at Shyboy. "No, I didn't know. I mean, I hoped, but he never said anything."

Shyboy was silent for a long moment. "Would it make a difference if he had?"

Mia shrugged. "I don't know. Yes... no... I don't know. Probably not."

Shyboy turned, listening intently. "I think the cavalry is on its way."

Mia groaned. "Fabulous." She turned her mare, gathering up the reins.

Shyboy put an arresting hand on her shoulder. "Mia, I'm really sorry. Seriously though — what are you going to do?"

"I don't know. I feel like I've fallen into a sand sink. My brain just keeps floundering around. I can't find anything solid to fix onto." Mia turned her head toward the sound of horses racing fast and furious across the sand. A strange emotion rippled through her. It was pride, love and a fierce sense of loyalty. Her people were coming to find her. They always would.

With a mighty effort she pushed Volta out of her head. What should she do? And then, as the sound of the approaching cavalcade swelled the night, all her confusion melted away. She turned back to Shyboy. "I'm going to do the only thing I can do — the best thing for my people," she said. She managed a tiny smile. "It's what my Da would do."

As the armed men arrived she lifted her head and gave the wild ululating call of her tribe. The riders wheeled around, swallowing her up into the heart of the herd. Then, a peculiar mood gripped her. A mixture of urgency and exhilaration, tinged with sadness and loss. With a squeeze of her legs she urged Whisper onward. Cutting like an arrow through the mob, Mia headed for home.

# CHAPTER 27

Shock waves ran through Volta's brain. His body felt
strangely weightless. The idea of Mia marrying Fidelus
Ferguson was bizarre. Shamay's return to the festivities and
her sudden announcement had sideswiped him. Sure as sand
was in a desert, he hadn't seen that one coming. He turned,
staring out into the darkness. Anxiety washed through him.
He had wanted to go with the mounted men to find Mia, but
sensed it was not his place. All that was left was to wait.
And watch. And wonder. What would Mia do?

He glanced at Shamay. If the charismatic woman was
disturbed she hid it well. Others were less restrained. Volta
turned toward the fire where Dart's angry profile flickered in
the light. Volta felt a flood of empathy toward the man
whom he had seen as a serious rival. How quickly things
could change. In an odd way, he felt a bond with the
Overlander youth. Dart was one of Mia's own. When it came
down to the nitty-gritty, Volta was forced to acknowledge
that the young man would be a good match for Mia.

Perhaps it was coincidence, or maybe Dart felt Volta's attention, for he turned and stared. His black eyes were wild with anger and hurt, his mouth set in a thin line of unhappiness. Volta felt no satisfaction in Dart's distress. He nodded his head briefly, a tiny gesture of understanding. After a second, the gesture was returned. It seemed that hostilities were suspended. The sudden intrusion of an outsider had unbalanced the picture. Volta could barely bring himself to imagine what Mia was feeling. The Sister Council had been evenly divided on the subject. The final decision now lay with Mia. He did not envy her.

While people chattered, gesticulated, argued and gossiped, Volta remained where he was. There was nothing left to do but wait. He was not sure how long Tully had been standing behind him when he sensed his presence. The bodyguard said nothing, for which Volta was grateful. People began to settle down to the serious business of eating. The noise levels dropped, eyes searching the black, hidden depths of the desert. The tension twisted and tightened. Music began. A single drum which seemed to beat in rhythm with Volta's heart. Slowly, other instruments blended in. The haunting call of a pipe, the deep throbbing of a didgeridoo and the soft rustling of maracas.

He heard the horses approaching before they became visible. Slowly the blurry forms clarified and Volta felt a surge of pride as Mia thundered past the lake with the others spreading out behind her. Some of his anxiety settled. Although her face was hidden, she sat tall and confident, her hair blowing behind her. One hand held the reins, the other resting easily upon her thigh. He couldn't help but remember the first time he'd seen her. A wild and elemental force that had captured his imagination so completely. Slowly the music petered out, voices settling to a subdued murmur.

Volta waited, his insides writhing like a pit of eels. He could feel a pulse galloping in his neck. The mounted tribesmen returned on foot to the fire in small groups. They did not fill plates and cups. Most were still wrapped in their robes, guns slung casually over a shoulder. The air was thick with expectancy as Mia finally travelled through the outer edges of the gathering. All movement ceased, except for the small cries and giggles of the young and the urgent hushing of their families. The wind rattled the fronds of the palm trees. The fire hissed and spat as the carcass dripped fat. Volta could just make out the soft scrunching of sand beneath Mia's sandal-shod feet. She carried herself with all the grace and composure of her tribe. As the firelight revealed her face she looked calm and assured.

Shamay stood and held out a welcoming hand.

Mia paused for a moment, as if unsure, but then stepped out confidently. She dropped her chin gracefully and touched forefinger and thumb to her forehead. "I see you, Shamay," she said formally. Her voice was soft but steady, carrying clearly.

Shamay returned the greeting. Then she observed Mia, and Volta felt she was seeking some sort of reassurance. Mia held the gaze steadily. Apparently satisfied by what she found, Shamay found her voice. "Mia, would you speak?"

For an instant Mia's façade wavered, her gaze sweeping across the crowd. In a moment so brief that it could almost have been imagined, her gaze grazed Volta's. And was gone. "I would speak."

There was a rustle of agitation amongst the tribe and a babble of conversation. Mia waited until all was still. "We have always been strong people. A people of deep traditions and beliefs. But there was a time when disease threatened to wipe us off the face of our homeland. We could only wait, filled with trepidation. And then an opportunity arose and our ancestors grasped it and became refugees in a strange world. And we survived. Our ancestors adapted and thrived. Today we face a new threat. We must adapt or decline. I choose to adapt." For a moment she paused, one hand lifting and fluttering gently on her throat. She looked slowly around the spellbound watchers. She closed her eyes and slowly opened them. "I will be Promised to the man from Alice. Fidelus Ferguson."

There was silence, and then a sigh of voices went rippling through the crowd. The sigh swelled into a murmur and then became a roar. Volta closed his eyes as a physical pain swept through him. His heart crushed in a vice. He wanted to leap up and protest. He wanted to charge in and sweep her away. Far away. It was not fair. It was not right.

But even as the thoughts formed, he was forced to acknowledge a deeper truth. For Mia it was the only choice. How could you not respect such integrity? How could you not admire such dignity? He looked at her again. It was still the same Mia, but there was some new quality, an air of quiet strength and authority. The child was gone — or subdued — below this new exterior. Volta tried to imagine what this decision had cost her. But all he knew for sure was that he was proud.

As the noise continued unabated he realised that her decision would create contention. There would be some who would be averse to her announcement. Many who may not comprehend the sacrifice that she made. Bowing to the inevitable, he put his pain aside. Mia would need all the support she could get. She would be able to count on him. There was nothing else he could do.

He left then and wandered blindly into the privacy of the night. He followed the gritty path around the lake. It was cold, the biting wind of the desert lifting his robes gently. Slowly the noise receded to be replaced with the gentle lapping of the water and the grating call of the katydids. He paused, looking out across the moon-dappled lake. He picked up a flat stone and set it skipping across the surface. When its silver wake faded he took a deep shuddering breath in. What good would his self-pity do? If he had anything to do with it, Mia's selfless gesture would not be in vain.

With renewed vigour he retraced his steps. Today seemed black, but there was always tomorrow. The moon's reflection smiled up at him from the water. But he did not smile back.

Mia, momentarily oblivious to the agitated tribe, watched Volta until his shadowy figure was swallowed up into the night. She felt a wave of longing and wanted to follow him and to explain. But she didn't. What was done was done. She would be Promised to the man from Alice. From this alliance new hope for a future would flower for her people. With deliberation she turned her gaze to Shamay. "It is the only thing to do," she whispered.

Shamay reached out and squeezed her shoulder softly. "I know, Mia. You are indeed wise beyond your years. There will be considerable discord for a while, but we are, perhaps above all else, a pragmatic people. They will reach acceptance, even approval."

Mia met the wise woman's gaze anxiously; ardently hoping her words would become the truth. Still, doubt trembled in her breast, for she was painfully aware of Dart's eyes burning into her like twin lasers. His rage had washed over her with all the fury of a westerly wind. She dare not look toward the fire lest she meet his scorching gaze. She could only hope that time would temper his anger. In the meantime, she must prepare for the future.

As if she had read her thoughts, Shamay interrupted her ruminations. "Mia," she said, "do not be overwhelmed. There is a full year before you can be Joined. In that time the doubts and fears you hold today will gradually ease. As the idea becomes more familiar, the prospect will seem less daunting. Most importantly, remember, it does not matter where you are, or who you are with. Inside here," Shamay tapped her chest, "you are always an Overlander."

Some of the knots in Mia's chest loosened a little. Shamay was right. When she had been imprisoned in Isbane she had never forgotten who she was. On the contrary, it had been her greatest strength. Nothing and nobody could change that. Her mind leapt to another point. While a Promising was binding, Mia was free to remain amongst her people until the Joining. She decided that she would not enter into a Joining until Da was free. She lifted her chin defiantly. Even if it took thirty years.

Mia could not face the rest of the celebrations. With a quick apology she headed back to her tent. To her relief she found Nonna already there, waiting for her. She pressed a cup of Melba into Mia's trembling hand. Mia stared miserably into the ancient face. "Nonna," she said, "what else could I do?"

Nonna tutted and pushed a strand of hair out of Mia's eyes. "Your Da would be proud," she said.

# CHAPTER 28

When Volta awoke light stabbed into his eyes like red-hot pokers. He groaned and closed them again. His mouth was dry as a fossil and his tongue felt several sizes too big. Apparently an army of termites had crawled through his ear while he slept and were busy excavating his brain. Tentatively he opened his eyes into slits and looked up, shading his face with a hand. Tully's grinning face came slowly into focus.

Volta unglued his tongue and forced out a barely audible question. "What happened?"

Tully observed him with all the happy satisfaction of a scientist observing an interesting new specimen. "What happened?" He chuckled and leant down toward Volta's prone body. "Ah... a good question... but where to begin?"

Somewhat disconcerted by this ambiguous reply, Volta pushed himself up onto one elbow. The back of his head felt strangely warm. Tentatively, so as not to upset the termites, he touched the hair on the back of his head. He looked at his hand. Yuk. "Why is there camel dung in my hair?" But a soft grumbling behind him supplied a reply. He blinked and looked around. Ashan, chewing gravely on his cud, eyed Volta disdainfully. Lines of puzzlement gathered on Volta's forehead. "Why am I here?"

"Too much Melba," said Tully.

Volta held out a hand which Tully grasped. With a groan of agony Volta lurched upright. His head swam and he thought he was going to be sick. Maybe he was dying. As he tottered along in Tully's wake, death began to feel like an attractive option. He discovered that if he concentrated really hard and kept his eyes really still, he could walk in a straight line. While he was aware that he was the object of some amusement, he couldn't summon the energy to care. If he could just make it to his tent, drink a pitcher of water and collapse onto his roll, he'd be a happy man.

Tully held the flap open and Volta stumbled gratefully in. The dim light brought some relief. "Water," he croaked. He yelped in shock as Tully chucked a cup full in his face. Gasping and spluttering, Volta glared at his bodyguard with a deeply injured air. "What'd you do that for?"

Tully handed him a clean robe. "Scrub up and get changed. You're going out."

Volta stared in dismay, he must be kidding. "I'm sick."

Tully sniffed. "Self-inflicted. No sympathy."

Volta glared. "I might die."

Tully raised an eyebrow. "A risk," he said, "that I am prepared to take."

Volta opened his mouth with a snappy comeback but a wave of nausea made him shut it smartly. For a minute he sank into the misery of his roiling stomach and thumping head, leaning heavily against the main tent pole. Finally the sickness passed. Too weak to protest, he slowly washed his hair and face and changed his clothes.

There was a gentle tap on the door flap. Tully strode over and peered out. Volta couldn't see who it was but it sounded like a young woman. For one glorious second he thought it was Mia, but then his brain lurched into action and the miserable memories of the previous day swamped him. After a minute of murmured conversation Tully returned and handed a steaming vessel to Volta.

Volta sniffed it suspiciously. "What is it?"

"It's a herbal infusion. Trina said that it will relieve your hangover."

Volta took a small sip. It wasn't too bad, quite nice really, fruity with a touch of spice. He took another drink and then paused. *Trina.* He knew that name. Then he recalled. Trina had done his makeup for him before his first trip to Alice. He looked at the drink. "That was nice of her," he said, a little puzzled.

"You think?"

Something in Tully's tone made Volta suddenly nervous. "What? I mean, I barely know the girl!"

Tully ran a hand thoughtfully over his beard. "That's tricky, 'cause she thinks she knows you very well."

"How's that?"

Tully sniggered. "Well, while you were spreading your charms around last night, that young woman seemed to hold your attention longer than most." He stopped, cogitating on the matter for a moment. "Mind you, that I can understand, she is very... nice"." Tully paused and grinned. "And easy on the eye too."

Volta stared at Tully, trying to decide if he were just baiting. He searched around in his mind, trying to draw out something to confirm or deny Tully's crazy accusations. But there was nothing. A big fat zero. His head slowly tilted to one side as he observed his companion anxiously. "Are you saying that me and Trina were—" He stopped, suddenly deeply embarrassed. "Were... you know," he finished lamely.

"Kissing and canoodling? Snogging and smooching? Loving and doving?" said Tully without a trace of empathy.

Son of Sol! It was worse than he feared. Panic filled him. "Does Mia know?" The words popped out before he could stop them.

Tully's expression softened. "I expect so."

Volta stared at him, stricken. Suddenly his pride utterly abandoned him. He had to know. "How did she seem?"

Tully shrugged. "Outwardly — unperturbed. Inwardly — who knows?"

Volta sat down, absent-mindedly drinking the brew. Then a horrible thought pierced his brain. His head jerked up, the hot liquid slopping onto his foot but he barely noticed. "Tully, this girl, Trina, you don't think I'll have to Join with her do you? I mean, have I made some sort of gesture that could be interpreted by the Overlanders as a proposal of sorts?" He had a horrible vision of Dart and a number of his equally determined relatives escorting him to a Joining under the scrutiny of several semi-automatics.

"I think you can rest easy on that score. Whilst your behaviour was not gentlemanly, it could not have been interpreted as a declaration of everlasting love either."

Volta felt weak with relief. And he realised, he felt better. The concoction had settled his stomach and the thumping in his head had reduced to a delicate tapping. "So, where am I going?"

"To Alice. Shamay has requested your attendance. They plan to formally accept Ferguson's proposal and to negotiate the bride price."

Volta's spirits crashed at this news. It made everything somehow real. He did not want any part in Mia's future union with Ferguson. But he could see no way out of it. He sighed. Still, maybe the negotiations would founder. Perhaps the Ferguson wives would change their minds. But deep down, he despaired. Somehow he knew that this was highly unlikely. There was too much at stake. Mia understood this only too well. He glanced at Tully, who observed him sadly. "Tully, is Mia going?"

Tully shook his head. "No."

Volta stood up, his mind slowly warming up. "What's with the bride price? I thought it sounded pretty generous?"

"It is. But the council doesn't want the horses. They want hovercraft instead."

Hovercraft? At first Volta thought he had misheard. The Overlanders and aircraft did not correlate in his mind. But, on further consideration, he concluded that it made perfect sense. After all, they used modern weapons and anything else that suited them. They took what they wanted and dismissed the rest. Times had changed. And so the Overlanders changed with them. Reluctantly Volta began to see the full potential of Mia's Joining. The Fergusons had been foresighted in admitting her into their ranks.

The sound of feet on the hard packed ground outside the tent alerted him to another visitor. A bit anxious it might be Trina again, he made Tully investigate. To his relief it was Shyboy.

"Volta," said the albino man, getting to the point. "Word is on the web that it was your mother who sent out the hovercraft to spy out the Overlanders. You know, the day Mia was breaking in the horse. Your sainted mother was looking for you."

The news, whilst unwelcome, was hardly a shock. Volta had suspected as much. But what her motives were he was less sure about. Was she simply searching for him to… what? Beg him to come home? It seemed unlikely. But he backtracked, examining the idea. Perhaps he could do just that. Go back to Isbane. Maybe then his mother would relent and agree to leave the Overlanders alone. He looked at Tully. "I should go back."

Tully snorted. "Do you really think that's an option? Do you honestly believe that your mother was hoping for a cosy chat?"

Shyboy chipped in. "Volta, it's too late. You know too much. And besides, could you really go back and just carry on? Become the next President of the Western Water Company? Do you think, even if you did, the Overlanders would be saved? Would you trust your mother and uncle to keep their word?"

Volta felt the full weight of their words. With a heavy heart he knew they were right. It was too late. There could be no turning back. Something inside him fractured as the last vestiges of loyalty he felt for his home and family dissolved. Oddly, he felt released. The sure knowledge that those who should have been his nearest and dearest might murder him in cold blood, set him free. A wave of fierce determination swept through him. If that was how they wanted to play, so be it. He would meet them measure for measure. He looked at his companions. "We'll accept no less than a dozen ships, latest edition, fully armed. Plus we'll need half a dozen dune buggies and three PCs."

Tully gave Volta a long appraising look and let out a low whistle. "That's a hefty request. He's only offering a herd of horses and sand guns."

Volta felt a painful tightening in his chest. His blue eyes narrowed slightly. "So Tully, tell me, what's Mia's sacrifice worth to you?"

Shyboy winced. "Ouch," he muttered.

Tully shook his head but made no reply.

Volta turned to Shyboy. "How are we getting to Alice?"

"Ferguson's sending his hover," said Shyboy.

Volta turned to the discarded costume lying on the mat. With a sigh, he picked up the corset and handed it to Tully.

He was grateful that Tully didn't smile or even make jest. The clothes no longer seemed amusing. "Shyboy, please go ask Shamay for some makeup. I'll do it myself." It was cowardly he knew, but he just couldn't face Trina. Not then. Later.

Dressed, wigged and corseted, Volta was finally ready. "Let's go," he said breathlessly.

With his companions, Volta strode through the camp toward the central fire. Several young women gaped at him. Volta acknowledged them with a polite nod of his head. As he passed the well he stopped involuntarily. Mia stared at him as water sloshed gently over the sides of the bucket clutched in her hands, splashing her robes. Her dark hair was loose, waving softly over her face, eyes wide, still darkened with kohl. Neither spoke, but Volta felt a strange connection, and knew that silently, they were saying goodbye. A leaden sadness filled him as the impact exploded in his head. What an utter fool he was. In that single moment he knew the truth. Mia felt as he did. But now, it was too late. Too late for declarations of love. Too late to talk of tomorrow.

Finally, he walked away.

# CHAPTER 29

It was an elegant office with blonde timber and acres of pristinely clean glass. It was a room to intimidate and Pavan squirmed. Actually squirmed. She stared up at the risen stage, at the six men presiding over her. She was sitting alone, perched stiffly on a small, upright chair in an ocean of bare floor. She felt ridiculously vulnerable. Like a naughty child. The room was silent. Pavan could hear the air rasping in and out of her dry throat. What were they waiting for?

Finally Senator Firth sniffed loudly, took a sip of water and looked over his glasses at Pavan.

Pavan subdued a snort of irritation. She knew full well that Senator Firth had perfect eyesight. The glasses were merely a prop. The idiot probably thought it gave him a scholarly air. Fat chance. He merely looked like a moulting owl. But she remained silent, afraid to speak and say the wrong thing.

"Pavan," Firth said finally. "Thank you for joining us, the Directorate appreciates your cooperation."

*The Directorate.* The words sent a chill down Pavan's expensively clad spine. She couldn't sweat. Her DNA didn't allow it. But the top of her skull felt as if it were melting and her teeth were numb. It took a full moment for her brain to identify the source of these distressing physical malfunctions. Fear. It was a long time since she'd been afraid. But she was now.

She forced a smile. "Senator Firth, how may I help you?"

Firth did not reply. Instead he flicked a switch on his console, perusing the hidden contents for a long, drawn-out moment.

Pavan could have screamed with repressed frustration. But she didn't. She waited, forcing her features into pleasant lines.

Finally, Firth looked down at her. "The Directorate would like you to tell us where your son is."

Pavan's mouth dried out. She just stared up at the senator, her mind scrambling for a plausible explanation.

There was a loud ping as a back window turned opaque and a vivid reel began running. Pavan stared in growing horror at the footage. A close up of Volta, sunburned as a savage, galloping across a desert. Then the scene swiftly changed. Volta again. This time eating beside a fire in the company of deviants and the green-eyed monster, Mia of the Overland. She sucked in her breath and dug her fingernails into her palms. Another scene. Volta again, this time in the company of Ferguson and his wives.

For the first time in her life Pavan wished she was not designed to live forever. A fatal stroke would have been welcome.

"Well?" Firth drawled maliciously. The other fat fools smirked appreciatively.

"Senator Firth," said Pavan. "Volta has, as you can see, fallen into bad company. But he is not a bad boy. He is merely young and naive. These monsters have brainwashed him. Turned him against his own kind. I am in the process of ransoming my son back," she lied. "Everyone has their price. The Overlanders and Ferguson are no different." Now she was warming up, Pavan almost believed it.

Firth breathed in and out. He glanced at his companions. None spoke but Pavan sensed this whole thing had been carefully orchestrated. "Very well," Firth finally said, "you have seven days to make this all go away." Firth gave her a searing look. "Do you understand me?"

Pavan nodded but inwardly she raged. How dare they! Didn't they know who she was? Didn't they know how important she was? How powerful she was? She wanted to liberally sprinkle their bloated bodies with bullets. That'd wipe the smug expressions off their faces, she thought furiously. She could not recall enduring such humiliation in her entire, unnaturally long life. She stood up stiffly, bowed and left the room on trembling legs.

Outside, her transport was docked and waiting. Pavan hurried up the ramp and slumped into the nearest seat. The machine vibrated and duly took off, but Pavan was insensible to all but the hideous outcome of her summons. Seven days! What was she going to do? One thing was for sure, she wasn't going to let those scumbags wreck her lovely life. She would destroy every Overlander in the solar system first. And Ferguson, the ungrateful swine. And his wives. And all the mutants and the deviants.

She sat back, her head throbbing. And then she thought of Wolfram and her foul mood curdled further. Why hadn't he been hauled in for an interrogation? The slippery snake was as deep in the mire as she was. Why should she take all the blame? Why should she be the one to suffer? She hardly dared even contemplate what would happen if she could not bring Volta home. There would be fines. There would be condemnation. And worst of all, they might strip away her water licence. Pavan closed her eyes, feeling physically ill at the prospect.

It did not take a perfectly engineered brain to grasp the ramifications of the latter. Total ruin. But almost worse was the prospect of Wolfram lining up gleefully to grab the licence for himself. She stiffened her spine, her lips compressing. Then she smiled grimly to herself. If she went down, Pavan thought viciously, then her brother was going with her. There were things she knew that were damning to them both.

But this did not take Pavan any closer to a solution. Delicious as it may be to exterminate all her enemies, it wasn't a practical solution. She needed to be subtle. Sneaky. If she could just get Volta home, she could deal with the rest. *Volta*. Her perfect nostrils flared in disgust. Her son seemed to be doing everything in his power to undermine her life's work. And to shame her. He was an unnatural, ungrateful little beast. Part of her wished he'd never been born.

Pavan had invested millions of sterls in him. He was supposed to be perfect! And look at him!

A balding waiter walked down the aisle, balancing a tray in one hand. He stopped, leaned over showing the wares and nodded politely. "Melba? Macadamia nuts?"

Pavan lifted up a hand and smacked the tray, sending the contents flying. The waiter blanched and bolted. Pavan wiped a splash of Melba off her hand and made up her mind. The Directorate had said she must 'make it go away'. So she would.

Volta was out of control. A danger to himself and the establishment. And to herself. She had tried to reason, hadn't she? In the end, it was his own fault if he refused to see sense. He was almost begging her to kill him.

With the suppressed thought finally aired, Pavan felt nothing but relief. Her brain went into overdrive. What she needed was to contract a couple of lowlifes in Alice. And she knew just the man who'd help her. In a flash she had the contact details. Yes, she thought, Senator Cruptor could be trusted. He was a twisted, degenerate man. Perfect for the job.

She didn't want to, she told herself. But — in the end — it was the best thing for everyone.

# CHAPTER 30

Inside the hovercraft the atmosphere was thick with expectation. Volta stared blindly out of a dirty window and watched the camp become a dot on the golden landscape. He glanced around at his companions. Tully and Shyboy were huddled close together talking in hushed tones. D2 occupied himself by breaking down a pistol, inspecting it and putting it back together again. Shoo sat beside him dressed in one of D2's old army shirts, a belt of bullets cinched at her waist. Shamay was with them to represent the Sister Council and therefore the Overlanders. The rest of the seats were taken up by several armed men, evidently in the service of Ferguson. They spoke little and moved less. Volta was painfully aware of Mia's absence. He wondered what she was doing and what she was thinking. Suddenly he found he didn't want the journey to end.

But of course, it did. With a deafening roar the machine began its abrupt descent. Volta could see a thick black fog swirling over Alice. A few of the taller buildings reared above the toxic smog. As the craft descended it became impossible to see anything beyond the range of the vehicle's spotlights. A soft thud announced they had landed. Slowly they all trooped out of the doorway and down the ramp.

"Blimey," said Shyboy, "what a stink."

Volta could only agree. The fog was most unpleasant and crawled over his bare skin with calculating, cold fingers. "What's it from?" he asked of no one in particular.

To his surprise one of the armed men, a fresh-faced fellow with a buzz cut, voluntarily opened his mouth. "It's from the factories. Happens when winds are down and production is up. Pollution's a way of life in Alice."

Poor Mia, thought Volta. But said nothing, the atmosphere oppressing him. There was something ominous in the dirty air. With hands on weapons they crowded together. Volta was very irritated to find D2 and Tully hemming him in beside Shamay. He scowled mulishly, lifted up his skirt and plucked a small pistol out of an ankle holster.

Tully glared at him. "You were told, no weapons," he hissed. "Put it away. It's unladylike."

Volta pretended not to hear. Out of the corner of his eye he watched Tully opening his mouth to follow up but then D2 grabbed their attention.

"Stop," said the hybrid.

Such was the weight of his authority that everyone froze. Safety catches on weapons clicked and aimed blindly into the smog.

"What is it?" whispered Volta.

But D2 did not reply. His stance was tense, his head turning slowly, searching. Then he looked into the waiting faces of his companions. "I'm not—"

But the rest of his words were lost as an explosion tore the air. A brilliant red light flared up, making everyone squint against the glare. Shyboy recovered first. "It's a tracer flash," he yelled. "They'll be on us in seconds. Run!"

For a scorching moment no one moved. Then D2 turned to the armed men. "Which way?"

One pointed and set off, booted feet hammering on the hard ground. Volta felt an urgent hand on his back. He looked behind. It was Tully.

"Move!" he said.

Volta looked around frantically for Shamay and Shyboy. To his relief they raced past in the lee of Ferguson's men with Shoo and D2 behind. Volta spurted after them, suddenly scared they'd disappear into the fog. It was not a second too soon. Behind, he could hear voices, muffled by the thick air, but still distinctive. A loud pop startled him. And another. Someone was firing at them. Inside his chest his heart seemed in danger of bursting through his rib cage. But then, a cold finger traced down his spine as a thought lodged in his brain. Unconsciously he began to slow.

A soldier bumped into him. "Move it!" he screamed.

But Volta barely heard. He stopped, trying to see through the eerie red light and the swirling, agitated tendrils of smog.

Ahead Shyboy came skidding to a halt and backtracked. "Volta, what's wrong?"

"Shyboy, where's Tully?"

Shyboy's face fell, but before he could respond another volley of shots echoed through the fog. It was hard to tell where the sound was coming from, but then a different weapon answered with the familiar tacca-tacca-tacca of an Overlander rifle. Tully. Volta took off in the direction of the gunfire, cursing the ridiculous pistol in his hand.

Again one of Ferguson's men intervened. He grabbed Volta from behind, both strong hands restraining him.

Volta whipped around in frustration. "For water's sake, we can't leave him behind!"

But the soldier hung on tenaciously. "He's doing this to give us all a chance."

Volta lifted up his hands and, with one furious movement, broke the man's hold. Then several more pops ripped through the air. Louder this time. The enemy was closing in. Again Tully's weapon replied, its distinctive chatter moving toward them. Volta took off. To his relief the soldier made no further attempt to stop him as he plunged into the gloom.

While it was frustrating to be moving blind, the red flare had nearly extinguished and Volta realised the enemy had lost their advantage. They wouldn't be able to see any better than him. His heart leapt up into his mouth as a gun rang out almost under his nose. A wave of panic gave way to profound relief when he spotted Tully crouching behind a garbage skip.

"Tully! Don't shoot," he screamed as he tore over. A barrage of shots lifted pieces of concrete off the ground around his feet. He hauled his skirts up around his thighs and practically flew, traversing the last few metres on his backside.

Volta scrambled up, peering into Tully's face. Tully put his finger to his lips. Volta tried to contain his breathing which sounded like a pair of giant bellows. Tully tapped him on the shoulder and pointed. Volta looked and nodded. He dropped and rolled beneath the garbage carrier. Tully followed. It was not a moment too soon. Lying flat, Volta heard feet hammering toward them, angry voices loud with vexation.

Breathing in the fetid air, Volta watched boot clad feet travelling closer. And stop. Two sets of boots. He could hear the men speaking but not what they said. Not that it mattered, their intent was clear. Their feet slowly turned in a circle. Then one set of feet went left and the other to the right of the carrier. Beside him, Volta felt Tully shift. Volta turned. Tully tapped his own chest and pointed right and tapped Volta's chest, pointing left. With almost imperceptible stealth, Tully began inching forward, elbows and knees digging into the ground, rifle in one hand. Volta followed his example, heading in the opposite direction. It was harder than he had anticipated, his skirt wrapping around his legs like a boa constrictor. When Tully finally

rolled out, Volta was still half a body length behind. He
wiggled frantically forward, swearing in frustration as a
deafening volley of shots filled the air.

Finally he was out, leaping to his feet, pistol at the ready.
But he was too late. Tully stood staring down at a man who
lay prostrate, blood pooling around his neck and shoulders.

Volta went closer. To his surprise the dead man seemed
familiar. He looked at Tully. "Do we know this man?"

Tully nodded. "Yes. Remember the fur factory?"

Of course he did. He reflected bitterly that they should have
left D2 to his own devices. The hybrid had had these scum
down to a tee. Volta stared around. "Where's the other
one?" Then the stink of death wafted up his nose. "Watch
out!" he yelled. Too late. Snarling with rage the second
furrier burst out from behind a large transportable container,
bullets spitting in every direction.

Tully lifted his gun. "Run!" he screamed.

Volta aimed his pistol and fired. Beside him Tully planted
his legs, meeting the enraged man measure for measure.
Volta watched the furrier collapsing slowly to his knees to
fall face down on the unyielding ground.

Volta turned victoriously to Tully, waving his pistol in the
air. But his wild exhilaration evaporated as Tully's rifle
slipped from his fingers, crashing to the earth. Tully opened
his mouth, but instead of words, he emitted a red froth of
blood. With an agonised cry, Volta reached for his man,
wrapping his arms around his torso. Warmth seeped across

Volta's chest; he looked down to see the front of his dress turning black with blood. He felt Tully's body sagging and Volta gripped hard, hugging him closer, as if the very act could prevent the inevitable. But soon he began staggering beneath the weight.

"Volta, let go." It was D2. "Let me help you." And without further ado, the assassin gently took Tully and lowered him to the ground.

Volta dropped down, his eyes searching the familiar, bearded face. He cried out with relief when Tully's eyes opened. Tully stared up and reached out to clutch Volta's hand in his own. Volta grasped the once strong hand, holding it hard. Tully's mouth opened and closed, his lips forming words, but Volta could not hear. He bent closer, his ear almost on his man's cheek. As Tully tried to speak a great spasm of coughing overtook him. Then Tully smiled, removing his hand from Volta's. The hand curled into a fist and Tully laid it upon his chest. Upon his heart. Their old, unspoken signal for love. Volta, crying openly, returned the gesture. Tully's hand relaxed and slid to the ground. Then his dark eyes widened, as if in surprise, and with a soft, bubbling sigh, he was gone.

For Volta the next few hours were strangely blurred. He knew at some level that help had arrived, willing hands carrying Tully. All the while Volta noticed there was something wrong with his eyes. He couldn't seem to focus. While he could hear people speaking, the words washed over him, as if they spoke some alien tongue. The room in which they lay the broken body was cool and clean. Vaguely

Volta knew that he was back in Ferguson's home. The wives kept coming in and looking at him. But leaving without speaking. For this he was grateful. He did not want to talk. How could he put into words the terrible sense of loss, the anger and the guilt that gripped his mind and heart? All sense seemed to have been sucked out of the world. Why Tully? Why? Why? Why? But of course, there was no answer.

He realised he felt stiff and wondered how long he had been sitting in the chair. Slowly he stood up, pins and needles fizzing painfully through his feet and legs. He looked at Tully. It seemed incomprehensible that he would never talk, walk, fight or laugh again. What would he do without him? Behind him the door sighed slowly open. Volta could not find the energy to turn around. A hand settled firmly on his shoulder and he turned his head.

It was Shyboy. He held a white robe in his hand."You've a job to do," he said.

Volta stared stupidly at his friend, and then took the robe. So clean. So white. And then a great lava of grief welled up and he began to shake. With the robe cradled in his arms he collapsed to his knees and he began crying in agonizing, convulsive waves. Shyboy crouched awkwardly beside him and embraced him tightly. Finally, Shyboy released him, and after a few minutes Volta's cries subsided. He rubbed his wet face with his sleeve and took a few deep breaths.

Shyboy waited until he had regained his composure. "Volta, shall the wives prepare Tully for burial or do you want to?"

Volta could not help the new wave of tears that leaked down his face. "Will you help me?"

Shyboy nodded. "Of course. I'll go get some washing stuff. I won't be long."

Shyboy was good to his word. He was gone for only a few minutes. Together they washed Tully, dabbing gently around the black wound in his chest. Shyboy strapped on a large plaster, for Volta found he simply couldn't. Then they dressed him in clean robes. Volta brushed Tully's hair and placed a gun across his chest. Finally satisfied, Volta stood back. It was all that could be done.

Shyboy moved to Tully and looked down at his old friend. "I see you, Tully of the Overland."

Volta was reminded of something that Mia had once said. "Shyboy," he said, "do you believe that he has gone back to Sol?"

Shyboy looked at him, eyes crinkling into lines of concentration. "To be truthful, Volta, I do not know. Which means that I believe it is possible."

Volta joined his bodyguard, and looked down at the familiar face. But even as he did so, he recognised that Tully was no longer there. His spirit, essence, soul, call it what you will, had moved on. Why not to Sol? Slowly he kissed his fingertips and lay them onto the cold brow. "I see you, Tully," he said softly. He turned and Shyboy accompanied him out of the room.

Volta stopped, pulled the door softly shut and looked at his friend. "We'll take him back to the camp. He would want to depart this world as an Overlander." He broke down again at the finality of his words but then dried his eyes. "It was his home."

Shyboy smiled. "I think he would like that."

Volta shook himself, like a bird shaking water off its feathers. "Let's get down to business."

He strode out of the room, grim faced and determined. The boy was gone. Forever.

# CHAPTER 31

Volta settled himself at the large dining room table. He looked briefly around until he found Ferguson. Pulling off his wig, he ran a hand through his sweaty, matted hair. He had had no time to change and was still dressed in costume. But he cared not. "The men who attacked us, the ones from the fur factory," he said, struggling to keep the emotion from his tone. "Was it connected to Isbane?" But of course what he meant was his mother.

Ferguson ran a hand across a dark beard of stubble. He looked tired. "I don't think so. Fact is, I think that, oddly enough, this was quite random. I'd say that having been put out of business, the furriers had settled on a spot of piracy to keep the coffers full."

Volta was quiet as he considered the information. Then he nodded. There was no more to be said. He sat back and waited, unwilling to disadvantage his bargaining power by starting the ball rolling. He noticed the wives exchanging glances and felt Ferguson's gaze upon him. He picked up a glass of water and drank studiously. Then he peered into a bowl of nuts and spent considerable time choosing one before popping it into his mouth. The silence stretched around them.

Palomino finally broke the stand-off. "Thank you for coming today. It is with great sadness that we must continue without the presence of Tully. Whilst ideally we would set business aside in respect for your loss, I think it fair to say that under present conditions this would be unwise."

"Tully would have expected nothing less," said Volta.

"So," said Palomino softly, looking around at her guests and family, "we thank you for coming today. We are delighted Mia has agreed to join us. In regard to our agreement we have already begun sourcing sand guns and the horses are yours on the word."

Volta sat up a little taller and tapped softly on the table. All heads turned. "I am afraid I have news that may not meet with your approval. On further discussion, the Overlanders have decided that the bride price is insufficient to compensate for the loss of a young woman of such status as Mia."

There was a marked hush. Ferguson looked sharply at Volta and the women exchanged knowing looks.

Ferguson spoke. "I see. So what does this revaluation amount to?"

"Sand guns as stated, twelve fully armed hovercraft, six dune buggies and three personal, speech activated computers," said Volta easily.

Ferguson twitched as if he had been stung by a bee. "Scorpion scrotums! Twelve craft! Do you think I'm manufacturing water bonds?" He ran a hand through his hair in agitation; it stuck up, while his jaw jutted in a stubborn line. His blue eyes were wide in entreaty.

Shamay interjected. "Mr. Ferguson, do you not have a child?"

Ferguson eyed the soft spoken woman with an air of deep suspicion. Finally he sighed. "Yes, Biddy."

Shamay smiled ingeniously. "Tell me, Mr. Ferguson, what bride price would you consider fair for your Biddy? To the Overlander way of thinking, Mia is priceless. She is a rare and precious jewel. Our flesh. Our blood." She paused and observed the renegade gently. "Just like your own child."

Volta watched Ferguson internally struggle. He was obviously furious but Volta thought more because he was being intellectually thrashed rather than by the financial implications.

A vein ticked on Ferguson's temple. He eyeballed his guests, the light of fight glinting in his eyes. "Twelve craft? P-lease, let's not be silly," he said.

Volta was unmoved. "Twelve," he reiterated calmly.

Ferguson tapped loudly on the table. "Six."

Volta shook his head. "Twelve."

Fidelus breathed heavily through his nostrils. "Seven, but no buggies."

"Twelve and seven buggies."

Fidelus's chest heaved with indignation. "But you said six buggies a minute ago!"

Volta smoothed the front of his blood crusted dress. "Changed my mind, woman's prerogative."

Ferguson turned, appealing to his wives. "Ladies — this is outrageous."

The Ferguson wives were all agreement and sympathy. There was a fluttering of reassurance and the women excused themselves, disappearing into the kitchen. A clinking of china could be heard and the low hum of conversation. While he strained his ears and tried to eavesdrop as discreetly as he could, Volta could not make out what was being said. He looked at D2, whose hearing was markedly better than his own, but this helped little. D2 was not in a position to share. Volta felt his nerves coiling tighter.

So Volta waited, occasionally glancing at Ferguson who sat with a faint smile on his lips, which Volta found troublesome. Sybil returned first, placing on the table a white china teapot and cups so fine they were almost translucent. She poured a cup of what smelled like herbal tea for her husband. He took a sip and after a few minutes the big vein retracted and the irate man seemed much mollified.

Coco and Palomino soon followed, balancing mugs of steaming cocoa on trays, which they distributed to their guests, with sugar and cream.

Sybil patted her husband's hand and turned to address her guests. "Shamay, we have listened with great respect to your words and — on discussion — can find no fault in your wisdom. So, on behalf of Fergie, Coco and Palomino, I would like to welcome Mia of the Overland into the Ferguson family."

For a moment Volta was quite wrong footed. What in Sol's name was going on? But a quick glance at Ferguson, who looked like he'd unwittingly swallowed a sword, sent a surge of triumph through him. He literally held his breath, waiting for an explosion, but the moment passed and Ferguson settled back in his chair and continued drinking his tea.

Volta took a moment to relish this easy victory. The Ferguson family had accepted the terms. All of them. The craft, arms, buggies and the computers. He turned to Tully to share the moment. But of course, he wasn't there. He dropped his head, took some deep breaths and forced himself to take control.

Beside him, Shyboy shifted softly in his seat. "Well done," he said quietly.

Volta gave him a grateful look. It gave comfort to know that someone else felt his loss. All of it. For on this day he felt that he had lost both Tully and Mia. And felt complicit in the loss of both.

Around the table the atmosphere lightened noticeably. There was a spontaneous wave of conversation. Palomino and Coco laughed and hugged, both obviously delighted by the outcome. For his part, Volta just felt exhausted now it was done. He wanted to go, the thought of Tully's body waiting for him made him anxious. Also, with the certain knowledge of Mia's Promising, he felt a renewed urgency to see her. He was on borrowed time.

Perhaps something of his state of mind translated to his hosts. "Volta," said Palomino, "I will go and organize a cooling coffin for you to transport Tully back to the camp. It will serve for burial if you so wish or you can return it."

Volta thanked her, touched by her kindness and couldn't help but think it boded well for Mia. There was a round of handshakes and goodbyes. They were escorted back to the craft by a dozen armed men. Outside, the fog still hung like a shroud across Alice. Volta shivered as they crossed the hard ground despite the exertion of shouldering the coffin with D2 and two of Ferguson's men. A dark stain marked the place of Tully's passing. Without being asked, the coffin bearers made a wide diversion around it. The party reached the craft without incident but Volta did not relax until Tully had been safely stowed in the hold. He boarded the ship and sank into his seat, sighing with relief. The craft shuddered and the engines roared into life. Slowly they lifted away.

For several minutes everyone was subdued, Tully's empty seat a stark reminder of their loss. Volta tipped his head back wearily and looked out of the window. As they lifted above the smog the bright sunlight jolted him. Somehow he had expected it to be night time. Dark and moonless. Perhaps this was due to the windowless, artificially lit environment of the underground city or perhaps it was the effect of the heavy, black fog. Maybe it was because it seemed like an eternity since they had left the camp behind.

It was Shamay who drew him out of his heavy thoughts. "I think the Ferguson wives were right about you, Volta." Then she turned to D2. "What do you think?"

"Right?" said Volta nervously. "What are they right about?"

D2 turned his black, stony stare on Volta, which made him even more uncomfortable.

Finally D2 addressed Shamay. "Yes," he said.

Shamay continued. "It was something the wives said in the kitchen. They said that you reminded them of Ferguson."

Volta stared. "Hang on a minute, that's rubbish. Just because we both wear a dress and wig, does not make us alike."

Shamay shook her head. "It's not that. Actually, what Palomino said was that you are as smart and determined as Ferguson."

Volta wasn't sure if this was better or worse. "Nothing like him," he muttered. Mind you, it was an interesting insight into the Ferguson family. The wives did not appear to take their spouse terribly seriously.

Then the craft lurched and began its slow descent. Volta peered through the small window at the brilliant blue lake and the spread of tents. Grief rolled over him as he beheld the rippling sand that would be Tully's last resting place. As land reared up to meet them, his eyes searched restlessly. Somewhere, Mia was waiting.

# CHAPTER 32

Mia knew that something was terribly wrong as soon as Shamay exited the craft. The wise woman looked grave and troubled. Shyboy hastened behind, his expression sombre. Impatiently, Mia waited for the rest of them. But after half a minute, when they did not materialize, she felt a premonition of disaster. She was not alone. Men and women slowly gathered, watching anxiously.

Finally Mia could stand it no longer. She ran up to Shamay. With great effort she stopped and touched her fingers to her forehead. "I see you, Shamay."

Shamay returned the greeting. "I see you, Mia."

"What is wrong?"

"Mia, I'm so sorry, but it is Tully." Shamay paused, her brown eyes welling with tears. "He's dead."

Mia was momentarily stunned. Dead? How could he be dead? Why, he had been there just that morning. She had spoken to him. "How?" she managed.

Shyboy stepped forward. "The men from the fur farm killed him."

And then she saw the rest of the men. They emerged from behind the carrier with a long box upon their shoulders. Volta at the front. They moved slowly, and Mia remembered what a big, strong man Tully was. *Had been.* As they passed, Mia found Volta's face. His eyes were dry but his mouth was set in a grim line of determination. Instinctively she stepped toward him, anxious to offer him comfort. But then she stopped. Was she not Promised? Instead, she did nothing.

From a distance she watched Volta and the other men settle the casket beneath a small stand of palm trees, on the outer edge of the camp. Her Nonna came and put an arm around Mia. And Mia laid her head upon her shoulder and she wept. She grieved for the loss of a good man. She grieved for Volta whom she realised was saying goodbye to a man that was both friend and family. And she wept for the barriers that stopped her weeping in his arms.

"Mia."

It was Shamay.

With a mighty effort Mia pulled herself together. "Yes?" she said.

"Mia," said Shamay, "we wondered if Volta would wish to send Tully to Sol, in our tradition?"

Mia was unsure. She looked over to the coffin and at Volta sitting slumped at its side. "I'm not sure," she said, "would you like for me to ask?"

Shamay looked relieved and nodded.

Mia waited for a few minutes, trying to think how to best approach the subject. But gave up and headed over. "Volta," she said softly.

His bent head lifted, his blue eyes dull and bleary. He looked so sad, he seemed somehow unfamiliar.

"Volta," Mia said. "I am so sorry. Tully was a good man. He will be irreplaceable." She paused, but when he did not reply she continued. "Tell me, what would you do with Tully?"

Volta frowned. "I think he would want to leave this world as an Overlander. That is, if you feel it would be right."

"Of course, Volta. Tully was one of our own. We would be honoured to help him travel to Sol. First there is the burning, where we send his most treasured belongings to Sol. We cannot have a pyre, there is not enough fuel here. But as the sun sets we will bury him in the desert and we will pile rocks upon his resting place, and say goodbye. Afterwards we will hold a feast in honour of his life."

Volta stood up. "Mia," he said gruffly, "can he be buried with his head facing toward Isbane? Tully was an Overlander but he was of Isbane too."

Mia nodded. "I think that this can be done." There was so much more she wanted to say. But she could only gaze and hope he understood. "I will go now."

As she turned he spoke softly. "I thank you, Mia of the Overland."

She stopped for a heartbeat, and walked on.

As she set out to find Shamay, Mia forced herself to address more personal issues. While it seemed self-absorbed to be focused on her own troubles, she could not set them aside. She found Nonna and Shamay at the fire. Mia sat down and watched Nonna preparing the drink known as 'kazza'. Nonna poured a measure of milk and spices into a round pot and deftly dropped in hot stones. The milk heated rapidly, bubbles racing up the sides. Nonna pulled out the stones and whisked the milk into a froth. Acknowledging Mia's presence, she poured out the resulting concoction into three cups. Mia smiled her thanks and sipped the drink, enjoying the nutty flavour.

The three women drank silently. When all the cups were empty, Shamay looked at Mia. "Mia, did you speak to Volta?"

Mia nodded. "Indeed, I did. Volta thanks you for the offer. He would see Tully buried as one of our people, but requests we lay Tully facing Isbane."

"Of course," said Shamay, poking at the embers of the fire with a stick until it crackled comfortably. The woman smiled at Mia. "Mia, your patience does you credit. You must be very anxious to know the outcome of the meeting with the Fergusons. A deal has been successfully made. The bride price has been negotiated at twelve, fully armed hovercraft, seven dune buggies, three personal computers and the supply of sand guns."

Mia was stunned. She glanced at Nonna who looked very smug indeed.

The old woman chuckled. "Mia, you must be the most expensive bride in the history of the Overlanders."

Shamay continued. "It was largely due to Volta, Mia. He negotiated the deal. Wouldn't give any quarter. And the wives wanted you at any price. Ferguson himself seemed to have surprisingly little to say." She reached over and squeezed Mia's arm. "The wives think you are wonderful."

Mia was horrified to feel hot tears brimming in her eyes. But it couldn't be stopped. Everything just seemed to overwhelm her. She hid her face in her hands and tried to muffle her sobs. It all flashed through her mind, all the details flickering and jostling for pole position. Volta's loyalty. Tully's death. The exorbitant bride price. She felt as if her head was exploding. Someone pushed something into her hands. It was a damp cloth. She held it to her face and took several deep breaths. When she finally looked at her audience, she found them observing her with great anxiety. "I'm sorry," she hiccuped. "I'm fine, really."

No one spoke.

Mia blew her nose loudly. "Honest, it's all good. I guess it's just a lot to take in."

Nonna and Shamay suddenly seemed very busy, moving empty cooking pots around. Mia tried to catch Nonna's eye, but the old woman seemed absorbed in scouring out the dirty milk pan with sand. To her dismay, Mia caught sight of a single tear trickling through the deeply corrugated surface of Nonna's cheek. She felt terrible.

"Shamay," she said, "will I talk to the men about the burial?"

"Thank you Mia, that's a good idea. There is much to be done before sunset."

Relieved, Mia set off.

The rest of the day passed swiftly as Mia threw herself into preparations for the burial. The frenetic activity helped keep thought at bay but she could not shut out the excited buzz of conversation that her presence seemed to trigger wherever she went. Nor could she ignore the speculative stares and — on occasion — words of praise and congratulations. Even harder was the furious look that she encountered from Dart. His mother wasn't pleased to see her either. Afterwards, Mia made a point of keeping out of their way. While their animosity made her angry, she dreaded a confrontation.

Despite the circumstances Mia felt relief as the sun finally began sinking. She joined her family and set off toward the burial site. There had been no burning. Tully had nothing. At the edge of the gathering Mia stopped, waiting for the coffin bearers to arrive. A soft, cool breeze blew her robes gently as a hush descended on the crowd. Everyone moved back a little to make way for Volta, Shyboy, D2 and Dart. The shiny silver lid of the cooler coffin reflected the burnt orange rays of the dying sun. Overhead, a peregrine soared on the thermal currents, its piercing scream resonating through the air. Slowly the coffin bearers approached the deep cavity and lowered it laboriously down with ropes.

Once done, the men moved back and Shamay stepped forward. "Today," she said, "we send Sol one of our own. Tully of the Overland. But we must not forget that Tully was also of Isbane. And so we bury him in remembrance of this also. Tully was a brave man. He died defending others. He was loyal. He was strong in body and spirit. It is how he will be remembered. We ask Sol to receive this man as one of her own sons." Shamay moved to the grave and touched her fingertips to her lips and then to her forehead. "I see you, Tully of the Overland."

One by one the Overlanders and Isbanites paid their respects. Volta was last. Mia could feel his grief as if it were a palpable thing. "I see you, Tully," he said, so softly Mia could only see his lips move as evidence of his goodbye.

And then the sinking sun set, spilling golden light across the horizon. The silence was broken with the wild ululating call of the Overlanders. Two dozen mounted men, swathed in dark head scarves, galloped to the mourners, circling them. As their rifles pointed skyward and shots assaulted the night sky, Mia felt in her heart that it was a fitting end for a truly good man.

# CHAPTER 33

It seemed to Mia that the burying of Tully marked a new beginning. As she looked around at the Sister Council she felt... comfortable. Previously she had felt accidental. As she waited for Volta, D2, Shoo and Shyboy to sit down, she realised she had grown into her new status. Perhaps it was the Promising, or maybe the loss of Tully. Or perhaps it was because she was at long last free to go north. Either way it didn't matter. Deep in her core she felt a new confidence and sense of purpose.

The meeting opened with due ceremony, Shamay picking up the speaking staff. "Sisters, Isbanites, our time here has come to an end. We must formulate a plan and decide how we can best aid Mia and her Isbanite friends in reaching the hospital in the north. Shyboy has brought his computer and will enable us to communicate with the Ferguson family, if no one has any objection." She paused and looked around expectantly. There were a few whispers but after a long moment no voice was raised. Shamay smiled. "Very well, if you would, Shyboy."

All eyes looked to the albino man but he took no notice, absorbed in his task. In seconds the 3D images of Palomino and Sybil appeared. They made a greeting and were silent, although Mia felt their eyes upon her.

Shamay looked at Volta. "Volta, we would welcome any thoughts you may have at this stage."

With a renewed wave of loss, Mia was reminded of Tully's demise. Anxiously she watched Volta, wondering how he would cope. But she need not have worried.

Volta acknowledged the request with a firm nod of his head. "I think that part of our success so far has been our number. We are few and so less visible. My instincts tell me that we should continue on as before, travelling light, moving swiftly and taking the hardest path."

Shamay glanced at the 3D images, but the wives waited wordlessly.

"I think Volta is right," said Mia. "But I also think that it would be wise to create a diversion. To keep the enemy occupied, so to speak."

Sybil spoke. "I think Mia is wise. This is not dissimilar to our own conclusions. Fergie has made a suggestion which may help gain some time." She paused as Palomino handed her a piece of paper. Sybil held it up. "This is an announcement of Fergie's forthcoming nuptials with Mia. If this were made public, it would have a twofold effect. It will put Volta's mother and uncle off balance, by subtly challenging their authority and secondly, by provoking speculation amidst the greater population. Hopefully it may prompt some to reassess their preconceived notions about the Overlander people. Make the Overlanders more visible and less vulnerable."

There was much animated discussion which ultimately created endorsement of the proposition. Sybil, obviously pleased, promised to go ahead with the plan.

Volta spoke again. "This is a good plan, but I feel that we must be prepared for the day that Isbane loses patience. My mother and uncle will not take the news kindly. They have much influence with the governing body, the Directorate. The Directorate may well be persuaded to mobilize the army. Therefore it is vital to be ready with a fighting force."

Sybil nodded. "Volta is right. Our alliance with Mia will be seen as a threat in Isbane. Threads will snap. The Ferguson family are now allied with Mia and the Overlanders. If it comes to war, we shall be with you."

It was true, Mia thought. Isbane would not relinquish its power willingly. Any threat, no matter how minor, must be crushed. With piercing clarity Mia knew Volta was right. War was coming.

Nonna spoke for the first time. "War is inevitable. It is a matter of time. So the Sister Council has been discussing how to best support Mia and the Isbanites with their plans. We have come up with a strategy."

Mia was dismayed and upset at Nonna's words. No one had talked to her. How unfair. But she bit her lip.

Shamay stirred and all eyes moved to her. "I have had a vision of the devourers. They will swarm soon. I believe that if we were to take an armed force east, we could lure the army of Isbane out into the devourers' flight path. A diversionary tactic, which, with luck, should result in minimal loss for ourselves."

This suggestion was met with tentative assent. Mia looked at Shamay with approval. It was a clever idea.

"'Excuse me. Excuse me!" It was Volta, looking thoroughly confused. "What — exactly — is a 'devourer'?"

Shamay explained. "They are an insect. In the breeding season they change colour from green, to red and black. They have strong armour and a sting in their tail. Some can grow to the width of a grown man's palm. When their numbers run to the millions they fly to find fresh forage. They devour all in their path and turn the day sky to darkness."

"And how does this help us?" asked Volta.

'Well," said Nonna, "Shamay has contacted the spirits of our ancestors, who have given guidance. When they fly, we will lure the army into their path and the devourers will defeat the opposition for us. They will get caught in engines, block periscopes, panic men and reduce vision to a few metres."

Mia watched Volta carefully, curious as to his reaction. She was amused to see disbelief struggling with his desire to be courteous.

"Sorry," said Volta, "but did you say that Shamay has contacted... spirits?" He lifted his arms high and made flapping motions. His tone said the rest.

Shamay nodded assent. "Of course. Do your spirits not help you?"

Volta's face was a picture. Mia giggled but managed to turn it into a cough. She could see Nonna grinning broadly at the young man's discomfort.

"Help me?" said Volta.

Shamay smiled. "The spirits of our ancestors come to our aid in times of trouble."

"So," said Volta, "are these spirits... reliable? You know, as a general rule?"

Shamay laughed. "Volta, there are no certainties in this world, but I am confident when I say that, to date, our ancestors have always given us wise counsel. Sometimes things may not unfold as we would expect, but then, the spirit world is not bound by human limitations. Sometimes, one must simply have faith."

"Faith," Volta repeated softly. His eyes travelled around the tent, searching the sea of faces. When he found Mia, his gaze lingered. "Perhaps," he said, "you are right."

His expression was so sad, so full of yearning, that Mia struggled to stay composed. She had the strangest feeling that his words held double meaning. Some hidden truth meant just for herself. But then, as his startling blue gaze moved away, doubt returned. Perhaps it was just an echo of what she wanted to see… even now. Which was no good.

"I am in agreement," said Volta, "if everyone is in agreement." He glanced at his companions questioningly.

"We are in agreement," said Sybil.

"Yep, works for me," said Shyboy.

"We agree," said D2, as Shoo nodded.

"And I," said Mia.

"So," said Volta, "we will head north, while the rest of you wreak havoc closer to home."

Discussion moved on. It was decided that Mia and her Isbanite companions would continue on horse and camel, heading across the shunned high country populated by dingo hybrids. The meeting finally ended and Mia hurried out to join her companions.

They were waiting beneath the shade of a stand of palm trees. Mia sank down onto the soft ground with them.

"When do we leave?" Mia asked eagerly.

"As soon as possible," said D2. "Tonight?" He looked around inquiringly.

Mia was pleased. She was desperate to get away. Da was depending on her. But… she was suddenly scared. With so much at stake, with so much uncertainty and peril, she feared for everyone. Although having the Fergusons on side gave her some measure of comfort.

The rest of the day was spent in preparation. Nonna packed so much food Mia was worried the camels would have hernias. The afternoon meal was tense and quiet and Mia sensed those around her were as apprehensive as she was at the prospect of saying goodbye.

It was Volta that stood and gave the request to be ready. Mia took her travelling robe from Nonna with a trembling hand. There was no need for words. They clung together like vines on a tree.

Finally Nonna extracted herself. "Look after yourself girl. I've packed your camel hair poncho. Make sure you wear it in the high country or you'll catch your death."

With a hollow feeling in her chest Mia went to Ashan. She hopped up onto his back. "Whooshka!" The mighty beast lurched up and soon the four travellers and the four horses moved into file. Just as she was about to urge Ashan on, a voice called out.

"Someone comes!"

Ever alert, all those that could, readied weapons.

"I hear horses," said Shamay.

Half a dozen mounted horses galloped into the camp, wheeling and slowing to a stop beside the camel train. Mia gaped. It was Fidelus Ferguson, Coco and a few heavily armed men. To her intense discomfort Ferguson rode up to Ashan.

"Mia, I would speak before you leave."

Mia nodded, horribly self-conscious as she appraised the man to whom she was Promised. She did not speak, for she could not think of a single thing to say.

Ferguson, however, seemed unperturbed by her tongue-tied state. "I have brought you something to remember me by."

Heat burned up her neck and face, and she wished she could sink into the sand as she felt the transfixed eyes of the entire tribe upon her. She realised that some form of response was called for. "I thank you," she said, feeling utterly foolish.

Fidelus turned and beckoned to his entourage. Mia watched as a man rode forward, leading another horse by its bridle. She couldn't believe her eyes. It was the bay stallion from Ferguson's stable. It was a mighty gift indeed. Startled, she looked at Ferguson, who was grinning broadly, obviously delighted with her response. His blue eyes twinkled with mischief but there was something else in his expression. It was the hint of a challenge. He was daring her to take the gift. To publicly show her acceptance. She considered refusing him. She looked at the stallion. He was magnificent.

"You are a generous man, Fidelus Ferguson," she said carefully. "And I accept."

Ferguson made no show of hiding his delight. "His name is Baha."

Mia turned to Volta. "I have no need for another horse. But Volta's steed is not swift and he would do well to have another mount for this journey." She turned, smiling at her future husband. She gestured, tips of fingers to forehead. "I see you, Fidelus Ferguson."

At this Ferguson roared with laughter. "I see you, Mia of the Overland," he finally replied.

It was not quite the response Mia had expected. Without any more fuss the stallion was handed over. Ferguson stopped briefly before her, his blue eyes and swarthy complexion alive with amusement. And suddenly Mia realised that she liked this complex man.

As the party stormed away into the night, Ferguson's voice drifted back. "Tell Volta that he bucks."

And then she laughed. She picked up the reins, and glanced around. Her own amusement was reflected in the faces of many of her people. Nonna and her mother smiled wryly, and she realised that Fidelus Ferguson had risen sharply in the estimation of many. But her smile withered as she caught a dark expression passing between Dart and Volta.

Suddenly impatient, she lifted her voice into the night. As Ashan led the way out into the desert, her people lifted their voices in the way of their ancestors, saying goodbye.

# CHAPTER 34

Wolfram stared at the electronic newspaper in disgust. Had the world gone mad? Or had he? He refused to believe what was written in plain print. Fidelus Ferguson betrothed to Mia of the Overland. It had to be a prank. Someone was toying with him. His heart jittered around his chest like a moth at a flame. He felt quite ill. The loud knocking on the door could not bode well. He waited while the mousey maid rushed to the door. His dear sister exploded into the room, nearly killing the help in the crush. Wolfram braced for the onslaught.

"Wolfram, have you seen the news?"

Wolfram sighed. "Yes, sweet sister." Despite his distress he couldn't help but reap a little gratification. Pavan looked distraught. "Of course, I don't know if it's true," he said, "but if it is, we are in trouble."

Pavan's aristocratic nostrils pinched in angst. "Oh, you don't say," she said cuttingly, "your insight is astonishing."

Wolfram felt her words fanning his fear into anger. "Don't act high and mighty with me. You are the one who sent surveillance to Alice. Alice, for water's sake!"

"Perhaps it was foolish," she snapped, "but what were you doing to try and rectify the problem? I don't think sitting on your fat bottom in a chemical stupor qualifies. You know as well as I do that the Directorate gave me a week to bring him back to the fold. If I fail to do so, what actions do they anticipate? Answer me that."

She was right, of course. The disposal of Volta was an acknowledged but unspoken agreement. Still, her timing was execrable. Now Ferguson was entrenched in the picture, things had become very complicated indeed. He looked at his sister. "This has passed out of our hands. We must go to the Directorate."

Pavan blanched, steadying herself with one hand upon the back of a chair. "They'll revoke my water licences."

Wolfram could not deny the thought had crossed his mind. He allowed himself a moment to gloat at the prospect. "If we try to cover up and things go pear-shaped, we'll certainly be in a black hole. But if we get there first, we can mould things to our own advantage. Ferguson's a minor player, with a very large armoury." The thought nevertheless unsettled him. With effort he collected his thoughts, "Ferguson lives on the edge. We must endeavour to push him over into the abyss."

Pavan was very still, her eyes boring into his. He could practically hear the cogs whirring in her head. "Very well," she finally hissed, "as long as you don't try and shove me over with him."

Wolfram's piggy eyes widened as far as it was possible in their folds of fat. He was all affronted innocence. "Pavan, I'm shocked. We are, after all, family."

Pavan smiled at him coldly. "So is Volta. Just remember that." And with that, she swept out.

Wolfram called for a quadruple Melba. The maid raced off and was back in minutes. As he took the crystal glass, her shaking hand caused the precious liquid to slop over the rim. He glanced at her in irritation, a sharp reprimand poised on the tip of his tongue. His gaze lingered on the swollen, black eye that she had arrived with that morning. It made her even more unattractive than usual. Instead of bawling her out he flapped a hand impatiently and she rushed away. After half a minute he checked to make sure she was out of sight and switched on his computer.

The foetus was now three months old, and while it was blobby, it no longer resembled a jelly bean. He sipped his drink and manipulated the womb, examining his prize from every angle. This triggered a wonderful daydream in which Volta was — tragically — deceased and the Western Water Company was sadly willed to his only child.

Reluctantly he closed the link and started on his mail. He must use all of his considerable cunning to compose a correspondence of calculated charm. It was time to let the Directorate know just how much they needed him.

He waited impatiently as the trolley rumbled down the corridor. When the flap opened he was already on his way over, smiling in anticipation. But when he peered out his smile vanished. Something was wrong. He inhaled deeply and his unique brain made an analysis. A soft wave of nausea washed over him, his forehead wrinkling in concern. As Tacker lifted the tray he observed her features anxiously. She looked unwell. Her coat was dry and brittle, her eyes bloodshot. And she was thinner than ever.

"Tacker, you are not well," he said directly. There was not enough time for the niceties.

She smiled. "Man of the Desert, I am fine. Just a little tired."

But the man's instincts told him otherwise. "Tacker, there is something bad in your body and blood."

She froze, her hands on the back of the tray, his on the front, the tray neither in nor out of the flap. He realised that he must have put into words something she already feared. He felt sorry for frightening her, but could not lie to her.

"Tacker, you should leave this place."

She looked at him then, and he could read in her eyes nothing but despair and sorrow. A rage built within him, fuelled by his own uselessness. At his inability to offer aid or comfort in the age-old way of his people.

Finally she took her hands off the tray. "Man of the Desert, where would I go?"

And of course, he had no answer. He watched helplessly as she moved away. The flap closed and he listened as the trolley trundled off. After a few minutes he carried the tray over to his bed and contemplated the contents. He lifted the plate of beans and smiled involuntarily. With gentle fingers he picked up a leaf. It was so green. So alive. The spicy aroma filled his nose and he closed his eyes. In his mind's eye he was transported to the desert. He could see the waves of rippling dunes and hear the piercing call of birds on the wing. He could see his mother deftly making sandals, her arthritic fingers red and swollen. And there were children playing tic-tac-toe in the shade of a coolibah tree.

The small gifts Tacker brought him would have been considered worthless to most. But to him, each leaf, pebble or seed pod was priceless. The humble offerings of nature bought him a fragile link to reality. They were almost as precious as Tacker herself.

But now he felt the weight of his fear upon him. Tacker was in trouble. Immediately his thoughts leapt to her children. Three fine sons. He knew their names. Bidgee, Paroo and Woomba. He had enjoyed living vicariously through their escapades. Over the weeks he felt he had grown to know them as well as Tacker. He sensed that whatever ailed her may also affect her children. And while the thought of losing her filled him with inconsolable grief, he knew somehow he must persuade her to leave.

As he mindlessly shovelled the food into his mouth his brain sought for an answer. Ultimately he concluded the only chance Tacker had was now in his possession. The lightning stone. After all, both Tacker and himself had been entranced by its magic. Why not someone else? Perhaps it had value. Maybe, if she could find a buyer, it would give her enough funds to get away and make a start somewhere else.

Footsteps rang hollowly down the corridor. He instinctively froze, but relaxed as they continued on by. This turned his thoughts to the staff. Would it be possible to bribe one of them into trading the stone? But he dismissed the idea immediately. They'd just steal it. No, Tacker must take it back.

When he had finished eating he went to his mattress and prized the stone out of the tiny hole he'd worried into the seam. Then he sat cross-legged on the bed with his back to the camera. He closed his eyes and began to chant, summoning the spirits. They gathered around him, their voices joining his. Slowly he let his body go, following them into the great void. All around him the lightning stone projected shimmering mirages of light. Something flew toward him. A dark, rapidly moving cloud. At first he thought it was a sand storm. He waited, senses questing. And then something small dropped onto his lap. A devourer looked at him with the deep, liquid brown eyes of his kind. And flew away.

Reluctantly the man returned to his body, bidding his ancestors goodbye. For many hours he pondered on the vision. He had sensed another Overlander had been in the void with him. With a rush of excitement he knew it must be the time of the devourer migration. It was early summer, still dry, but heating up. The goats would be birthing. The Melba would be brewing. There would be grouse roasting and yam baking. Out there his people still lived and communed with the spirits. His tribe. His family. His world.

# CHAPTER 35

They had set up camp in the shelter of a cliff. A small
hangover of rock gave some protection from the elements.
To the south lay the desert. To the north the sand
begrudgingly gave way to scrub country which seemed more
hospitable. Volta shifted his weight from one buttock to the
other, wincing. It occurred to him with a pang, that Tully
would have been highly amused. Fidelus Ferguson had
definitely had the last laugh. Baha was a devil in disguise.

"What are you glowering about?"

Volta was jolted out of his reverie by Mia's question. In the
few days they had been travelling it was the first time she
had addressed him directly, other than to dish out an order.
Or laugh at him. Acutely aware of the change in her status,
Volta had been at a loss to know how to respond. He had
withdrawn and waited. Now, eager to re-establish something
of their old rapport, he answered honestly. "I was just
thinking Tully would have been amused by Baha's

behaviour. Personally, I can't decide who I'm more annoyed with. You. Ferguson. Or Baha."

Mia looked outraged and Volta watched the tips of her ears turning pink. A sure sign of an imminent meltdown. A surge of relief ran through him. Perhaps anger was not the emotion he desired to elicit, but it had to be an improvement.

Mia's narrowed eyes were as sharp as cut stones, her chest heaving with indignation. "Me! Why would you be mad at me? I'm not the one who keeps falling off their horse."

"No, that's true. But you were the one that nearly peed herself laughing on each and every occasion."

She tried to keep her furious expression in place, but a smile was tugging at the corner of her mouth. Volta raised an eyebrow which was the final straw, causing the last of Mia's self control to crumble.

She collapsed helplessly into gales of laughter. She gasped for breath, her features contorted with glee. "I'm s-s-so sorry," she gasped. "But it really was funny."

Funny! Volta gaped at her. Why, it was a miracle he still had the use of all of his bodily functions.

Mia flapped a hand at him, taking deep breaths as she fought for control. "That last time — when you slid right over Baha's bottom — the look on your face—" She lost it again, shrieking with laughter.

As he watched, she shook her head helplessly, clutching her side as if she had a stitch, and suddenly he saw the funny side. His lips quivered and he chuckled. A wave of happiness poured over him like caramel sauce over sticky date pudding. Infected by Mia's helpless hilarity he too slid away into laughter and he almost felt affection for the bucking beast.

Finally they regained their composure. Volta looked around the landscape in a fit of self-consciousness. Where to from here? A flicker of anxiety ran through him, suddenly afraid Mia would withdraw again. But his worry was unfounded.

"Ferguson," said Mia, "knew Baha bucks. He told me so. I believe it's something the horse has been taught. A kind of built in equine security system. I suspect that if I had taken the horse for myself he would have given me the key to its prevention."

Volta shifted uncomfortably again and frowned. "Perhaps so," he said, "but meanwhile — I'm in mortal peril."

Mia smiled. "Don't worry. Soon as the sun goes down we'll figure it out. It will be something simple."

Volta could not see how, but did not pursue the issue. He was just pleased to be back on speaking terms. Both he and Mia turned at the sound of voices. The others had taken the computer further afield to try to get a signal.

Hot and sweaty, D2, Shoo and Shyboy collapsed in the shade and passed the water around. D2 had a huge snake slung over one shoulder.

"What's the snake for?" asked Volta.

"Dinner," said the assassin.

"Snake to bake," said Shoo in her sing-song voice.

"Oh," said Volta, wishing he hadn't asked. He turned to Shyboy. "Any luck?"

"In a manner of speaking," said the albino. "Ferguson's ploy seems to be holding off the storm. All's quiet on the Isbane front, but one of our MLF members tells us that the catchers are unusually active in the Poor Quarter. Could be coincidence of course."

Volta gathered by the expression on Shyboy's face that he, at least, didn't think so. "If it's deliberate, what do you think the motivation would be?"

"That's easy," Shyboy continued, "they'll crack down hard, saying we've created a high security risk. People always love to have someone to blame. The powers that be will give the populace our names in big print."

D2 nodded. "Sounds about right. Subtle start to a propaganda campaign."

Volta thought of Beatrice. "Well," he said grimly, "they're still one step behind us."

Shyboy nodded. "When we get to the hospital we'll get some footage. That should up the ante."

They chatted for a while but soon the heat overtook them. The temperature continued to rise, and everyone slumbered fitfully. It was only in the cool of the evening that the group awoke, groggy from the debilitating heat. Mia rose first and busied herself at the fire. Volta's nose sniffed the air appreciatively as he roused himself. When he sat down to eat he blanched as he remembered it was snake on the menu. Looking around at everyone else digging in, he tentatively took a bite. To his surprise, the snake was good.

"Volta, go tack up Baha," said Mia when he had barely swallowed his last bite.

Volta took a quick drink of water and gathered up his gear. He found Baha glued to Whisper's side as usual. The stallion barely twitched an ear as Volta threw on the saddle and cinched up the girth. He looked, Volta reflected ruefully, the image of domesticity.

As he slipped the bridle over Baha's ears, Mia arrived. Wordlessly he handed over the reins. Mia led the stallion away from the rest of the herd and, in one fluid movement, was in the saddle. She gave Baha his head and walked around. The stallion moved easily, with no sign of resistance. After a few minutes she pushed him into a trot, making a few wide circles. Again, nothing. Volta was just beginning to think that the fault must be his when Baha exploded into a frenzy of bucking. Awestruck, Volta watched Mia clinging on like a limpet. Baha cranked things up and began leaping with all four feet off the ground. Mia came off. Baha sauntered back to Whisper.

Volta rushed to Mia just in time to help her back on her feet.

For a minute she seemed winded, her breath painfully laboured.

"Are you alright?" said Volta anxiously.

She nodded. "Volta, it's when you ask for canter," she said breathlessly.

And Volta realized she was quite right. But before he could say anything, Mia was off after the stallion again. She vaulted up and this time the tornado of activity happened in seconds. Seriously alarmed he raced over to her prone body and rolled her over, convinced she had broken her neck.

She opened her eyes. "Think I've got it," she said.

Despite Volta's protests, Mia set off, apparently oblivious to the blood trickling out of her nose.

"Mia—"

But it was too late; she was back in the saddle. Volta could barely bring himself to watch. But to his amazement this time the stallion popped into a canter like a well trained rocking horse.

After a few neat circles Mia brought him up and walked over. "No leg aid for canter," she said. "Just bring your upper body back a bit. It's when you bring the lower leg behind the girth that he goes off."

Volta was mightily impressed. "You are brilliant," he said.

Mia sniffed and dismounted, but Volta was sure he caught sight of a small smile as she turned away.

Volta took the reins from her and eyed Baha suspiciously. The stallion's black eyes twinkled at him through the heavy forelock. "He's enjoying this," Volta grumbled. Slowly he climbed back into the saddle, his aching body reminding him of the accumulated damage. But he sat up and legged the stallion into his flowing trot. For a couple of circles Volta put it off, but seeing Mia's anxious face he took a deep breath and leant back. Baha promptly moved into a canter. After a few more tries, Volta reined Baha back in. "Brilliant."

Mia smiled up at him, green eyes blazing with triumph. "Well done!"

Volta felt his heart quickening. She was so beautiful. And he ached to tell her so. But remained silent as the seconds stretched painfully between them, their eyes locked upon each other.

"Volta! Mia!"

They both startled and turned as Shyboy waved. "It's time to go."

Wordlessly they headed back to the camp.

# CHAPTER 36

As dusk descended and the group set off once more, Mia felt some of her anxiety melting away. It was good to be on the move. Good to be heading north at last. Her heart rejoiced at the prospect of being reunited with her Da. And the tense, loaded moment with Volta seemed less worrying now. After all, nothing had happened. She felt resigned to the future, accepting even, and would not shirk her responsibilities or betray the bonds which lay upon her. So why should she freeze Volta out? She had tried that, but his confusion and distress had filled her with shame. And in the back of her mind, Farro's and Tully's deaths clung like cobwebs to her conscience. What if Volta were killed? She could not bear for him to die estranged from her. After all, he had done nothing wrong.

Defiantly, she told herself they were just friends. No one could possibly interpret their relationship in any other way. Her thoughts were interrupted by a frenzy of activity behind her. Concerned, she looked around. Volta was on the ground again, Baha still bucking.

He lay still for a minute and then sat up. "Forgot," he said, by way of explanation.

Mia caught the stallion and took him back to Volta. He stood up stiffly and took the reins.

"That'll teach me to daydream," he said with a sigh, as he climbed back on board.

Mia laughed. "What were you dreaming about?"

Volta's mouth opened but nothing came out. He looked in every direction but Mia's. "Nothing," he finally mumbled, sending Baha into a canter.

Mia watched him go silently. She urged Whisper on, but at a safe distance. She knew she had blundered and wanted to make things right. Some things though, just weren't fixable.

For his part, Volta was furious with himself. He had made a promise to let go. Mia was beyond his reach. The past. Yesterday's news. But sometimes he forgot. It was easy to slide back into old habits. Especially now, back on the road. If it weren't for Tully's absence, he could almost imagine they'd never been to Alice. He wished he could hate Fidelus Ferguson. But he couldn't. He had to admit he had a grudging respect for the man. Indeed, there were times he had to fight hard not to actively warm to the renegade. In different circumstances he would have probably wanted to get to know him better. And he had to concede that if Mia had to be Promised to anyone, Ferguson was not a bad candidate. Not for the first time, he wished he'd spoken out, told Mia how he felt about her. But would the outcome have been any different? Life was very confusing.

"You alright?"

Without realising, Shyboy had caught up with Volta. "Sure, I'm fine," he lied.

Shyboy stared speculatively. "You don't look fine. You had an upset with Mia?"

"No!"

Shyboy sighed. "I'm really sorry, Volta. Listen, I don't want to make your life any more difficult—"

Volta butted in. "Good, please don't."

Shyboy ignored him and ploughed on. "I've got something for you." He groped around beneath his robe and grunted in satisfaction. "Got it." He held out something in his hand.

Rather reluctantly Volta took it. It was a band, woven in a yellow, red and blue zigzag pattern. It was very fine. "What is it?"

"It's a wrist bracelet."

Volta looked at it again, wondering why Shyboy had made it for him. "Thank you," he said, "it's really nice."

Shyboy laughed. "It's not from me, dimwit. It's from Trina."

"Trina?"

"Yes, remember Trina — she of the pleasing curves and dimpled chin — oops, of course you don't remember Trina. But she certainly remembers you."

Volta shifted uncomfortably in his saddle. While he could not remember the specifics of his encounter with the young woman, he had not been oblivious to her ongoing, discreet attention. A couple of times he had been aware of her observation. She had taken every opportunity to sit near or with him. They had exchanged a few words and smiles. Volta had felt obliged to return her attention, to do otherwise would have been impolite. He looked at the wrist bracelet again. "Does it mean anything... specific?" he queried carefully.

"Don't be dim. Yes, of course it means something specific. It means that she likes you."

Volta squirmed. "No, that's not what I meant. I mean, if I wear it, does it have some sort of tribal significance?"

"No, it's just a gift." Shyboy paused and caught Volta's eye. "She's a really nice girl, Volta. You should think about it."

Volta carefully put the bracelet away into his saddle bag. Of course, Shyboy was right. Trina was a really nice girl and pretty and smart.

But she wasn't Mia.

# CHAPTER 37

In the privacy of the cave Tacker slowly readied herself for work. It was late. Outside the birdsong had silenced and night crouched on the horizon. She could hear her sons laughing and tumbling in the undergrowth. She smiled, warmed by their childish antics. But in her heart, she knew it would not be long before they left their brief childhood behind. When that happened she feared maternal bonds would begin fraying as their natural desire for independence asserted itself. A sudden wave of dizziness overwhelmed her and she leaned against the wall. If she had felt less exhausted she would have cried. She knew Valley was right. She was not well. Worse, she feared whatever it was that afflicted her, would spread to her young. Every day she observed them with dread. Was it her imagination, or were they less energetic?

The dizzy spell passed and she picked up a water bottle, weighing it in her hand. She undid the lid and sniffed it, her nose wrinkling up. It did not smell good, despite being boiled. Perhaps she should start drinking the bottled water she bought for the boys despite its exorbitant price. It was dawning on her that the dark pool of water she had been so delighted to discover deep in the cave might not be such a boon after all.

After a brief clash of wills she bribed the boys back into the cave, with the promise of a hunt the next morning if they were good. She knew she would not be able to coerce them in such a manner for much longer. Perhaps they should go. Just leave. Go back to the wilds, just the four of them. After all, they were older now. Were the risks any greater than in this terrible place?

As she walked through the camp at the foot of the mountain, it was quiet. She did not have to endure the usual barrage of lewd comments, barely veiled threats and hostile watching eyes. It must be Friday. The sounds of muted catcalling and occasional yells confirmed her assumption. Friday evening was the night that residents suspended hostilities while they squeezed around a large screen to watch a fuzzy episode of The Game. Tacker cheered up, her footsteps a little lighter. The staff at the hospital would also be engrossed in the big screen. This meant a rare opportunity to spend a little more time with the man. She put her hand in her pocket and drew out the small flowers. The tiny, star-like clusters of red blooms were pretty, although they didn't smell pleasant. Lantana was one of the few flowers that still bloomed in the scrub. It had become a daily challenge to find something new for the Man of the Desert.

Security was practically nonexistent, the guards barely lifting their eyes from the show which they watched surreptitiously on small wrist screens. Tacker hurried to the kitchen, grabbed her trolley and hauled it to the lifts. In the ward the staff were gathered around a 3D screen, making no pretence of work. Tacker raced down the ward, aware that she only had about twenty minutes left. She was out of breath by the time she reached his door. She grabbed the tray and flipped open the flap.

His vivid green eyes met hers. "I see you, Woman of the Desert." He took the tray and put it on the bed, returning quickly. "Is the show on?"

She nodded and pulled the flowers out of her pocket like a conjuror. He took the posy and sniffed it.

"It doesn't smell the best," she said.

He smiled. "It does to me."

She glanced up and down the corridor. No one in sight. She looked at him again, aware that despite all of his urging, he would be sad when she told him her news. She realized then he was part of the reason she had stayed so long. "You are right," she said softly, "I must leave this place."

For a minute he just looked at her and then he turned away. She was taken aback, thinking he was angry or upset. She was just about to close the flap and go, when he returned.

"Tacker, you must take this with you."

She looked at the lightning stone, drawing in her breath in wonder. She had forgotten how powerful it's magic was. But she backed away nervously. "I cannot, it is yours."

He thrust his hand through the flap, proffering the lightning stone. His voice was urgent. "Tacker, we don't have time for an argument. The lightning stone has spoken to me through the spirits. The spirits want you to take it. It is their will. If you take it to Isbane or Alice, it will have worth. It would trade well for water bonds. Take it, I beg you."

Tacker was nearly beside herself. What should she do? She did not want to take it back. It was a gift. But he seemed so sure, and his talk of spirits filled her with superstitious fear. She already had enough to deal with, without inviting trouble from the other world. In a panic she took the stone and thrust it in her pocket. "I must go," she whispered, glancing fearfully down toward the nurse's station. Time was nearly up.

"Goodbye, Woman of the Desert."

"Goodbye, Man of the Desert," she said.

With a trembling hand she locked the flap down. The memory of his green eyes lived with her for a very long time.

Wolfram and Pavan waited stiffly side by side at the transport station. They did not speak. Both were preoccupied by the forthcoming meeting with the Directorate. Transportation was on its way. For both of them it would be a first flight on one of the latest Fast Force Fliers (FFF's), a gyroscopic sphere that created a gravity resistance-free path through which it travelled. It could reach the speed of galactic ships within the earth's atmosphere, making it the swiftest transportation available.

Normally Pavan would have been preening at the Directorate's preferential treatment. But today she was terrified that she was just racing to her own destruction. Fidelus Ferguson was the only other person outside herself and Wolfram who knew of the full treachery of the Western Water Company. Volta remained an unknown quantity. It did not take a genius to understand the inflated value of water on a dry planet. But if the truth came out, disaster loomed. Decades ago, Fidelus Ferguson had helped create and then manage an underground dam that held an ocean of water. Water that had been surreptitiously rerouted, effectively creating drought throughout the region. Global warming had ensured that the old water courses had never replenished. Only now did Pavan consider the possibility that they may have created a monster in Fidelus Ferguson. He could bring them all down.

Wolfram's state of mind was highly charged. His biggest fear was that the Directorate would change allies. If he were in their shoes it would seem a reasonable option. Extinguish the water company and do a deal with Ferguson. After all, with one of the Overlander diviners practically in his lap, a wealth of inside information, three well-connected wives and a sharp business brain of his own, Ferguson was an attractive proposition. The only thing keeping complete panic at bay was the hope that Ferguson would prove to be uncooperative. In which case, they were saved. The Directorate would have no choice but to declare war. Wolfram wouldn't get another night's sleep until Ferguson, Volta and the Overlander tribes were erased from Earth.

He glanced at Pavan's disdainful profile. It comforted him to know that she was suffering. After all, when it came to water, she had more to lose. Whilst he, on the other hand, had a finger in several sticky pies. Though water had been good for him, there was more to his portfolio. Things would be tight, admittedly, but on the whole he'd manage. And it seemed that whatever the outcome, Volta's future didn't look rosy. He could only imagine the breadth and depth of his sister's fury when she discovered his little piece of precious. His new heir apparent — to everything.

Pavan felt the arrival of the scheduled FFF seconds before it arrived. A sudden rippling of air that pushed her back a step or two before the transporter landed silently in its PVC ring. She hurried through the circular door and looked around, curious despite her anxiety. The interior was sleek and shiny, with moulded red chairs, lime green cushions and black, spongy floor coverings. She sat down and fastened the seat belt. There were no windows, but she did have the latest entertainment software at voice command. As soon as Wolfram was settled the computer announced the ETA. Fifteen minutes. A slight vibration announced their departure.

"Wolfram," she said, finally breaking the silence, "we must convince the Directorate that the Fergusons are traitors. A threat to international security."

Wolfram opened one eye lazily. "How, dearest, do you propose to do that?"

Her eyes narrowed. "We tell them that we have evidence Ferguson is affiliated with the MLF. And that this alliance with the Overlander is as good as an admission of his guilt." She smiled grimly to herself as her brother's other eye popped open.

"What evidence?"

She smiled slyly. "How does intercepted mail between that deformed dancer wife of Ferguson's and a suspected MLF insurgent in Isbane sound?"

Wolfram's pretended indifference washed away. "Can you produce the goods?"

She pretended to be offended. "Naturally," she said coldly. "The Agency is always willing to oblige. For a price."

# CHAPTER 38

The man awoke, instantly alert. He jumped up and padded to the door, listening. Footsteps. Voices raised in anger. Nurse Elapid, the man mused, recognizing the bullying tone at once. And two of his cronies. Then sounds of struggle. Clearly one of the inmates was resisting strenuously. The man grinned. It was a rare but most edifying event.

"Let me go, scum eaters!"

A new voice! A woman.

"Hands off, dirt bags!"

Then a muffled thud and a scream. The man's smile faded as he leaned his forehead on the door.

"I am Beatrice!" said the voice, breathless but undeterred. "I am Beatrice!"

Then the buzz of a laser. And a groan.

"Leave her alone you cowardly cockroaches!" yelled the man, hammering on his cell door. "Get off her!"

A door slammed followed by an ominous silence. Broken by Beatrice. "MLF! MLF! MLF!"

The man shook his head, breathing out a ragged sigh of relief. Whoever she was, Beatrice was clearly unbroken. The man felt a surge of savage delight at the woman's insurrection. "MLF! MLF! MLF!" he chanted. Louder and louder, slamming his fists on the walls. He had no idea what MLF was. And didn't care much as other inmates joined in, the sounds thundering up and down the corridor.

The heady moment shattered as the flap on his door opened and the man found himself eye to eye with Elapid. The man took a hasty step back, expecting an invasion. But the nurse's slack mouth twitched into a smirking grimace.

"Enjoying yourself?" Elapid said, grinning widely now.

That was new. And unnerving. The nurse had never before shown even a hint of humour. The man did not reply, but his skin felt as if it were crawling with ants. Since their last run-in, the nurse had lost no opportunity in making his life miserable. Elapid had not dared accost him again, but the man had experienced more subtle abuse. A decrease in water rations. Loss of shower privileges. Sleep deprivation. Slowly but surely eroding the man's depleting resilience.

Elapid licked his lips. "We've got a special treat in store," he said.

The man felt his throat tighten. He'd been expecting it. All his most recent wounds were healed. Even the scab on his spine had dried and fallen away. But he gazed steadily at his tormentor, forcing his expression to be calm and his tongue to be still.

"Oh yes," Elapid breathed ecstatically. "Not blood or bone. Not skin or serum." He leaned closer and lifted his hand, tapping the front of his forehead. "This time they're going to drill a hole and dig out a bit of brain." The nurse began to laugh soundlessly. Then, clearly with some effort, he sobered up. "Can't imagine you'll be quite... yourself, afterwards." He looked over his shoulder, checking they were still alone. Then he leaned in close. "But don't you worry, I'll be here to look after you."

The flap snapped shut. And for the first time, the man felt hope beginning to fade.

# CHAPTER 39

Mia halted Ashan, scanning the landscape to find a viable way forward. It was a barren, desolate looking place, uneven, rocky and full of fissures. A death trap for the animals. Plus, there was no plant life. No grasses, herbage or shrubs. Nothing to sustain the life of the livestock. Her heart sank. The horses would never make it across. The camels she wasn't sure about. But it was too dark to make a decision.

"What do you think, Mia?" said Shyboy, his face shadowed in the moonlight.

Mia turned and sighed, aware of all the anxious eyes upon her. "The horses won't make it across. But I'm not sure about the camels. It'll be light soon and then I shall know."

Understandably her news was not met with enthusiasm. Volta looked over at the herd of horses. "But what shall we do? We can't leave them behind!"

Hearing the note of panic in his voice, Mia hurried to reassure him. "Volta, they will be fine. This is their home."

"But Mia," said Volta, a little desperately, "how will we find them again?"

"We will return this way. They will not go far. If our calculations are right, we are not far from the green lake D2 told us about." Mia looked questioningly at Shyboy.

"It's not far," Shyboy agreed, "say four klicks as the bird flies."

"We shall not be gone long," said Mia. But even she could hear the unspoken words "if we are lucky" hanging in the air.

Volta didn't speak but Mia sensed his distress. "Volta, they will find the nearest water source. We will find them." She looked over at Whisper, her silver white coat ghostly in the night. "I would not abandon them, Volta."

His mouth relaxed into an apologetic smile. "That I believe," he said.

"Let us rest until sun up," she said.

Soon they were settled, sipping water and chewing on dried dates. Shyboy hauled out his PC and began scrolling madly, muttering under his breath. No one interrupted but Mia realised everyone was tense, worrying and waiting for news.

Shyboy stiffened and turned to the waiting group. "Message from the MLF in Canberra." He glanced at Volta. "Seems your mother and uncle have been there for a meeting with the Directorate. Word has it they went away looking pleased with themselves. No details though. Otherwise, everything is strangely quiet."

Volta grimaced but said nothing.

No one spoke, eyes focused to the east, waiting impatiently for the light. As the sun finally rose, they all stirred. Mia walked slowly, preoccupied. Talk of the outside world reminded Mia of how vulnerable they all were. She wondered about her family and her people. They too were travelling. Heading to Isbane to draw the full might of the army upon themselves. She felt her heart jittering inside her chest. It was a necessary distraction, she knew. But she wished it wasn't. In retrospect, the plan seemed terribly fragile. What if the devourers didn't swarm? What if the army decimated her people first? What if… She took in a sharp breath and forced herself to stop. It did no good. They were committed. She must have faith.

She stopped and surveyed the landscape once more. D2 and Shoo stood beside her and gave her a questioning look. Mia gloomily shook her head. If anything, the bright light of day only served to reinforce her fears. It was a fearsome country. As brutal as any Mia had ever encountered. "We must go on foot," she said.

D2 nodded. Shoo shrugged. Shyboy sighed. Volta grimaced. But no one argued.

It was with a heavy heart that Mia unloaded and unsaddled the camels. They seemed unconcerned however, ambling off without a fuss. The horses were harder still, Mia's throat contracting as she slipped Whisper's head collar free, hugged her, and let her go. It had to be done.

"What about all our stuff?" said Shyboy.

Mia considered for a moment. "We'll just have to leave everything we can't carry." Everyone looked unhappy. Mia empathised. It was gutting, but there was no alternative. And there was more bad news to impart. "We cannot travel at night," she said, regretfully. "This country is riddled with ravines and potholes. To travel at night would be almost suicidal."

Everyone seemed to accept her words, for which she was grateful. It took several more moments to gather the meagre possessions that they could carry. Water, dried meat and weaponry in the main. They moved on quickly, all clearly as eager as she to reach their destination. Mia tried to contain her growing excitement. Her Da suddenly felt so near. Soon they would find the green water, and then the hospital. And then—

"Stop!"

Mia halted, turning to D2 whose hands were softly releasing the safety catch of his semi-automatic. "What's wrong?" D2 turned to her with a snarl, causing Mia to step back.

"Dingo!" he hissed.

Mia's spirits plunged. She could recall only too clearly their last disastrous encounter with dingo hybrids. She looked around carefully but could see nothing. But then she startled as a high, sad howl reverberated across the craggy land. The hairs on her arms stood to attention as another dingo replied. The group exchanged tense looks.

Volta jerked his head forward. "Best keep going."

There was really no other option. They went on, scrambling, sweating and puffing with exertion. Despite the rough terrain the group put on a spurt of speed. Mia could see the sunlight glinting off the surface of the terror toxin bazooka that D2 carried, seemingly effortlessly.

After several moments, they heard no more. D2 shrugged but kept his weapon primed and ready. The pace, however, did not relent. The threat was enough. They paused a few times for much needed water and chewed strips of dried camel meat as they travelled. And then, as she scrambled up to the top of a high crag, Mia's heart leapt with joy. "Look!" she cried.

For, down below, lay an emerald green lake. They were nearly there. At last.

# CHAPTER 40

Volta gazed down at the water. It was incredibly beautiful. The exact green of Mia's eyes. Which was ironic as he knew full well the water was cradled in an ancient quarry. Centuries ago, large quantities of uranium had been gouged out of earth with little or no respect for the radioactive waste that subsequently polluted the landscape.

Finally he dragged his eyes away, looking across the water. His eyes settled on a less hostile environment. It was not pretty, but there was vegetation, shrubs and even trees. Signs of life that seemed lush after the desolation of the dingo country. It also offered more cover. Travelling in daylight over the barren and brutal rockface made him feel exceedingly vulnerable. He couldn't shake off the feeling they were being watched.

Beside him Shyboy let out a small cry of jubilation. "Look."

Obediently Volta trained his eyes onto Shyboy's pointing finger, his eyes travelling swiftly up a tree-studded mountain. And there it was, stark and ugly against the sky. The prison hospital. Volta turned to Mia, eager to share his elation. "Mia, there it is!" Her eyes met his, blazing with emotion. He had some idea of what she was feeling. Her father was now practically in plain sight. At this moment all their plans seemed to finally have substance.

"We must find cover," said D2.

Volta glanced at the assassin and his mood sobered. The look on D2's face was ugly. And no wonder. He had suffered cruelly in this place. It would elicit no warm fuzzy feelings for D2. But more than that, Volta realized he was right. It was plain madness to linger in this place, exposed as they were. They had been lucky so far. But that wasn't a reason to tempt fate.

Without a word of argument they set off once more, climbing down now, all eager to enter the relative safety of scrub country ahead. But it was slow going. It was very hot and despite their eagerness the pace steadily slowed. Volta himself was very weary. But when he turned to check on Shyboy, he was disconcerted to find Mia lagging behind. "Mia!"

She lifted her head and waved at him. "I'm fine," she said. And so saying, she hurried to catch up.

As she did, Volta felt a frisson of alarm, noting the pallor of her face and the black rings beneath her eyes. Why, she looked... unwell. It was ridiculous but Volta was shaken by this conclusion. He had never known Mia to be anything less than robustly healthy. It was very worrying. "Mia, are you alright?"

Mia glared at him. "Of course!" she snapped.

Volta said no more. Her tone was a clear warning to back off. But it didn't stop him worrying. And then his anxiety doubled as he caught sight of D2, who had stopped ahead of him. The assassin was observing Shoo with a tense expression on his dark face. It was a look of deep concern. Immediately Volta honed in on the little hybrid who was travelling at the front of their group. He watched her progress carefully but could not discern anything untoward. Shoo seemed fine, covering the rough ground with no apparent difficulty. He glanced back at D2, but he was on the move again, seemingly unperturbed. Yet Volta couldn't shake off the bad feeling that shadowed his mind. He found himself constantly checking on both the young women, fear building in a tight band around his chest. Out here they were absolutely alone. If any of them were to succumb to illness, there was no one to turn to.

It was a huge relief to finally reach the scrub. The soil was thin and stony but the plant life still thrived somehow. Trees grew sparsely but shrubs and lantana flourished in the sunlit spaces. Galahs shrieked and flapped in the canopy and cicadas shrilled. It stank though. Even the sharp tangs of eucalyptus and lantana could not override the stench of rot and human filth. They had found civilization it would seem, Volta thought ruefully.

Shyboy stopped. "Let's find somewhere to camp. We can do no more until we have had contact from Ferguson. And we don't want to accidentally bump into anyone."

Shyboy's words gave Volta a nasty turn. The man was right. They must find cover. Lie low until nightfall. He looked around, half expecting to discover someone spying on them. They walked on, heads turning rapidly as they searched for a safe haven.

"Here!"

Everyone turned and hurried over to where Mia indicated. Volta smiled involuntarily as he peered down into a dried-up riverbed, almost completely invisible in the scrub. He'd not spotted it himself and doubted anyone other than Mia would have seen it.

Within minutes they were all secreted in the natural hide. They sat silently, passing a water bottle around, adjusting to their new environment. The ground was sandy and soft which was pleasant but alive with large, leggy ants which was less so. Volta subdued a yelp as one bit him. It hurt.

Mia hissed and began slapping her bare legs energetically. Shyboy grunted, dug around in his backpack and withdrew an aerosol. Gratefully Volta took it and sprayed himself liberally with the repellent. Thankfully the ants withdrew to find other victims.

"Best get some sleep," said D2, who promptly lay down, closed his eyes and seemed to fall instantly into a slumber. Shoo yawned, showing small sharp teeth and then curled up beside her friend, purring softly.

"I'll keep guard," said Volta. He didn't think he would sleep. Whilst his body was twitching with exhaustion his mind was in fast forward. A million things streamed through his brain like shooting stars. He tried not to stare at Mia, although his concern for her was intensifying. She was not herself, being unnaturally subdued. Was she ill? Or just worn out with exertion and worry? After all, the past few days must have been tough. To say the least. And now they were so close to their goal, perhaps Mia, like himself, was starting to feel the strain.

Volta wished for the umpteenth time that Tully was there. His friend and bodyguard had been his confidante. And his conscience. The weight of responsibility sat heavily upon his shoulders. But perhaps, he thought wearily, that was what being grown up was all about.

He sat still, senses questing. As he waited for the night, Volta was forced to acknowledge part of his sadness lay in the certainty that this quest would soon be at an end. And then, one way or another, he would have to say goodbye to Mia. And he knew that when he did, his designer heart would be breaking.

# CHAPTER 41

Mia awoke with a jolt and started to get up. That was a mistake. She slumped back down as her head swam and her tummy did somersaults. She felt sick.

"Mia, what's wrong?"

She opened her eyes to find Volta looking down at her, his face taut with anxiety. Slowly she sat up, and managed a weak smile. "I don't feel well," she admitted. There was no point denying it. Her sickness was not going to go away. "It's this place, Volta. It is poisoned. The water from the radioactive lake has polluted everything. My mind and my body feel it."

Volta crouched down, peering at her minutely. "Can I do anything? Do you need to leave?"

She swallowed down another wave of nausea and shook her head. "There is nothing to be done. I will be alright. Once we get inside the hospital the sickness will abate."

Volta nodded but still seemed troubled. "As long as you are sure…"

"I am." She looked around and saw that the shadows were long. "Where is everyone?"

"D2 and Shoo have gone hunting. And Shyboy went to find a higher spot to access his mail to see what's happening."

"Someone taking my name in vain?" said Shyboy, materialising from the trees.

Seconds later D2 and Shoo slipped back into view. D2 had a goanna slung across his back. Volta hoped it would prove to be as tasty as the snake. Their rations were very low and fresh meat would be welcome. But his hopes were crushed.

"No fire," Mia said.

Any protest was effectively cut off by Shyboy. "I got mail."

All heads swivelled his way.

"Well?" said Volta.

"A message from Ferguson. He says, 'The devourers fly. It must be tonight'."

Mia felt her mouth go dry. The Overlanders and Ferguson were armed and on the move. War was imminent and they must do their part while the enemy's eyes were diverted.

"Time for a recce," said D2 in his deep rumbling voice. "Shoo and I passed close to a camp. It's a dirty, disorganised place. Stinks."

"Smelly poo, so bad for you," said Shoo sadly.

"Staff?" asked Volta.

"Yes," said D2. "But not medical or nursing I think. Domestic. Maybe security."

Mia considered this information for a moment. "It would be wise to detour the place. If our cover is blown we lose our main advantage." Everyone agreed. "D2, Shoo, we'll follow your lead. You have the best night vision."

The two hybrids made no comment but proceeded to ready themselves. D2 soon resembled a mobile armoury. Shoo wrapped a belt of bullets around her narrow waist.

The rest of the group followed suit. Mia reluctantly left her sling and stones behind, shrugging her crossbow over one shoulder and pocketing the bolts. It was not a more accurate weapon but it certainly had the deadly edge. This was not a time to indulge in whims. They fell into single file, and climbed as quietly as they could up into the scrub.

Mia trembled slightly as she scrambled up the steep slope. But it was not due to the sickness. It was from excitement and fear. So much was at stake. So much could go wrong. But as she glanced around at her companions' determined faces her jangling nerves began to settle. She trusted them implicitly. And as Volta gave her a quick smile, she smiled back and realised how glad she was to have him here. Volta had been there from the start. It seemed fitting that he was here now.

There was a hiss from the front as D2 and Shoo stopped. Everyone instinctively froze, all eyes on the two hybrids, almost invisible in the shadows.

"What?" whispered Shyboy.

D2 turned slowly, gun cocked. Shoo's lantern eyes glowed gold. D2 held up a warning hand, touching his lips with his finger. Mia could hear nothing above the rapid breathing of her companions and the pulse hammering in her neck. A soft growl of fury rumbled from D2. Mia felt a prickle of fear. She jumped as a twig snapped in the darkness. With steady hands she plucked her bow free and slid a bolt softly home. It weighed little in her hands as her eyes darted around the forest. There was something out there. She sensed it. She sucked in her breath as she realised what.

"Dingoes," said Volta softly in her ear.

Mia glanced at him and nodded.

D2 snarled and yelled. "No!"

Too late. A group of armed people came bursting out of the sparse foliage, jaws wide with fury, teeth bared to the gums. Guns eyeballed guns and Mia's finger trembled on the trigger. The five faced off the four.

# CHAPTER 42

As she faced off the trespassers, memories washed over Tacker, dark and dreadful. Grief tightened like a noose around her heart. She had not always been alone. Once there had been a father. Bennalong. Her mate. Her man. He had been hard, it was true. But he had been loyal too. And brave. Together they had made a life. They had managed. But then these trespassers had come and killed him, leaving his body bleeding on the desert floor. And she hated them for it. And she ached for revenge.

She cocked her gun and hissed. "Trespassers!" Her sons moved closer, teeth bared, a deep resonant growl emanating from their young throats.

Mia eyed the dingo woman with trepidation. She looked the same. Although she seemed ill. She was gaunt, the muscles clearly visible over her bones. The loaded gun gripped in her hand looked lively enough though. And her young were no longer pups. Nearly full grown they were about as cute as their dead father had been.

D2 spat. "I told you we should have finished them off,'" he said.

The dingo woman's eyes honed in on D2, her lip curling into a snarl.

It was hard to say which of the hybrids loathing was the most intense. Mia felt panic rising, sensing violence was but a hair's breadth away. Hostilities seemed inevitable and would end in a blood bath. There would be no winners.

D2's wrist ratcheted off his safety switch with a stark click of sound. Four answering clicks cut the air. Mia sensed Volta and Shyboy tensing beside her as they too lifted their weapons in readiness.

"Trespassers!" howled one of the dingo boys. Bang! His gun went off. Mia ducked. There was a crack and thud as a branch blasted off a nearby tree.

Shoo let out a yowl and D2 roared with rage.

"Stop!" Mia screamed, hurrying forward, her hands held up in supplication.

"Mia!" Volta yelled after her.

But Mia barely heard. She only knew she must stop this thing before they were all destroyed.

Then the dingo woman turned, her gun shadowing Mia as she moved. "Trespasser!"

"Don't! Please! I'm sorry! Sorry that he died!"

Tacker did not really hear the words. Her heart pumped vengeance through her blood and she thirsted for a kill. She frowned in concentration as she trained the barrel of the gun up the girl's dirty white robe and into her hated face. She wanted to look into the trespasser's eyes and watch the light of life extinguished. Her finger gently stroked the trigger in anticipation. The girl was close. So close she couldn't miss. So close she could see the brilliant green of her eyes.

Tacker twitched and stepped back, dropping the muzzle of the gun. "You!" she whispered.

Mia skidded to a halt, her skin flinching with fear, anticipating a barrage of bullets. But none came. To her amazement the dingo hybrid had lowered her weapon and was staring at her with the oddest expression. She took an uncertain step forward.

The dingo woman paused for a moment, her amber eyes searching. "You are… Mia," she finally said.

Mia was flummoxed. "How do you know?"

"You have the eyes of the Man of the Desert. He talks of you often."

It was Mia's turn to stare. There was only one other person in the world who had eyes like her own. And yet — "Who are you?" said Mia.

"I am Tacker," said Tacker. "Woman of the Desert."

Mia was trembling. "You have seen my father?"

"Yes," said Tacker. "He is my friend."

There was such honesty and dignity in the simple statement that Mia was utterly disarmed. She glanced around at her companions and found varying degrees of doubt, indecision and simmering anger. "Put your guns down!" she ordered. She turned, her eyes skimming over her companions, urging them to comply.

Volta was first, gently lowering his gun. Shyboy quickly followed suit. Mia heard the dingo woman speak sharply and caught sight of two of her sons disarming in the periphery of her vision. D2 and one of the pups reluctantly gave in last, eyeing each other with undisguised loathing.

Tacker, shivering with fatigue and adrenaline, found the green-eyed girl once more. "We must talk." She shouldered her gun and jerked her chin at them before turning away. She wasn't sure they would come. And wasn't quite sure that she wanted them to. But they fell into line and followed her through the prickly, stony path down to her camp.

There she stopped awkwardly, acutely aware of the hostility and suspicion emanating from her guests. If one could call them that. She did not trust them. But she owed the Man of the Desert this much and more. She would not sully her honour with the blood of his child. She had not sunk so low.

Aware the truce was tenuous at best, Mia sat down on the cool earth. She only breathed again as she watched the woman, Tacker, put down her gun and settle beside her. After a second's hesitation Volta sat opposite. Slowly, they all assembled, D2 and Shoo at a distance.

Mia leaned forward to the dingo woman. "Tell me everything, please."

And Tacker did. Finally she finished. "Tonight I plan to leave." Her eyes locked onto Mia's. "Your father says this land is filled with sickness. If I do not leave I will not survive and neither will my sons."

"Where will you go?" said Mia softly.

"Back to the desert," said Tacker.

Mia was silent for a minute. She bit her lip. "Tacker, if you stay one more night and help us release my father, I will help you find your people. I swear it."

Mia waited breathlessly. This woman's aid would be invaluable. She had legitimate access to the hospital. And knowledge of the exact location of Valley, Mia's father. Mia felt sure she would say no.

Tacker looked at her sons. Torn. They watched her anxiously but did not interfere. She looked back at Mia. "You have seen my people?"

Mia frowned. "No, not exactly. But I am sure we can find them. We have both computers and a vast network of contacts. It should not be hard. And we have water," she added.

Tacker picked up her gun. Mia tensed, but the woman simply rested her face against its hard surface and closed her eyes. Mia could sense her weariness.

Abruptly, Tacker put the weapon down. Once more she observed her sons, who watched her intently. "I will stay," she said.

Mia closed her eyes in relief. "Thank you." Then she smiled.

The woman smiled back.

And so the deal was done.

# CHAPTER 43

In the cool of the cave Mia looked around at the others. "Where are D2 and Shoo?" No one seemed to know. She decided they'd probably gone hunting. Her mouth felt dry with nerves and she breathed deeply as another wave of nausea overcame her. She glanced around. "One more time," she said.

There was a universal groan.

Mia stood firm. "One more time."

Shyboy started. "We leave as soon as The Game starts. We skirt the camp and go straight to the employees' entry at the back. D2 and Volta will overcome the guards while I access the computer and locate the emergency systems. Meanwhile, Tacker, Shoo, Mia, Volta and D2 will go up the lift to find Valley."

Volta pitched in. "When the alarm goes off Shy should be able to open all the cell doors. We find Valley and — in the subsequent chaos — we get the hell out."

Sitting beside Mia, Tacker unscrewed an old bottle and poured water into a cup. Dry retching, Mia slapped the bottle out of Tacker's hand. "Don't drink that. It's toxic."

"The Man of the Desert knows this too," Tacker said softly.

Wordlessly Volta passed over his own water.

Tacker hesitated and then took it, drinking a small amount. "I thank you."

Mia waited until the nausea passed and carried on. "Then we head back the way we came." She smiled at Tacker. "Then we find your kin."

Tacker nodded curtly, but said nothing.

Mia sensed Tacker did not fully trust them. She could understand why, but could think of no way to reassure the woman. "So — that's it then?" She looked around inquiringly.

"Piece of possum poop," said Volta. He stood and stretched. "Must be time for a nap."

Mia was not the only one to jump like a jack rabbit as D2 came storming in. Alarmed by the furious expression on his face she feared they were under attack. "What's wrong?" she gasped.

"Shoo's sick," he snarled.

Immediately Mia's mind jumped to the poisonous water. "What is wrong, D2?"

"She vomits. And has bad pain, here," said D2, slapping a hand low on his abdomen.

There was a silence as everyone absorbed the news. Mia jumped up. "What can we do?"

D2 turned on his heel and without looking back he yelled, "We're leaving. Now. She needs a doctor."

Mia looked helplessly at the others. "Where in Sol's name are we expected to find a doctor?" But the answer hit her almost spontaneously. Oh crap! "He's taking her to the hospital, isn't he?"

They all scrambled to their feet.

"Why can't anything be simple?" grumbled Volta, but even as he spoke he grabbed his gun and began loading it.

Outside they found D2 with Shoo in his arms. Mia forgot her fear as she gazed at the glazed eyes of the young hybrid. She could hear Shoo's shallow, panting breath. D2 was right, something was very wrong. "Let's go," she said. "We go now. Same plan."

Despite their protests, Tacker would not consent to allowing her sons to accompany them. They all set off, almost running to keep up with D2. It took barely twenty minutes to arrive at the hospital's back entry. Tacker strolled in ahead of them, a large knife secreted in her waistband. She walked through the scanner which began flashing and wailing. Just as the guards began a body search, Volta raced in, lifted the huge terror toxin bazooka and let rip. In less than a second the guards were squirming and gibbering on the ground.

Mia, vaccinated against the toxin, watched as Tacker cheerfully clouted them over the head with the butt of her knife.

Shyboy locked the door behind them and began feverishly inspecting the security system. He looked up frowning. "Go," he said. "This won't take long."

No one questioned him. They surged down the corridor to the lift. Mia thought they were in luck, all seemed quiet. But as they watched the lights of the console slowly working downward, a voice called out. A white-uniformed nurse raced toward them.

"Hey! What are you doing?' he yelled.

Volta heaved up his bazooka, eyes swivelling from the lift to the irate nurse. A soft ping announced the lift's arrival. They all surged in. Just before the doors closed Volta let another canister go.

Mia covered her ears as the alarm went off. "Good work, Shyboy," she said. But then her heart twisted as Shoo let out a deep groan of agony.

Volta hit the wall. "Hurry up!"

Finally they reached the sixth floor. They burst out into an empty corridor. Tacker led them on. At the entry to the operating theatre Volta freed his gun and blew the door away.

The three resident theatre staff were so shocked, they made no resistance. A man dressed in green stared at them in dumb amazement.

D2 slid to a stop in front of him. "Hello, honey," he said softly, "I'm home!"

There was no doubt in Mia's mind that the green man recognised D2.

Volta stepped up. "D2's wife is sick. She needs help."

The green man sneered and then actually laughed. "I think not."

Volta moved in and stuck his gun in the man's face. "Actually, I think you do."

The laughter switched off. The man's mouth opened but no words came out. Beside him one of his offsiders made a dash for the demolished door.

Mia lifted the crossbow D2 had given her, slotted in a bolt and focused down the sight. Just as the nurse reached the door he screamed and dropped to the floor clutching at his leg, through which a bolt was now wedged. She raced over, grabbed the man and towed him away from the exit.

The surgeon in green scrubs seemed to have a change of heart. He pointed to the surgical bed. "Put her there."

D2 concurred, settling Shoo onto the hard surface. He whipped around and grabbed the surgeon by his green collar. "If she dies. You die. I'll personally remove your organs one by one… without anaesthetic."

The surgeon obviously believed D2. He turned to his remaining staff and began barking out instructions, beads of sweat popping up on his forehead.

Without taking his eyes off the surgeon, D2 spoke. "Volta. Mia. Tacker. Go!"

Mia cast an anguished look at Shoo, whose face had disappeared beneath a black, shiny mask. But she realised there was nothing more to be done. Her heart began beating wildly in her chest. The moment had arrived. She plunged out of the doorway, racing after Tacker, Volta at her side.

Outside the theatre, the world was wet, liquid gas misting down. Tacker stopped at a door, swiped a card and they were in. It was a brightly lit passage, with doors lining its length on both sides. There was a loud clunk and Mia watched as the rows of cell doors simultaneously opened. Slipping and sliding they raced headlong down the corridor. Half way down Tacker began to slow. Mia reached out to brake herself on the wall, but her feet got left behind. She fell, sliding head first. A pair of bare feet arrested her flight. A pair of strong hands lifted her up.

"Mia. Daughter of the Desert."

She looked into a pair of emerald eyes. "Da! My Da."

And then she collapsed into his arms. She breathed in the goodness of him. Felt the softness of his beard tickle her cheek and heard the strong beating of his heart. And for one tiny, fragile instant of time, all was right in the world.

# CHAPTER 44

The resemblance was uncanny. The same eyes, the high cheek bones and the dusky skin. Only the hair was different, Valley's being white and Mia's dark. Volta waited, moved by the outpouring of emotion. Both were weeping uncontrollably.

It was Tacker who broke the moment. "We must go."

Volta looked around. The corridor was filled with people, all dressed in the distinctive uniform of the inmates. Some moved purposefully toward the exit, others seemed overwhelmed, staring around wild eyed. Volta turned to Mia. "Mia, we must go."

Mia stared at him, her eyes unfocused. Then she pulled back from her father. "Da, we must go."

Quickly they grouped and headed back for the theatre. They all swept in anxiously. D2 was waiting beside Shoo, who still looked unconscious. Shyboy stood close beside them.

"How is she?" said Mia.

"She will be well," said D2. "Explain later."

Volta felt a huge weight lift off his chest. "Thanks be to Sol."

Mia stared down at the floor where all the theatre staff appeared to be sleeping. "What happened to them?"

Shyboy looked rather pleased with himself. "You know, I really think I have a future in anaesthetics."

"If we don't hurry, none of us will have a future," said D2 grimly, scooping Shoo into his arms.

They hurried out, heading back down the corridor. Ahead, the lift was nearly invisible behind a crowd of people.

"We'll take the stairs," said Tacker. She stopped. "Wait a minute."

Volta watched as she ran down the corridor and into a cell. When she came out she carried a small child. She did not explain. "Let's go."

"What about Beatrice?" said Shyboy.

"We don't know where she is," said Mia. She turned to Tacker. "Do you know Beatrice, she's a hare hybrid, shaved head, tattered ears?"

"Yes," said Tacker, who turned back and went darting into a cell.

They rushed after her, all crowding around the open door. But it was empty. Shyboy swore.

Volta realised they could not help. "We must go, and hope for the best. At least now she has a chance to escape."

From the lift end of the corridor there came a scream. The doors had opened and two men were shoving their way brutally through the crowd. There was a loud buzzing and the smell of burning flesh.

"Time to go," said Volta.

Tacker took off, hugging the child to her chest, the rest close behind. At the end of the corridor was a small door. They raced through into a narrow, musty staircase. Volta had to physically drag Shyboy and his recorder through the doorway. Mercifully the stairs were dry, else they'd have collectively broken their necks. Tacker travelled swiftly despite her burden. D2 seemed inexhaustible.

At the bottom they all stopped, anxiously eyeing a closed door.

"Where does it go?" said Volta.

"The laundry. There's an emergency exit. If the alarms have been set off, it should still be open," said Tacker confidently.

"Many staff?"

Tacker shook her head. "Not at this time of the day."

Volta mentally braced himself. "Let's do it." He shoved the door, which swung open, banging against a wall. To his relief the vast laundry was empty, except for a dozen wheelie carts piled with washing. If anyone had been there, they'd sensibly left. They filed out. Volta glanced at Shoo. She appeared to be asleep or unconscious. He couldn't help but wonder if D2 proposed to carry her all the way home. Still, no point worrying yet. Home seemed a long way away.

As they filed past the laundry carts, Volta let out a yell of shock as he was attacked by a pile of sheets.

"Die, you perverted pisspots!" screamed the sheets, knocking him to the ground.

Someone ripped the smelly washing away from his face and the tip of a large kitchen knife nearly poked his left eye out. He blinked. "Beatrice?"

The knife retreated. Beatrice backed off. "What the…" Then she let out a yip of delight. "Shyboy! I should've known!"

Volta stood up, watching while the members of the MLF made a brief but happy reunion. Then they were outside at last. It was strangely serene after the chaos inside. The only sounds were the muted screaming of the alarm and the harsh cawing of a crow. They followed Tacker into the scrub, which offered some cover at least. As they rounded the building they heard human activity. People were pouring out of the hospital. Volta stopped, anxiously seeking for signs of violence, but either the guards had been overwhelmed or they'd headed for the hills. Reassured, he hurried after D2's broad, receding back. They did not stop until they gained the camp. Tacker's sons burst out of the cave and nearly suffocated her with their enthusiasm.

"Wait boys," she chided them gently. Her sons backed off reluctantly. Tacker walked over to Beatrice and smiled, gently easing the small, quivering body from her chest.

Beatrice took in a hoarse breath of air and took the little hybrid girl who snuggled into her neck. Gently Beatrice stroked her long, velvety ears.

Tacker smiled.

Beatrice smiled back. "I thank you. I will find her family. Take her home."

Volta turned away, unwilling to intrude. He went to Shoo. She lay on a rough bed with D2 hovering at her side. "D2, will Shoo be alright?" D2 stared at him stonily and Volta inwardly quailed.

"They will all be well," the assassin finally rumbled.

Volta exchanged eyemeets with Mia and Shyboy. "They?" he mouthed, silently.

Mia's eyes were wide with shock. "D2," she said nervously. "By 'they' do you mean…"

"I mean Shoo and the kittens," D2 replied.

Before anyone could respond, Shoo finally stirred. D2 bent down, helping her sit up. Shoo reached up with a small hand and stroked his head.

Volta startled, ears on stalks. He could hear the loud humming of an engine. He caught Shyboy's eye. "You hear that?" he asked quietly.

Shyboy laughed. "Yep."

Volta's heart thudded in his chest. Approaching vehicles did not bode well. "Better check it out."

Shyboy pointed to D2 and raised an eyebrow. "Rather you than me."

And then it dawned on Volta. It was not an engine at all. D2 was purring. Volta shook his head. "Wonders will never cease."

Volta realised his mouth was bone dry. He had a raging thirst. He found his bottle and took a long, satisfying drink. As he paused for breath Shyboy hurried over.

"Do you hear that?"

Volta listened. "Shit," he said, "that's not D2."

# CHAPTER 45

Mia and her father heard the fast approaching hovercraft at the same time. Too late she realised she should have insisted they go inside. But Da had begged to be able to sit in the sun. And she had been unable to refuse him. Although she knew it was too late, she grabbed her father by the hand and raced for shelter.

"I'm sorry!" she gasped at the sight of everyone's stricken faces.

"It's not your fault," said Volta. "They probably have heat seekers anyway."

"Perhaps they'll pass over," said Shyboy.

The sound of the engines was loud now, whipping up a wind and blowing dust into the cave. Mia held her breath and willed the craft to keep going. Her heart sank as the wind turned into a hurricane, blasts of sand scudding through the opening. The sound was deafening.

Mia screwed up her eyes and edged to the exit. The hovercraft hung some ten metres above the clearing. Two large rockets made a bright splash of colour beneath the dark vehicle. She scurried back and relayed her findings.

"We must fight," said D2.

Mia looked at Shoo, at Beatrice and the little girl and at Tacker's three half grown boys. She thought about the rockets. And didn't know what to do. The wind speed increased and in her mind's eye she saw the craft settling on the stony ground.

Her father stepped toward her. "Mia, find me a gun, for Sol's sake!"

His words galvanized them all into action. D2 scooped up Shoo and disappeared into the dark recesses of the cave. He was back almost instantly. He pointed at Beatrice. "Stay with her, please."

Mia held her breath, sure Beatrice would protest. But to her relief the woman settled the little hybrid girl more firmly on her hip and nodded.

This time Tacker's sons would not be told. They ignored their mother's furious demands and anguished pleas.

They all shook their heads, and repeated one word. "Trespassers."

Tacker gave up.

Armed to the wisdom teeth, the group gathered. Mia prayed it would not be for the last time.

"Where's Shyboy?" said D2.

Everyone looked at everyone else. No one seemed to know.

Mia took a deep breath. "We wait until the craft is down and the soldiers show themselves. Then we go together. All guns blazing." She stopped, eyes skipping around the group. "Unless anyone has a better plan?"

No one did.

"May Sol go with you all," said Valley.

They moved cautiously to the front of the cave. Mia could hear the distant cry of a kestrel and the rapid breathing of her small army. Her eyes found Volta. Briefly his hand wrapped around hers. She could feel the warmth of his skin and the hard calluses on his palms. His eyes reminded her of the sky. He squeezed her hand and let go.

"Make every bullet count," he said softly.

Mia tensed, sensing the time was close. She saw D2 lifting his gun and she clicked a bolt into her bow. She stepped forward then startled back, holding up a warning hand as Shyboy slid into their midst.

"Stop!" he screamed. "Don't shoot!"

Volta looked deeply offended. "We're not going to shoot you!"

"Not me," Shyboy gasped. He pointed outside. "Them."

"Who?" said Mia.

"The Fergusons."

They all looked at Shyboy stupidly.

Volta lowered his gun. "You mean, that's Fidelus Ferguson out there in one of his craft?"

Shyboy grinned. "Our craft, you mean."

Mia leaned weakly against the wall of the cave. "But how?"

Shyboy waved his computer at her. "He mailed me. Said he was on his way."

Mia knew then the war to draw the eyes of Isbane from the prison hospital was over. Ferguson was here, safe and sound. But what of her people? She took her father's hand and together they hurried out of the cave, her mouth dry with dread. The craft had settled, the engine winding down. A door yawned open and a set of steps slid out. Fidelus Ferguson emerged and descended in two easy strides. Sybil followed.

"Hello, Mia," Ferguson said.

"I see you, Fidelus Ferguson," she said formally. She noticed his sharp appraisal of her. She realised she must look like an absolute fright. But she did him an injustice.

"You're not hurt?" he said.

She shook her head and watched the lines around his eyes relax. He looked behind her to the others. "Is anyone hurt?"

They reassured him not.

"We must make haste then," Ferguson said. "Your little jaunt has created quite a stir."

Mia could bear it no longer. "Fidelus, what of my people? Are they alright?"

He nodded. "All went according to plan. A few flesh wounds, but no one killed. They have returned to the winter camp."

Mia suddenly felt feather light. She closed her eyes and gave thanks. Then she made formal introductions, starting with her father and ending with Beatrice and her little bundle.

Sybil, very clean and elegant in a pale yellow jumpsuit, addressed her husband anxiously. "Fergie, it will be a squeeze. We had not anticipated so many."

But Mia intervened. "I will not be boarding. I have vowed to take Tacker and her sons to her people."

At this several voices were raised in consternation. Mia blithely waited for the furore to wane. She turned to her father. "Da, an Overlander's word is the law, is it not?"

"It is," he said softly.

Before anyone could argue, Mia pressed on. "Besides, I left Whisper behind. I will not return home without her."

Ferguson looked exasperated. Sybil amused. Ferguson turned to her. "Why must I always choose women with the willpower of an out-of-orbit meteorite?" he demanded.

Sybil glanced at Mia. "Perhaps it's just good luck, Fergie," she said mildly.

Mia could have hugged her.

Mia turned to Volta. "Will you make sure everyone gets home safely?"

"No," he said.

Mia felt utterly flattened. Her hurt was almost unbearable. For a horrible moment she thought she might cry.

"I can't," Volta continued steadily, "because I am coming with you. I have two horses to collect."

"Fine," she snapped, to cover up her confusion, desperately trying to hide her relief.

"I'm coming too," said Shyboy.

Ferguson was silent for a moment. "Very well," he said.

Mia sensed he was unhappy, but she could do no less than she had promised. She clung to her father as she said goodbye.

"I am proud of you, Daughter of the Desert," he said softly.

With everyone onboard, Ferguson came back to Mia. He took her hand gently. "Come home safely," he said.

His eyes were sky blue. Just like Volta's.

"I see you, Fidelus Ferguson," she said.

"I see you, Mia of the Overland," he replied.

Without a backward look he swung aboard. As the craft lifted skyward Mia took a deep breath, Fidelus Ferguson's last words echoing in her head. *Come home.* But where was home? Was it Alice?

She was intensely aware of Volta standing silently beside her. So familiar. So strong. And, in a moment of clarity, she understood that no matter where she roamed, there could be no home without him.

# ABOUT THE AUTHOR

Born in Britain, Jenny went to Australia as a young woman for a holiday, and returned to England 32 years later to resettle in Devon. She started writing down her imagings whilst bedbound following a back injury. On recovery she continued to write and was published by Escape (Harlequin).

Printed in Great Britain
by Amazon